Wishing you a happy holiday—and many, many happy reads.

She's coming home for the holidays...and there's gonna be hell to pay.

Last Christmas, Melody Mage vanished without a trace. The wealthy socialite was presumed dead by her loved ones. But on the anniversary of her disappearance, Melody appears on the doorstep of her family's estate. Her memories are fractured, her past shrouded in fog and confusion, but she knows one thing—someone attacked her. Left her for dead. She just has to figure out *who* the guilty culprit is. Then she'll make the person pay.

In other words, Melody has to solve her own cold case mystery.

And she's going to do it—no matter what it takes. No matter how many skeletons she has to drag out of her wealthy family's closet. And no one will get in her way. Not even her father's intense—and dangerously attractive—protégé, Victor Alexander. Victor has just taken over as the company's new CEO. He's driven, powerful, and he stares at her with eyes that glitter with far too much...longing?

He ripped apart the world looking for her, and the love of his life just casually knocked on the front door.

Except Melody doesn't know that Victor had his heart carved out of his chest when she vanished. Their relationship had been secret. On the outside, he and Melody had appeared to barely tolerate each other. In private, they'd touched—and ignited. She'd been his obsession. He'd been her personal attack dog. Now she's back, saying she's looking for justice, and he's going to give it to her. He will give her *anything*. Unfortunately, Melody has no idea that she once promised to love him forever—or that when she vanished, she was wearing the engagement ring he'd given to her.

He never stopped loving her. Too bad she believes he's the enemy.

Victor has been working with the Ice Breakers, a cold-case solving crew, and he suspects that Melody's attacker is someone in the family's inner circle. He also knows that there is no way on earth he will ever let Melody vanish again. He'll protect her, he'll win her heart once more, and he will see to it that the person who hurt *his* Melody is buried in an icy grave before the new year dawns.

Author's Note: It's Christmas and cold-case solving time…only for this book, the heroine is the case. Melody can't fully remember her past. She doesn't know if she can trust Victor—or if he might just be a villain she should fear. No worries on that score. While Victor may have a dark side, he's only a villain to the rest of the world. Never to her. Let's deck the halls, solve a cold case, and fall in love this ICE COLD CHRISTMAS.

Ice Cold Christmas

Ice Breaker Cold Case Romance
Book 15

Cynthia Eden

HOCUS POCUS
PUBLISHING INC.

Published by Hocus Pocus Publishing, Inc.

2

If you have any problems, comments, or questions about this publication, please contact info@hocuspocuspublishing.com.

Prologue

"I'm done being your dirty little secret." Melody Mage's breath heaved out as she glared at the far too sexy jerk before her. All big, bold, and seductively dangerous—*and the man who just kept breaking her heart.* Victor Alexander.

Her father's protégé.

Her long-term nemesis.

The lover who made her quake and shake in all the right and wrong ways.

Christmas music played softly in the background. The lights from the twelve-foot Christmas tree gleamed. They were at the company's big holiday party. A party where he'd barely spoken to her all night long.

He wore a perfectly cut tux.

She wore a bold red dress.

Her father had just announced that Victor would be taking over the company. There had been shock from the attendees. Then, after a stunned beat of time, applause for Victor. Victor—the genius who'd snuck past everyone's guard. The hardcore predator who knew how to attack corporate enemies.

The lover who stole my heart.

Very, very slowly, Victor put down the champagne flute that he held. They were alone, for the moment. And maybe she should have held onto her control, but...

Control had never been her strong suit. They'd been playing games for far too long, and she was done.

Her gaze darted to the Christmas tree. It was probably over the top, but then again, that was the way of things in her family. Big. Over the top. *Too much.* There were seven different Christmas trees in the building, and this one—this one was in the main boardroom at Mage Industries. A gorgeous angel, strumming a harp, perched on top of the boardroom tree. Dozens of ornaments—all colors, red, blue, green, gold, white—hung from the limbs even as twisting, silver ribbon trailed down the branches.

The tree was massive, and the boardroom itself was huge, too, but as her stare slid back to Victor, the space somehow felt far too small as she faced off with her lover. A lover who denied her in public even as he made her scream with pleasure in private.

Oh, we are so done. If he didn't stand by her side in public, he didn't get to fuck her in private.

"I wasn't aware that you were interested in telling people about our involvement." Victor's voice was very, very careful. That was the thing about Victor. He was *always* careful. Always controlled. Her total opposite. Even when they had sex—phenomenal sex, by the way—he was still controlled. Still seeming to hold part of himself back even as she splintered into a million pieces. That was hardly fair. It wasn't right that she was completely lost to him. In *love* with him. But he could still maintain perfect control without so much as a small break in his chilling veneer.

He took a step toward her. The light hit the darkness of his hair, and his hard gaze raked her. "You seemed happy enough with our arrangement. Pretty sure you were screaming for more just last night."

He had *not* just gone there. Melody stomped toward him in her two-inch, red heels. The heels still left her several inches below his towering height. "Don't be an asshole."

"Why not?" A cool reply. "Everyone says I'm so very good at the task. Pretty sure that's the entire reason I'm taking over Mage Industries. Your father wants a real asshole at the helm. Someone who won't take shit from the competition."

She swallowed. "You're breaking my heart." Something she had *not* meant to say. Because she wasn't supposed to admit that she cared. From the beginning, it had just been sex between them.

Right?

Only...

No, no, from the beginning, it was more. Always more, to me.

"Didn't think you could break a heart that someone didn't have."

She sucked in a breath and felt pain blast straight to her heart as he delivered those emotionless words. A heart she very much possessed. "No more. We're done." She had to get out of there. Had to escape, as fast as she could.

Blindly, blinking away tears, she rushed for the door.

Only for his hand to curl around her wrist. That warm, strong hand. His touch always sent a charge burning through her blood.

"*We're not done.*" Lethal. Low.

She looked at his hand. The golden skin. The crisp, white edge of his shirt, then the black smoothness of his tux sleeve. Her gaze slowly rose to collide with his, and when it did, for just an instant—

Desperation.

She could have sworn that she saw a crack in Victor's careful armor. Melody swallowed. Had she really seen it? Or just hoped that she had? "Why not? You have everything you ever wanted."

"The hell I do." Grim. "But I will." A vow. He let go of her wrist.

She should probably finish her dramatic, fleeing exit. But...

He reached into his tux pocket. And he dropped to one knee in front of her.

Melody blinked. "Why are you taking a knee? What is happening right now?"

"I was going to wait. Had this whole scene planned out. But with you, nothing ever goes according to plan."

Was that an insult? It felt like one.

He opened a small, red box. "I don't want you to be a secret. I just want you." He stared up at her, unblinking. "Marry me."

"What?" Her hands fisted at her sides.

"I didn't want anyone to say I was fucking you in order to get the company. The company *will* be mine. And I want you, too."

Her brow furrowed.

"Not like you're a damn bonus prize, that's not what I meant. Fuck, I'm screwing this up." Victor kept the box extended even as he huffed out a frustrated breath. "You're it, Melody. You're what I want. Not a secret. I want you with me, always."

He hadn't said he loved her.

Then again, she hadn't told him those words, either.

He's offering me a ring. She should take it. Throw her arms around him and tell him how thrilled she was. But, something felt off.

Because he hadn't said he loved her.

"I love you," Melody blurted.

And...something changed. In his eyes—the darkness flared ever bolder. On his face—a flash of savage satisfaction. In the next instant, he was on his feet. Towering over her again. His mouth crashed onto hers, and she shouldn't kiss him back, Melody knew that she shouldn't, but she did. Because she truly loved him. With every part of her being. Even though she feared that she should not. She loved him.

Her mouth opened beneath his. The kiss was frantic. Passionate. Hungry. Possessive. His hands were suddenly around her waist. *What had he done with the ring? The glittering, gleaming ring?* But she stopped wondering when he lifted her up. Victor put her on the edge of the big, intimidating boardroom table, and he pushed her legs apart.

Her dress hiked up. A shiver skated over her even as her hands grabbed for his shoulders, and she held on with all of her strength.

They weren't going to fuck right there. No way. Not with all of those people right outside. Her family. Her friends. Strangers. Enemies. Surely, they weren't—not *there?*

But one of his hands slid between her legs. Went right under the skirt of her dress. He caught the edge of her panties even as his mouth continued to claim hers in a primal possession and then he was brushing his callused fingertips right over her clit—

The squeak of the door. Laughter. "Come on, we can go inside and—" The male voice broke off, shocked.

Victor had gone statue-still. For just an instant. But in the next moment, he wrenched away from her. Spun for the intruder. "*Out, now!*" Nearly a roar.

The person—people? Because she thought she'd heard the sound of feminine laughter—so maybe a man and a woman—got out. Immediately. The door clicked closed.

Melody's heart raced too quickly. Her breath came too fast. Had she been spotted? And what would happen if she had been? *No, no, Victor shielded me.* She didn't think anyone had seen her face...

Victor spun back toward her.

She should get off the table. Maybe close her legs. Both acts seemed like excellent ideas.

"Marry. Me."

She smoothed down her dress even as she slid off the table. "Is that an order? Or a request?" Her stomach was in knots, and her knees felt far too weak. "Because it sounded like an order."

"You love me."

With her entire heart. The heart he'd accused her of not having. But he hadn't said how he felt. That was Victor. Always keeping things close to the vest. Always spinning and plotting. She could never quite figure him out. Truth be told, maybe that was part of his appeal. She liked a man with some mystery about him.

"They're going to rush back to the party," Victor warned her as he watched her with his intense gaze. "That was Trey and Eleanor."

Eleanor was her stepbrother's secretary. She was also

one of the biggest gossips to ever grace the planet. Trey was a VP of accounting and Eleanor's current flame.

"If they saw your face, they'll say I'm fucking you. I don't want that gossip spreading. I'd rather tell the world I'm marrying you."

He had the ring again. He'd plucked it from his pocket.

"You are not my secret."

She stared at the ring. "They didn't see my face." He'd been in front of her. Blocking her. Protecting her? The ring gleamed. She reached out for it.

And realized that Victor was holding his breath.

Her fingers paused in the air. "Why do you want to marry me?"

"Because *you're* everything I've ever wanted."

He was the only thing she did want. Melody took the ring. Slid it onto her finger. "How about that? A perfect fit."

"*Melody.*"

She eased out a breath. "I'm going home. I want you to follow. I want you to make love to me all night long. And I want you to tell me, over and over...how much you love me." There. Done. She'd said the words. Put it all out there. The ring was a light weight on her finger.

No more secrets.

She smoothed her hair. Nodded. "Don't keep me waiting." She brushed past him. Headed for the door. She couldn't face the big crowd again. Not that night. She wanted Victor. Away from everyone. No interruptions. No whispers.

She didn't look back as she left the boardroom. She retrieved her coat and her bag, and a fast elevator ride had her in the parking garage. Her fingers pressed the remote for her vehicle, and the lights flashed on her blue Benz. She slid inside. Pulled the door shut.

And then her shaking fingers curled around the steering wheel. Her gaze caught the ring. The beautiful, wonderful ring. Three diamonds. So gorgeous. *I am going to marry Victor. He is going to say that he loves me. We will be happy.* No matter what rumors she'd caught. No matter what the detective who'd come to see her a few weeks before had said, how he'd tried to make her fear Victor, no matter—

"Start the car."

Melody jumped because that rasping voice had just come from *the back seat of her vehicle.* She started to spin around.

But something pressed to her temple.

"This is a gun, Melody. I can blow your brains out here and now, or you can start the damn car."

Trembling, heart nearly bursting from her chest, she started the car. But her wild gaze swung toward the bank of elevators. She'd told Victor to follow her. He should be appearing. He would help her. He would—

"Victor sends his regards," the rasping voice told her. *"Drive the fucking car."*

❄

THE ELEVATOR DINGED. Cursing, Victor hurried out. He'd been delayed. He should have been in that parking garage much, much sooner, but Melody's dick of a stepbrother had held him up. Dario had jumped into his path. Demanded to know Victor's plans.

My plan is to go fuck your stepsister. Then to marry her. But he hadn't said those words. Too many eyes had been on them. Too many ears listening. So he'd bullshitted about the company. Developments. Expansions. Then he'd rushed the hell out of there.

Now he was in the garage, and automatically, he searched for the blue Benz. Melody's car.

Already gone.

His jaw locked. He marched forward, pulling out his own keys and hitting the button to unlock the sleek black car that waited.

He'd meet Melody at her place. He'd fuck her all night long. *While* she wore his ring. And tomorrow, they'd tell the world that they were getting married.

My dirty secret?

Hell, no, she was not. Far from it. She was the end game. Screw the business. Melody was his goal. She always had been, from the moment he'd met her. The woman had no idea that she was his obsession.

He drove to her place. Let himself in with the key she'd given him. He expected to find Melody waiting. Maybe naked. Oh, but a man could dream. Only...

She wasn't there.

An hour passed.

She didn't arrive.

He called her. She didn't pick up. He just got her voicemail. Over and over.

Over.

And...

Over.

THE TEXT CAME to him at six a.m. After a frantic night of looking for her, Melody finally contacted him.

Don't look for me. Her text message.

Not look? In what universe? He texted back, *Where the hell are you?*

But there was no response. No matter how many times he tried... *No. Response.*

Victor did not give up. He kept texting. *Melody. Where are you?* Fear and rage twisted inside of him. This couldn't be happening. Not now. Not when he was so very close to having her. To having everything he needed. He'd worked so hard. Things could not explode on him now. He'd been so careful. Always keeping his control. Hiding his darkest parts. Keeping his past secret. He'd tried to be perfect so that she would fall for him. So he could claim her.

When he stormed into her father's house, when he demanded to know where the fuck Melody had gone...

Victor learned that her father had also received a text.

I want to try something new. See you soon. Don't worry.

Seven days before Christmas. Melody Mage disappeared seven days before Christmas.

Victor called the cops. They came. Dutifully listened to him. But...there was no sign of foul play. A grown woman had decided to leave town for a bit. No big deal. Camera footage from the parking garage showed her entering her vehicle. Leaving alone. A street cam even picked her up, driving out of town.

The days passed. Christmas came. Went. Melody didn't return. It was as if she'd vanished from the face of the earth.

Victor hired PIs to find her. They turned up BS leads that led nowhere.

Victor lost his fucking mind.

And by the time everyone else realized the truth...that something very, very bad had happened to Melody Mage, it was far too late.

She was gone.

Chapter One

One year later...

He wasn't sure that he would be able to make it through the night without killing someone.

Victor Alexander held the wine glass in his hand, he stared at the glittering Christmas tree, and he heard the voices rising and falling around him. Laughter grated in his ears like nails on a chalkboard. Anger twisted in his gut as he thought about all of the ways that he could commit his murder. It would really be quite easy...

"She has to be dead," Dario Mage announced with a dramatic sigh. Not a Mage by birth, but by marriage. Though he'd taken on the last name as fast as possible. "I mean, come on, this is my sister we're talking about here..."

Actually, he was talking about his *stepsister*. An important distinction that the guy seemed to be missing. Though it was a distinction that Dario had made the time he tried to fuck Melody.

I hate the sonofabitch and his smug face. He'd be an easy

enough one to kill. Victor tried to ease his grip on the fragile wine glass. If he wasn't careful, he'd snap the stem.

These days, he just wasn't good at being careful. Or good at handling fragile things. Or, well, *good.* At all. Darkness had swallowed him whole, and only rage lived and breathed inside of him.

"Melody hasn't touched any of her bank accounts in the last year." Dario's voice kept right on grating. "The woman cannot survive without her expensive accessories."

Cannot survive.

Dario ambled toward the fireplace. Gas, not wood. The flames flickered and danced. "Not like she's taken up a lifestyle waiting tables some place. If she could have accessed the money, she would have done it." Dario braced his forearm against the mantel. His black hair was perfectly styled. Just like the trousers were perfectly pressed. The white shirt perfectly ironed. "We have to face facts. She isn't coming back."

A twitter of nervous laughter followed his pronouncement. Victor clenched his back teeth even as his gaze darted toward the source of that laughter.

Olivia Hatcher—Dario's current lover and Melody's one-time best friend—had bright patches of color staining her cheeks. Probably from the wine she'd been downing. At last count, she'd had three glasses.

Olivia weaved in her heels before announcing, "Just because she hasn't touched the money, it doesn't mean Melody is *dead.*" She beetled her eyebrows toward the quiet man sitting in the corner, Sebastian Mage.

Melody's father.

"Melody lived—*lives,*" Olivia hurriedly corrected, "for adventure. She probably found a new lover, hooked up with him, and for all we know, they're sunning it up in the south of France right now. She hasn't touched her money because she doesn't *need* it. You don't have to take a doom-and-gloom perspective."

Sebastian stared into the fire. "It's been a long time."

It had been one long-ass, painful year.

"My Melody was many things," Sebastian continued in his deep, but slightly shaking voice. "But she wasn't cruel." His fingers trembled slightly. The tremors had been getting worse lately. "She wouldn't vanish. Wouldn't just disappear without ever talking to me again." He shook his head. "No, something more is at play." His gaze slowly turned from the fire and landed on Victor. "You haven't said a word all night."

Because he hadn't wanted to be in that damn house. Everywhere he looked, Melody haunted him. Her picture was on the mantel. A smiling image of her at her college graduation.

He refused to look at that picture.

He was already feeling murderous enough. One fucking year had passed. A year where he'd been living with his heart cut out of his chest.

"Victor, do you think my Melody is dead?" Sebastian asked him.

He didn't want to answer that question. Because if he answered it, then there would be no going back. No more pretending. No more thinking that he'd turn around, and Melody would just *be there*. Smiling her mischievous grin, the one that made the dimple in her right cheek flash. Just the right cheek. She didn't have a dimple in the left. Her green eyes would sparkle. Her full lips would tempt him, and, just like that, he'd be wrapped around her little finger. Not that he could let her know. Not that he could say—

"Oh, come on," Dario scoffed. "Victor and Melody

barely tolerated each other. The man doesn't give a shit one way or the other, am I right? He's got the business. He's got plenty of money, and he has Melody out of his hair. Wins all around for him." Bitterness underscored every word.

The bastard had been drinking way too much. His mouth was too damn loose.

Victor was highly conscious of the drumming of his heartbeat as it echoed in his ears. He turned his attention to Dario. Let that attention linger.

Dario yanked his arm away from the mantel. "What? No need for the ferocious glare. I'm just stating the obvious. We all know the cops even interviewed you several times over the last year. You and Melody hated each other."

No, he had not hated her. But, yes, the cops had interviewed him. When they'd finally come around to the idea that Melody might not have vanished of her own accord, he'd been their chief suspect.

Even though *he'd* been the one trying to find her the hardest. He'd hired five different PIs over the last year. They'd turned up jack shit. A woman shouldn't vanish into thin air.

Definitely not my woman. She shouldn't have vanished. I should have kept her safe. Savagery beat beneath his surface. His control was far too thin these days. Probably because nothing mattered any longer. Nothing but finding the sonofabitch who'd taken Melody and putting the bastard in the ground.

"We have to face facts," Dario continued with a sage nod. "Time to sell her house. Time to change the will. Look, I've investigated. It takes five years to declare a person dead without a body. *Five years.* We're only on year one and I'm not so sure that..." A telling glance toward Sebastian's hunched figure. "I'm not so sure that everyone in this room has four more years left."

A sharp gasp from Olivia.

Dario had never been a tactful bastard. Mostly, he'd just been a whiny prick. One who'd always gotten on Victor's last nerve.

It truly would be easy to kill him.

A chime echoed in the house. Not really a house. A freaking mansion. A country *estate* outside of Richmond, Virginia. The chime meant another guest had arrived to join their party from hell.

Why in the world had Sebastian organized this horror show of a night? Especially with an impending snowstorm? But, oh, no, despite the weather reports, the guy had *insisted* that everyone show up. Said he had urgent matters to discuss.

This mansion was the last place Victor wanted to be. The snow had been falling heavily when he arrived, and, unfortunately, since the snowfall didn't seem to be letting up any, Victor knew they'd all probably be stuck in the house until morning. Fucking hell.

He'd be stuck with more memories of Melody everywhere he turned. As if her ghost didn't haunt him enough.

"Victor." Sebastian's weak voice. "Do you think my daughter is dead?"

He forced his back teeth to unclench. *Don't say it. Don't.* He'd held on to hope. At first, he'd been so sure there was a mistake. Melody couldn't really be gone. She'd planned to meet him at her house. She'd been wearing his ring. She'd...

The doorbell rang again.

Dario turned toward the sound, frowning. "Just how many people were invited out here this weekend?"

"Hatterson will answer," Sebastian waved away the ringing bell. He also didn't answer Dario's question. "Hatterson is on top of things like that."

Hatterson. The butler, assistant, guard—all of the above. He tended to constantly be lurking around. Yes, he'd get the door. If the visitor hadn't been invited, Hatterson would block access to the inner sanctum. Hatterson always got rid of problems. Snowstorm or not.

"*Victor.*" Sebastian's voice was stronger than it had been in ages. Maybe the new medication was helping him. "Do you believe my daughter is dead?"

Is that why Sebastian had called for this little gathering? Maybe he was finally going to give in to Dario's urging and change the family will. *Yeah, right. Good luck with that.*

Victor lifted the wine glass to his lips. Barely tasted the two-hundred-dollar-a-bottle wine that had come from some lush vineyard somewhere in France. Then he said the words that he knew would haunt him forever, "Yes, Melody is dead. Probably fucking buried somewhere." *I will find the sonofabitch who took her from me. Even if it's the last thing I do, and I will bury him. But first, I will make him hurt. I will make him bleed. I will make him beg.* "So we have to stop expecting her to show up." He had to stop expecting to just turn around and see her. She was never going to walk in a room again and flash her dimpled smile his way. Her green eyes weren't going to light up when she looked at him. "I'm sorry, Sebastian." Each word tore from him. "But Melody is never coming home again."

Never.

And it was time for him to accept that stark truth, too.

Damn...but he really wanted to murder someone. *And I*

will. As soon as I find the bastard who took my Melody away, I will murder him.

SHE RANG the doorbell for a third time as she stood on the stone porch, with snowflakes swirling around her. The wind kept kicking up and tossing them her way. Every breath she took had a little patch of white fog appearing in front of her mouth because it was positively frigid outside.

Would it *kill* the people in the giant *mansion* to open a door when they had a visitor? She was just about to go for ring number four when the door finally flew open.

She pasted a bright smile on her face. "Thank goodness!"

The man in the doorway—silver threading through his hair, a neatly trimmed beard on his face—blinked at her.

She barreled inside before he could speak. "I was turning into a popsicle outside." Snow fell onto the floor as she stomped her boots. Then she hauled off her coat and put it on the rack near the door. A battered wool coat she'd picked up from a thrift shop. She loved that coat. It had kept her warm on plenty of cold nights. More snowflakes sprinkled down onto the floor, though they quickly melted in the warm room. Voices rose and fell from a room down the hallway, drawing her attention. "Is that where everyone is?"

He didn't speak. Just stared. Kinda gaped.

"Right." She flashed another broad smile at him. "I'll just go greet them, shall I? Could you do me a major favor and bring in my bag? It's on the porch. Thanks so much."

She didn't give him a chance to respond. Hopefully, the bag grabbing would keep him busy.

Her steps double-timed it as she hurried down the narrow hallway. She didn't glance inside the room to the right. *The library.* Or look up at the massive staircase. Her gaze remained directed dead ahead.

"Eventually, a body will be discovered." A man's deep, rumbling voice.

She shivered and tried to pretend the shiver was just from the walk through all the snow. Her worn boots hadn't exactly protected her feet. Her toes felt icy. Come to think of it, her entire body seemed to be encased in ice. *Because I am terrified.*

"Melody is gone," that voice continued, making her heart twist, "and she's not coming back."

For just a moment, she paused on the threshold of the room. A big, too-fancy room with lots of leather furniture, a crackling fireplace, and a tree that had every single limb decorated. She sucked in a deep breath and then... "Merry Christmas, everyone," she announced.

Every eye in the room was immediately on her.

Shock came first.

Some jaws dropped.

Shock, horror and...

Glass shattered.

Her gaze followed the sound. She saw that the big man to the right—the man who'd been standing near the elaborately decorated Christmas tree—had just broken the wine glass he held. As their gazes collided, she could have sworn an electric shock whipped through her blood.

Victor Alexander. She knew him by sight, thanks to her careful research. The man who'd worked as Sebastian Mage's protégé. The man who had taken over the company. The man who—

Was rushing toward her. Staring at her with glittering

eyes. With a handsome face that seemed to have been carved from granite. Shock. Rage. Desire? So many emotions flashed in his eyes and on his face as he reached out to her with his big hands.

And she realized…"You have blood on your hands."

His dark eyes widened.

Then he looked at his hands. Or, rather, at his right hand. The one that had held the wine glass before it shattered.

She locked her knees. The urge to turn and flee was nearly overwhelming. But…

"Melody!" Sebastian Mage rose to his feet. Almost fell but caught himself. "Melody…my God!" He gaped at her, as if she had to be a ghost.

Fair enough, considering that was exactly what she was.

Melody Mage smiled at her father. Then she let that smile sweep to the others in the room. "Hello, everyone. Guess who's back?"

Silence greeted her.

"The Ghost of Christmas Past," she said into that silence. *And this ghost is here to wreck your world.*

Ho. Ho. Ho.

Chapter Two

A DRAMATIC ENTRANCE HAD SEEMED LIKE THE BEST approach. But, wow, it sure had been hard to pull off.

Four hours later, Melody paced the confines of the guest room that she'd been given at the Mage Mansion. Yes, that was how she thought of the place. *Mage Mansion.* Not home, because it wasn't home to her. The whole place felt intimidating. Scary.

Everything about the room she'd been given was fancy—and cold. Paintings on the wall that held no soul. A million pillows artfully arranged on a big, white bed. A settee. White, wood furniture. Kinda looked like it had all come straight from some decorating website.

A completely alien environment.

But a place that was supposed to be part of *her* world.

"Where were you?"

"Why didn't you call?"

"Why didn't you text?"

"You vanished!"

"How could you be so heartless? You abandoned your family! You abandoned everyone who loved you!"

She'd expected all of the questions. And even the anger. The accusations. After all, there had to be confusion and rage from her family.

As for the questions, she'd had answers ready. She'd spent plenty of time rehearsing her responses.

I had to get away. Please understand, I needed time on my own. I regret that I caused any concern...

Such utter bullshit. She didn't think they'd bought her words. And that was fair, because the words had not been the truth.

Not. At. All.

Everything she'd said that night had been a lie. From the minute that she'd walked into the house, it had been one giant lie after another.

Her arms wrapped around her body. She rocked forward. "You can do this," she whispered. More like, *you have to do this.* Because there wasn't any choice. The game had started, and she had to finish it, no matter the cost.

She hadn't expected Sebastian Mage to look so...fragile. In the photos she'd seen online, he'd been robust. Almost larger than life. In that den, though, he'd been too thin. His body shaking. Too pale. She'd wanted to run to him. To wrap her arms around him and say—

A door opened. One to the left. It squeaked and sent her heart racing into a panic as it swung open and a big, shadowy form filled the doorway. A doorway that connected to the guest room next door, not to the hallway.

She hadn't thought anyone was in that room. But now the big, dark shadow was moving toward her, and Melody didn't believe that screaming would do any good. Too many people in the home were out for her blood. Her hands fell as she automatically took a step back.

"Where the fuck were you?"

Victor. Victor Alexander was in her room. He shut the door behind him. *Click.* He glared at her. Seemed even bigger. If Sebastian Mage had been smaller than she anticipated, then Victor—he was a whole lot *more* than she'd expected. Taller. Stronger. More...savage. His eyes glinted and held an icy darkness that seemed to pierce straight to her soul.

Victor wore dress pants. Gleaming shoes. A white dress shirt. No coat. No tie. The top buttons on his shirt had been yanked open while his sleeves rolled up to reveal powerful forearms.

Hatterson had brought her coat into the room. Her coat and her bag. Automatically, she inched toward that coat. It had been tossed onto the foot of the bed. She'd done the tossing. Her fingers grabbed for the coat, and her hand slipped into the front pocket.

"Where the fuck were you?" Again, same question. Lethal intensity.

Her breath shuddered out. She turned toward him, and at the same time, Melody tucked her hands behind her back. "I don't remember inviting you into my room."

"I don't need a fucking invitation."

She cleared her throat. "You say 'fuck' a lot."

He blinked.

"And I'm pretty sure you do need an invitation." Melody kept her chin up. "You can't just burst into a woman's bedroom without asking. That's not done."

He stalked toward her. *Stalked.* The only way to describe his movements. His hands were clenched at his sides in powerful fists. Tension held his body in a fierce grip. A muscle flexed along what was a very strong and square jaw as he closed in on her.

She didn't retreat. Mostly because the bed was behind

her. But fear bloomed in her heart. She didn't know this man. Couldn't predict what he might do next. Her research had indicated he would be a dangerous adversary.

How dangerous? What will you do to me, Victor Alexander? Or, better question...What have you already done?

He stopped right in front of her.

Her head tipped back. The better to stare up at him. Into the darkness of his eyes. He was a brutally handsome man. Emphasis on the brutal part. All hard edges and angles. No softness at all. Thick, almost jet-black hair. Strong nose. Sharp cheekbones. And that hard, clenched jaw...

"You think I'm going to buy that you just had to get *away?*"

She wet her lips.

His gaze locked on her mouth.

"A lot was happening," she murmured. "You'd gotten control over the company..."

He growled.

"I-I needed to find my place. I had to go—"

"Find your *place?* Your place? You had a place! That makes no fucking sense." He reached for her. Caught himself. His hands lingered in the air. She'd been wrong before, when she thought that he'd cut his hand on the broken wine glass. That had just been dark, red wine on his skin. Not blood.

She could not breathe because Victor stared at her as if he'd very much like to commit murder. *Is it going to be this easy? Will he just admit the truth?* This easy...or this crazy. Because she was alone in the opulent room with him. And he was so much bigger than she was. Could he kill her before she could even cry out for help?

"You had to go...away from me?" Victor bit out.

She didn't move. "Why are you in my room right now?" *Do not show fear. Do not.*

"Oh, I don't know, Melody, maybe because I've spent the last year of my life tearing the world apart *looking* for you? Could that possibly be it?"

Her heart raced even faster. She was surprised that he couldn't hear its frantic beat. The hard pounding certainly echoed in her own ears. "You looked for me?" He'd just stunned her.

"A slew of private investigators couldn't find you."

Probably because they'd been looking in the wrong places.

"No trace. That's what they turned up. *Nothing.* False leads and bullshit. You drove away, and you weren't found."

Her lips pressed together.

He growled. An animalistic sound. His gaze slowly rose to pin her eyes. "You left *me.*"

"Uh, newsflash." She needed to be aggressive. Sharp. Melody had never been a pushover, or at least, she didn't think she had been. "I left everyone. I hardly see why my dad's business partner or protégé or whatever you want to call yourself—I hardly see why you'd get your silk boxers twisted up over me taking some time to go out and have myself some fun."

The last year had not been fun. The last year had been a nonstop nightmare. But she had a role to play, and she was going to play that role to perfection.

Melody Mage had been a bored socialite. Always flitting from one bit of drama to the next. She'd loved the high life. She'd been self-absorbed. She'd partied with rock stars. She'd dated artists. She'd caused havoc and mayhem, and her own father had long since sworn she'd never get her hands on the family business. Or at least, those had been the stories flashed online so frequently.

In other words, Melody Mage had been...*someone I don't know. Someone I don't understand.* A woman with her face. Her body. But someone she only knew through online research. Research she'd started after bits and pieces of the past had begun to flit through her mind. For a while, there'd been nothing in her mind when she tried to focus on the past. Nothing but darkness and fear and screams.

Then she'd begun to have flashes of...more.

"You hardly see..." Victor blinked. Stared at her as if she had two heads. "You thought I wouldn't look for you?"

From what she'd seen, no one had looked. Was she supposed to just buy his story about the PIs? "There were no major news reports about me vanishing. Clearly, you knew I wanted time for myself."

"I got the fucking text, Melody."

Her heart slammed into her ribs. "There's that word again. You are naughty, aren't you? Guess you just have a very dirty mouth."

"Don't look for me."

Her body jerked.

"That's all you told me. One text. In a year. Then your phone was turned off a day later. It never turned back on. Not in a whole year."

Goosebumps rose on her body. It was so cold in that room. Cold in the house. Cold outside the house. She could hear the roaring of the wind. Heaving and twisting. With the news of the heavy snowfall, she'd almost canceled her plans. Almost turned tail and run away at the last moment. But...then she'd seen Victor arrive at the house.

Yes, I was watching outside. I saw you arrive, Victor. I

shivered in the cold, and I hid and I watched you and Dario and Olivia. She knew the players in this game.

"Where is your phone, Melody?"

Excellent question. She had no idea. "I...threw it away."

His left hand reached out. This time, he touched her. His fingers slid beneath her chin, tipping her head up even more, and she didn't expect the charge of absolute heat to flood through her body at his touch. But it did. So much heat. A sensual electricity flooded her veins, and she was suddenly, completely terrified.

Because he stared at her as if...as if...

"You threw it away?" Victor breathed. "The same way you threw *me* away?"

This wasn't what she'd anticipated, not at all. His rage was a palpable force in the bedroom. Rage and something more. So much more.

"I was ready to kill for you," he told her.

What? Terror crashed through her body, driving away the strange warmth that had filled her with the brush of his fingers against her skin. Now those fingers—now his strength—frightened her to the marrow of her bones.

"And you threw me away? Threw us away?" A hard, negative shake of his head. "It doesn't work that way, Melody. *You have to give me more than that.* You *will* give me more than that or by God—"

Her hands flew between them. "I need you to back up, right now." Fear made her words quiver.

His dark brows snapped together. He looked down, between their bodies. Blinked. "Melody." Softer. "Is that a knife in your hand?"

It was. Her fingers clenched tightly around the handle. She'd snagged the knife from the pocket of her coat. She wasn't stabbing him, she was *not*. But the blade pressed roughly over his heart. "I didn't give you permission to touch me."

"I didn't give you permission to pull a knife on me." No emotion at all in his voice now.

"You broke into my room."

"I opened a door."

"A door I'd locked." As if she would have left any doors unlocked in this house.

"I had the key." A pause. "Fine. That's a lie. I picked the lock."

Her mouth was desert dry. So much about Victor Alexander's life had been a mystery. Too many blank spaces when she tried to dig deeper past the faint details she'd unearthed. Details that had seemed too perfect. "You picked the lock," she whispered. "Just where would a fancy lawyer-slash-MBA type like yourself learn such a skill?"

If possible, his eyes narrowed even more. "Just where would a pampered princess like yourself—born with a silver spoon in her mouth and a staff at her beck and call—have learned to hide a knife *and* to pull it so easily on a...friend?"

She did not lower her knife. "Are you my friend?"

His lashes, oddly thick and so dark, flickered. "What else could I possibly be?"

"My enemy." An immediate reply. "Everyone knows we hate each other. Common knowledge. You stole my father's company from me."

He took a step back. Shook his head. A faint furrow remained between his brows. "Common...knowledge," he muttered.

Why were they just repeating each other?

"I'm not your friend. I'm your enemy. Nothing more." Victor nodded. A steely mask had covered his face. No emotion showed at all. "Strawberries."

She was utterly and completely lost. She was also just holding a knife in the air because he'd moved so far back that the blade no longer touched him. She should lower the weapon. "Why on earth are you talking to me about strawberries?"

"Why, indeed?" Hard. No, brittle.

Melody lowered the knife. "I was just defending myself."

"From your enemy. Right. Heard it the first time." He turned away from her.

She thought that he'd stalk from the room. He didn't. Victor began to prowl around. Very much like an angry lion. Meanwhile, Melody just stood there, still gripping her knife, uncertain what to do or say.

He eyed the bag near the door. A slightly battered, black, luggage bag that she'd picked up at the same thrift store where she'd gotten her coat. His shoulders tensed as he stared at the bag. Then, slowly, he glanced over his shoulder to peer at her. "Your hair is different."

Should she put the knife down on the bed? She was afraid to let go of her weapon. Trusting anyone in this house would be a major mistake.

They don't care about me. None of them do.

"It's so much shorter than it was before," he noted.

Not like she'd had much choice on that.

"The cut suits you, of course. Everything always suits you." He turned fully toward her. His gaze raked over her body. "You've lost weight. That I don't love."

"I don't care." Why in the world was he criticizing her appearance? She'd taken special care with her damn appearance before coming to the Mage Mansion. She'd found designer jeans at a secondhand shop. A soft, white sweater. She looked wealthy enough, didn't she? Her boots were a bit scuffed, but she'd done her best to polish them.

"You're at least ten pounds lighter, and you didn't have the weight to lose in the first place." He stalked toward her. Yep, stalking again. His stare rose over her, inch by slow inch, until he was carefully assessing her face. "Sharper."

What was sharper?

"Could be from the weight loss." His head tilted. "But something else is...slightly different."

Yes, something else was slightly different. Her left cheek bone had been fractured. Her nose broken. The doctors had patched her up, and she thought they'd done a very good job. When she looked at the pictures, she truly did look like Melody Mage. *Almost* an exact match.

Victor stopped right in front of her and ignored the knife that she still gripped. He reached toward her face.

Automatically, she lifted the knife, as if bracing for an attack.

"Have fun with that," he told her, voice flippant and mocking. "My heart has already been carved out once by you. By all means, feel free to do it again." Instead of touching her face, his hand dropped, quickly, and his fingers curled around her wrist. He hauled her hand up and forced the tip of the blade against his shirt-front, right over his heart. "Want me to help?"

Her breath heaved out. "Let me go." Was he crazy?

"No. I'm never fucking doing that again. You'll be lucky if I don't *chain* you to my side. Handcuff you. Wherever you go, I go. You will *never* get away again."

He was pushing her hand against him too hard. If he wasn't careful, she'd cut him with the blade. "Stop."

He didn't.

"Stop, or you'll be bleeding! I-I don't want to hurt you."

"How the fuck do you think I felt when you left me before?"

Her eyes widened at the savage pain that suddenly flashed on his face.

"Oh, sorry." A mocking smile curled his lips. That smile never reached the darkness of his eyes. "Am I cursing too *fucking* much for you? Since when did you become such a prude?"

"I—" She stopped. She was playing this scene wrong. Melody Mage wasn't a prude. Far from it. There were even rumors that a sex tape of Melody had once been about to leak, only for the tape to vanish.

Just like I vanished?

"You look different. You *act* different." His hold on her wrist sent heat streaking though her. "What else is different about you? After the year from hell, what else is different? I am dying to know."

Everything. She wanted to say that. To admit that everything was different and that it would never, ever be the same again. That she would never be the same.

"Let's find out what's different," Victor growled. Then his head lowered and his mouth crashed down onto hers.

Chapter Three

She had a knife pressed over his heart. Fair enough. His heart belonged to her, so if she wanted to cut it out while it still freaking beat, that was her prerogative.

Melody is back. Melody is back. He couldn't believe it. Was half convinced that she truly was a ghost. Or maybe he'd just lost the last bit of his sanity, and he was imagining her. He'd finally gone that far off the deep end.

But, no, he wasn't lost to madness. She was real. He could *feel* her. He could also feel the edge of her blade as it cut through his shirt and pushed into his skin.

Melody is back.

She'd rang the doorbell at the mansion. Walked inside the den with snowflakes still visible in the darkness of her hair. Her much shorter hair. Hair that used to tumble halfway down her back but now skimmed her jawline. Her heart-shaped face was thinner, her cheekbones seeming sharper. As crazy as it seemed, even *higher*. The shorter hair made her green eyes appear bigger. Deeper. And there was just something...*different*. Off.

But his body didn't care about something being off. He

responded to her. Melody. His Melody. Back. A heavy, aching arousal flooded through him, and, who cared if she had a knife pressed to his chest? He was going to kiss her. He was going to taste her. He was going to have his Melody back in his arms again, and if this whole night turned out to be some twisted hallucination, then so be it.

So the fuck be it.

There I go again, cursing even in my fucking head.

His mouth took hers. Her lips were soft beneath his. She gave a little gasp. Stiffened. His tongue swept inside her mouth, and, damn, but he'd missed her. Missed her taste and the wildfire of desire they could always ignite when they kissed. The way they'd go from zero to one hundred miles an hour, and she'd moan and arch into him and he'd have her naked and coming for him in about two minutes flat—

The knife pressed harder into his chest. A quick flash of pain.

In the next instant, Melody shoved him away. "What in the world are you doing?"

He looked down at his chest. There was a drop of red blood on his white shirt. The blade had broken his skin.

"Oh, no." A frantic shake of her head as she, too, saw the blood. "I cut you. I'm sorry! I-I didn't mean—"

"You didn't kiss me back." His heart was leaden in his chest.

She still gripped the knife. "Why would you kiss me?"

"Why?" Victor ignored the blood.

"You hate me." She looked around the room, seemingly confused. "You hate me. Everyone knows...and you come in here to kiss me?"

He'd come in there to fuck her. To reclaim his *fiancée*. Except Melody was staring at him like he was insane.

His spine snapped straight. His shoulders rolled back. "Strawberries."

"Why do you keep saying that? There are no strawberries in here. If you want some, I'd suggest you check the kitchen." Her nose scrunched. "I think you need to leave my room. Now." Her voice cracked a bit around the edges of what should have been a hard order.

"Where were you for the last year?" His nostrils flared. Melody had always smelled like a blend of champagne and vanilla. With a hint of honeysuckle. Her signature fragrance. She'd had the special perfume imported from Paris.

She...didn't smell like champagne and vanilla. No trace of honeysuckle. She smelled crisp. Clean. Maybe she carried the faintest scent of jasmine.

"Traveling." A vague reply from her. "I was taking time for myself. Clearing my head."

Utter bullshit. "You didn't contact your family once. Your father has been sick." Sebastian Mage's condition was far worse than most people knew. Tonight had been one of his good nights. A very, very good night.

Most nights—and days—weren't so good. Some of them were pure nightmares.

Melody flinched. "I...didn't know that he was ill. It wasn't in any news reports."

He was sick before you left, Melody. It's the whole reason I finally took over the company. How the fuck could you not know that about Sebastian? How the—

He stopped the thought. Studied her again. The shorter hair. The thinner body. The cheeks that were far hollower and more pronounced than he'd ever seen before. Melody, but...different. He just hadn't quite realized how different.

Why would she need to check the news to learn about

her father's illness? She'd gone with Sebastian to all of the original doctors' visits. She *knew* what was wrong with Sebastian. Another reason why her disappearance hadn't made sense. Despite her issues with her father—and there were certainly plenty of issues—Victor had never thought that Melody would leave Sebastian in his time of need.

Not willingly.

The rest of the world might have believed that Melody Mage was spoiled. Fickle. Narcissistic. But Victor had known the real woman.

No one's heart had been as big as Melody's. On her own, with zero help from her family, she'd created two shelters for women and abused children. She'd opened two food pantries. She'd stopped for every lost dog she'd seen in the road. Been constantly fostering animals as she found them the perfect home.

It was only those who didn't truly know her who believed Melody was cold and uncaring.

"Why are you looking at me like that?" Her right hand gripped the knife.

Melody had hated knives. Mostly because, a few years ago, she'd been mugged. The bastard who'd slashed her bag right off her shoulder had cut her with his blade. She'd been bleeding in the street.

She'd called Victor to help her.

He'd gotten her stitched up. He'd made sure the mugger was handled. In other words, he'd beaten the hell out of the bastard. No one hurt Melody on his watch. Not ever.

"Do you mind taking off your sweater?" Victor asked, and he thought it was a very polite question. Especially since he was feeling far from polite. In fact, he was holding onto his control by a thread.

"Are you quite insane?" Melody returned as her eyes

widened. "Yes, I one hundred percent mind. I'm not about to take off my top for you! Get *out*. I don't know what you think is going to happen here, but you're clearly confused."

He nodded. Yes, he had been confused. *I needed Melody back.* "Just wanted to check. Make sure you still had the scar. About two inches long, faint, along your right shoulder, pointing toward your collarbone."

She wet her lower lip. "I'm not taking off my sweater for you."

Another nod. "Fair enough. I do apologize if I frightened you." It would be simple enough for her to pull her top to the side and show him the scar. To prove such a simple thing existed on her body.

But she made no move to reveal the scar that she should possess. Instead, her chin notched up even more. "It's normal to be frightened when a stranger breaks into your bedroom. Even if it *is* a guest bedroom."

A stranger. Yes. That was what he appeared to be. Before he did something that he would regret, Victor needed to get out of that bedroom. "Be sure and lock up after me."

"Don't worry, I will. Though a lock hardly prevented your entrance the first time, now, did it?"

No, it had not. Victor turned on his heel. Marched for the connecting door.

"Why did you kiss me?"

The question cut right through him. But it shouldn't have. The answer was really quite obvious. "Because I thought you were someone else."

She gasped.

He opened the connecting door. Strode forward. Shut the door behind him with a soft click. He pulled in a deep breath. Then one more. With determined steps, he crossed the guest room he'd taken for the night. Screw the snowstorm. He would have driven right through it in order to get home, if *she* hadn't been there. But she had been. Melody Mage had walked out of the snowy night, and everything had changed.

He yanked off the cut shirt. A small cut from the tip of her knife. There were drops of blood on the garment, so he threw it to the side and hauled a fresh, white, dress shirt from his bag. A bag he always kept in his car, just in case. Then Victor exited his room. Hurried for the staircase. His feet thudded down the stairs. At the landing, with no hesitation, he turned and advanced for the den. He threw open the door. The little group was still there. Waiting.

Dario, drinking and glaring near the fireplace.

Olivia, pacing near the Christmas tree.

Sebastian, still hunched in his chair.

Sebastian's nurse, Tracy Ryder, had joined the group. She hovered near Sebastian, faint worry on her face.

Even Hatterson lurked nearby, twisting his hands in front of his big body.

All eyes locked on Victor.

"Well?" Dario bit out.

Victor's fingers curled too tightly around the doorknob. "We need a DNA test. Immediately."

Dario's breath expelled in a rush. "I told you, I *told* you all! I don't think that's Melody. She looks different. She acts different."

Yes, she did. She looked different. Small differences. She acted differently. Big differences. She'd called him her enemy. A stranger. She hadn't kissed him. Had seemed shocked that he'd ever want to kiss her.

She'd refused to show him her scar.

"I know my daughter." Sebastian was adamant. "That's *her.*"

Victor wanted it to be. He did. But... "DNA test. There's too much money on the line. You can't just accept her into this house without proof." But he didn't really mean *into this house.* He meant...*You can't accept her into the family. We can't bring her into our lives.*

I can't—

"She is Melody!" Veins bulged in Sebastian's forehead.

Was she Melody? Or was she just a very carefully produced look-alike? "She wanted to know when you got sick," he told Sebastian.

Sebastian's lips parted. He didn't speak.

"When I questioned her, she said she didn't know about your illness. That it wasn't in the news."

"Well, of course, it's not in the news," Dario muttered. He slammed down a shot glass. It clinked when it hit the mantel top. No more wine for him. He'd advanced to the whiskey. "We're keeping it secret from the Press. Had mergers to deal with. Millions of dollars were on the line. Can't let the info leak because then you'll have panicked investors and—"

Victor just stared at him.

"Oh." Dario nodded. Cleared his throat. "She should know. Right. Yes. Understood. Check."

Considering that Melody was the one who'd first noticed the small signs that indicated Sebastian's condition, yes, she should know.

But she didn't.

Just as she didn't seem to know that she and Victor had been lovers.

Just as she didn't know the meaning of *strawberries.* That had been their codeword. If they'd been at a party or a company meeting and she'd wanted to leave, she'd brush by him and whisper, "*Strawberries.*"

Or, if others had been present and she'd been in the mood to torment him, she'd make up some vague statement and say it right in front of everyone. Something like... "You know what would make this dessert extra decadent?" She'd stare at him with her incredible eyes. "Strawberries." And he'd known she wanted to get away with him. That she wanted to be in private with him so they could close out the rest of the world.

So that they could fuck like animals and get lost to pleasure.

But the woman upstairs had seemed clueless when he uttered the one word that Melody had relished using so often with him. *Their* private codeword.

She hadn't known what the word truly meant.

She hadn't known her father was sick.

She hadn't known that she and Victor were lovers.

Not Melody. Not Melody. Not Melody. The refrain blasted through his head. Made the hope he'd felt earlier taste bitter on his tongue. *She is not my Melody.*

And that posed another big question. If the woman currently in the guest room right above him wasn't Melody Mage, then who the hell was she?

Chapter Four

She'd made a tactical mistake. Melody could feel it in her bones. She'd heard Victor open his bedroom door and then storm downstairs. It wasn't as if the man had quiet footsteps. He just pounded and pounded down the steps with an angry stomp.

She'd tiptoed out after him. Not like she wanted to alert the man to her presence, but she knew trouble when she heard it. Especially when that trouble stomped so furiously.

So she ditched her boots and socks and slipped down the stairs barefoot. She crept toward the den. Stayed out of sight and quite clearly heard the words that chilled her.

"We need a DNA test. Immediately." Victor's rough, angry voice.

Followed by Dario's, "I told you, I *told* you all! I don't think that's Melody. She looks different. She acts different."

Her heart nearly jumped from her chest. The very first night, and already, they were ready to kick her out of their world. What were they going to do? Toss her into the snow? Let her freeze in the darkness?

She'd hired a driver to bring her to the mansion. A

deliberate choice because, well, one, she didn't have a car. And, two, because she hadn't wanted the people in the mansion tracking her back to where she'd been staying before tonight. *No sense in them learning I arrived in Richmond three days ago and have been staying at the shadiest no-tell-motel imaginable.* At night, she dragged the old chair beneath the door in her motel room and lodged it in place for a bit of extra security.

Now, though, she was at Mage Mansion and left with a big problem. If they kicked her out—

No, no, that can't happen.

She had to stay. She had a job to do. A mission. And she wasn't going to be thrown off *or* out. Her original plan had been tricky, yes, but she could change gears. She could do this.

She just had to figure out her next step.

Except, in that instant, her next step came charging toward her. Victor rushed out of the den and stormed straight toward her.

"Thought I heard you," he rumbled in the deep and dark voice that seemed to sink straight through her. Anger flashed in his eyes, igniting the darkness and stealing her breath. Victor was intimidating and dangerous, and he'd kissed her like he'd been starving for her. Something that made no sense. None at all.

But, evidently, Victor was the one in control at the mansion. Not Sebastian. Not Dario. *Victor.* The others seemed to follow his commands. And if she wanted to stay...

Then Victor had to be on her side.

Hell. She grabbed the bottom of her sweater, and she lifted it up. She yanked the sweater over her head and dropped it to the floor. "I have the scar." Her hand gestured toward her right shoulder. "Happy now?"

His eyes widened. Then they dropped—they dropped to her right shoulder. To the curve where a faded, white line cut across her skin. The scar on her shoulder pointed toward her collar bone.

But his gaze didn't stop on her collar bone. Instead, that dark gaze of his went down...down to the long scar that cut across her stomach. A slash that wasn't quite as faded as the one on her shoulder because it was far more recent.

"What in the fuck..." Victor began.

"Hey!" A shout from behind him. Dario. "What's happening?" The shuffle of footsteps. Then he was shoving his head—followed by his whole body—out of the doorway. "Holy shit, is she stripping?"

A growl broke from Victor even as he surged toward Melody. His arms wrapped around her, and he hauled her forward, shielding her with his body. Curling himself around her. "Get the fuck back inside!" Victor blasted.

"You love that word," she murmured, even as a shiver skated over her. "I think *fuck* must be your favorite."

He said it again, and she wondered if he'd done it just for her, but then he was yanking off *his* shirt. Shoving her arms into it. Buttoning it crookedly and then, *what in the world?*

Victor lifted her into his arms. Started carrying her back toward the staircase.

"What is happening?" Dario yelled after them. "You tossing her out?"

Fear coiled within her. "Don't." A breath. "Please."

"You're not going any fucking place. You'll stay here. You'll stay *with me.*"

Aw, he'd said the fucking magic word again.

Then, louder, Victor announced, "I'm taking Melody back to bed. She's tired, and she's confused."

She was tired. She was not confused. Well, maybe a bit. *Why do I feel so strange each time Victor touches me?*

"Tell everyone to get to bed!" Another command from Victor as he mounted the stairs. Mounted them carrying her and the man wasn't even slightly out of breath. "We'll talk in the morning."

"Shouldn't you be kicking her ass out?" Dario's steps followed them.

Victor stopped midway up the staircase. His gaze fell to collide with hers.

Melody held her breath.

"She's not going anywhere," Victor said, and the words were a vow.

Her arm lifted and curled around his neck. It was a tentative movement, one mostly borne out of fear because she worried that he might drop her. But at her touch, he stiffened. His hold became even stronger, even more determined, and then he was double-timing it up the rest of the stairs with her. He didn't stop, not until they were back in her guest room. He kicked the door shut behind them. Stood just beyond the threshold with her in his arms.

His shirt felt soft against her skin. It carried his scent. Masculine. Woodsy. Her nostrils flared as she drank in that scent. There was something familiar about it. Comforting? Her head tilted a bit closer to him. She *almost* put her head on his shoulder, but stopped at the last second. He wasn't some sort of safe port for her.

What on earth was she thinking? He was dangerous. Everyone in that massive house was dangerous. She couldn't trust any of the people there.

Melody cleared her throat. "Are you satisfied now?"

"This is not my fucking satisfied face."

She peeked up at him. Nope, he did not look satisfied. Far from it.

"Though you do know that face."

Uh, oh. Yep, this was what she'd feared. After that kiss, after the way he'd looked at her. Even the fiercely possessive touch of his hands as he covered her in his shirt...All of that info pointed to one undeniable conclusion. Melody swallowed. "We're lovers?" The question came out husky and breathless.

And, crap, she'd made another mistake. Her words had definitely sounded like a question. She tried again. "We're lovers." There. More definite. Maybe?

A muscle jerked along his jaw. He strode across the room. Headed straight for the bed. She expected him to drop her on top of it. Instead, he gently lowered her onto the soft bedding. Victor didn't let go right away. His hands lingered.

She felt that linger in every inch of her body. Heat and electricity surged through her. A touch truly should not impact her so strongly. Yet, his did. Then again, it had really been one hell of a day.

A week.

A month.

A real nightmare of a year.

He finally let her go. Straightened, but didn't back away from the bed. "How the fuck did you get that scar on your stomach?"

She gave a little eye roll as she sat up and swung her legs to the side of the bed. Melody didn't rise. Instead, she perched on the edge of the mattress and peered up at him. A variety of potential responses spun through her mind, but Melody finally settled on, "It takes a lot to satisfy you, doesn't it? I mean, one moment, you're demanding I take off my shirt. I do it, only for you to immediately cover me up in *your* shirt."

"I didn't want that dumbass Dario staring at your chest!"

She'd been wearing a bra. Still was. A plain, white bra beneath his white dress shirt. "I don't think my *brother* was going to be overwhelmed by seeing—"

"Stepbrother, sweetheart. He's your freaking stepbrother, and he's been obsessed with you for years. No sense waving a red flag at the bull, not unless you want me to beat the shit out of him."

Tension slithered down her spine. Victor had just revealed two very important things to her.

First...*sweetheart*. He'd called her sweetheart. And his voice had deepened even more and hitched with possessiveness when he dropped the endearment. You didn't call your enemy *sweetheart* in quite that tone. Did you?

And second...*What. The. Hell?* Dario was obsessed with her? Her stepbrother?

"But you didn't know that." Victor nodded, as if he'd just had a confirmation that he actually expected. "Just like you don't know how you got that scar on your shoulder, am I right?"

She needed to bluff. Immediately. "I got it from a knife."

One dark eyebrow quirked.

"The *blade* of a knife," she added. "A long time ago. Accidents happen."

"It was no *fucking* accident. You were mugged. You'd just started that food pantry on West Lake, and you were coming home too damn late at night. You were mugged. The prick cut your purse strap and took the bag right off you. You were bleeding and scared, and you ran into a gas station, and you called me to come and get you."

She'd called him? "Why would I call you?"

He blinked. Those dark eyes—obsidian. She knew the color because she'd been in a souvenir shop not too long ago, and she'd seen a chunk of obsidian for sale. She'd reached out and touched the black rock. It had felt smooth and strong beneath her fingertips. She'd stared and stared at it, even as the sales clerk had come by and started telling her that obsidian was a volcanic rock. It was supposed to offer protection. Truth. Some believed it even shielded its carrier against negative energy. She'd bought the small rock. Been drawn to it by a pull of familiarity that had seemed overwhelming.

She often kept it tucked in a pocket. When she was nervous or stressed, she'd reach for it.

The rock was currently in her bag, near the door. Her knife was in that bag, too. She'd shoved it in the bag before hurrying down the stairs.

Victor's eyes were obsidian. Nearly a perfect match for the rock.

Nervous, her hands reached for the buttons on his shirt. The incorrectly matched buttons and holes. She began to undo the wrong buttons.

His hand flew out and stopped her, mid-button.

She sighed. A long, put upon sigh. "One minute, you're telling me to take off my shirt. Now you're trying to stop me from properly buttoning up?" She could feel the roughness on the tips of his fingers. Calluses. "You need to make up your mind." She should probably go downstairs and get the sweater she'd left behind. Not like she wanted to lose that garment. It had been a lucky find.

"The scar on your stomach is new."

"I think I left *my* sweater downstairs."

"How the—"

"Fuck did I get the second scar?" she broke in, knowing those were the exact words he'd intended to utter.

Victor nodded.

Her lips pressed together. She had no answer for him. Wasn't that the entire reason she'd come to this monstrosity of a home? Back to the people she instinctively feared? Because she did not know how she'd gotten the seven-inch-long slash across her stomach. Because she didn't even know how she'd gotten the two-inch slash near her shoulder.

Because she didn't know hardly anything at all when she thought of her past.

"Someone hurt you." Victor's voice had gone low and lethal.

A chill skated down her spine.

"Give me a name," he continued in that same tone. The one that promised hell. Lots of carnage and pain. "And I'll put him in the ground for you."

She felt her eyes widen. Knew they had to be huge. But Victor Alexander had just casually offered to kill for her, and she was sure that was not the way things were normally done. Or, maybe, in this new, twisted world she'd entered, they were.

"Why so shocked?" His hand left hers. But only so it could rise. Cup her cheek. "You think because you walked out, left me insane for a year, that I'd ever let anyone hurt you?"

She'd left him insane?

"No one hurts you." Flat. His thumb brushed over her lower lip. "Whether you're mine or not, I'll still annihilate anyone who dares to hurt you. And when someone makes you *bleed?* When someone puts a mark on your skin? The sonofabitch is going *in the ground.*"

Okay. That was utterly chilling. She should be terrified. She was, for the record. But she was also leaning toward him. Her lips had parted, and she might have just licked his thumb.

Why, oh, why had she just done that?

But she had.

And he'd stilled. And the darkness of his eyes seemed even more powerful. As if the obsidian would absolutely swallow her alive.

"Are you playing with me?" Victor asked her. Still in that lethal tone.

She had come to the Mage Mansion in order to play a very dangerous game with him—and with the others downstairs.

"That would be a dangerous game," he warned her.

She knew it. Was fully aware of the risks. What she hadn't been fully aware of, not until Victor touched her, was the way he made her feel. Need and desire surged through her. A heady, dangerous mix. She should not trust him. She should not trust anyone in the house. And yet...

The tip of her tongue touched his thumb once more.

He hissed out a breath. She thought he'd surge toward her. Kiss her. And then she could kiss him back this time. Fully. See what it felt like and if the desire would surge even hotter inside of her.

But he stepped back. Lots of steps back. He whirled, turning away from her, and she rose slowly to her feet. Uncertainty filled her. Quickly now, she finished undoing the mismatched buttoning job. She put the small buttons in the correct holes. His shirt fell past her thighs. Swallowed her. But somehow, the shirt felt good. His masculine scent clung to the fabric and seemed to envelop her.

He didn't speak. The silence stretched too far. She looked toward the window. The curtains were parted, and she could just make out the heavy fall of the snow beyond the window panes. By morning, everything would be covered in a mound of white softness.

She'd woken in snow once. Only it hadn't been white. It had been red. Soaked by her blood.

"I will gladly take a DNA test," she told Victor. Mostly because she had to say something to break the terrible silence that filled the room. And because she wanted the test. She'd like her own definitive proof. "But I am Melody Mage."

Her gaze darted over his back. His bare back. She was highly conscious of his body. Powerful shoulders. Rippling muscles. He turned toward her.

She swallowed.

The man did not spend all of his time behind a desk. Oh, most assuredly, he did not. He had a big, broad chest. Sculpted muscles. Abs on top of abs. She should probably not be gaping. And, honestly, she'd done a stellar job of not gaping, until now.

But now...

Wow.

"You look at me like you've never seen me without my shirt before."

Her eyes whipped up to catch his.

A furrow appeared between his brows. "But you have. Over and over again. Kinda have to see me that way, when I'm buried balls deep in you and fucking you."

Her breath froze in her chest.

"Fucking you in an elevator. Against a wall. In that

four-poster monstrosity you call a bed at your place." His head cocked. "You've had my dick in your mouth, Melody."

Oh, wow. Someone was being exceedingly blunt.

"I've made you come against my tongue more times than I can count."

He could not be serious. Automatically, she shook her head.

"Okay, you got me." A faint smirk curled his lips. "I'm lying."

Her breath whooshed out.

"I have counted," Victor revealed without breaking eye contact. "I know exactly how many times you've come against my mouth."

Boom. Boom. Boom. Oh, that was just her heart. Pounding out of control by this development that she had never, ever expected.

He closed in on her. He'd turned away, seemingly regrouped, and now was coming in with an attack that had her totally off balance.

"The first time you came against my mouth, it was in my office. At Mage Industries."

At the office? Heat singed her cheeks.

"You were arguing with me. Telling me what a total dick I was. I'd chased off your latest dumbass boyfriend. Chad. Seriously, *Chad?* He was after your family's money. I got compromising photos. Chad was shown the door and you—you were so furious with me." He was back to standing directly in front of her. "But something changed in the middle of our fight. Fury and lust. They can go hand in hand, can't they? One minute, you were about to slap me. Probably had that slap coming, by the way."

He'd probably had a slap coming? Good to know.

"I caught your hand. Pulled you close. Then in the next

instant, your mouth was on mine. Mine on yours. Hell, I don't know if I kissed you or if you kissed me. All I know was that I'd wanted your mouth on mine for too long, and I finally had you. I wasn't letting you go."

She didn't have chill bumps. She was overheating.

"I fucked you right there. Shoved everything off my desk. Spread you out. Had you coming against my mouth. Then around my dick."

Okay, this was...*a lot*. She swallowed. "I...see."

He frowned at her, the faint lines deepening around his eyes. "I don't think you do." Then he reached out. His hands curled around her shoulders. "Call me a liar."

Why? Was he?

"Or tell me that you remember the first time we fucked. Tell me that you remember what happened that very first time."

She could not. Because she did not.

And the knowledge was there on his face. "You don't know."

She couldn't even shake her head. She'd intended to bluff her way past everyone. But she couldn't bluff past this. She'd never expected *this*.

"You don't know if I fucked you on my desk. You don't know if we were ever lovers at all." He tugged her closer. "Because you don't know me, do you?"

"I know you're Victor Alexander." She'd looked him up online. Studied him as best she could. Her research, after all. Not like she'd walked into this thing totally blind.

"Do you *know* me? Do you *remember* me?" His gaze searched hers, frantic. Desperate.

So she gave him the truth. "No."

His grip tightened on her, almost bruising in its intensity.

"But if it makes you feel better..." Though she doubted it would. Melody confessed, "I don't remember me, either."

❄

Victor shut the connecting door softly. Stood with his back against the wood even as his heart raced far too fast in his chest.

Fury and fear tangled inside of him. Fury—because he knew something bad had happened to Melody. He should have been able to protect her. He'd failed.

And fear because...

She's still not safe.

He knew it. But this time, he would not let her down. She would not be hurt again. No matter what the hell he had to do, Melody would be safe.

He sucked in some deep breaths. They didn't do a single thing to calm him. Hell, the only thing that had ever calmed him? *Melody.*

He edged away from the door. Victor pulled out his phone. Yeah, it was helluva late, but he didn't care. He dialed his contact. Let the phone ring. Once. Twice. Three times. Four.

"Ho, the fuck ho," a grousing male voice answered. "Do you own a clock? If not, should I gift you one this holiday season?"

"Memphis." A growl of the other man's name. Memphis Camden. Former bounty hunter. All around asshole. Also, an Ice Breaker.

The Ice Breakers were in the news all the time these days. A cold-case solving group, they were able to solve mysteries that had stumped law enforcement for years.

They brought justice to those long dead. They locked away murderers.

They found the missing.

He'd gotten the group to take on Melody's case. In order to get them involved, he'd had to apply one hell of a lot of pressure on the Ice Breakers. The waiting list for their services was insane. As in, thousands of people wanted their help. Because they could produce actual results.

He'd waited too long already. So he'd done whatever was necessary to get their cooperation. They'd been helping him figure out who had taken Melody. *I know she was taken. I know she didn't just walk away from me and never look back.*

"Victor," Memphis sighed his name. "I get that you like weekly updates. Trust me, everybody on the team gets that fun fact about you, but I don't have anything new to tell you so can't this chat wait until tomorrow? Until a semi-reasonable hour?"

"She's here. Melody is back." The words rushed out.

Silence. Then, "Yeah, I was asleep. Curled up in bed with my lovely wife. So I'm gonna need you to say that again. Very, very slowly."

"She's here," he repeated. "Melody. Is. Back."

"Victor." Softer this time. With a hint of sympathy. "Have you been drinking? Because we've been over this. I told you that, after this length of time, you have to be realistic. Melody—hell, there's been no contact in far too long. You have to face the possibility—the very real possibility—that she is dead. That she has been dead ever since the night she vanished."

Screw that shit. "The dead woman knocked on the front door tonight. She came home. *Melody is back.*"

Chapter Five

She was cold and wet.

Something brushed against her cheek. So chilling. The icy touch of death. Why was death so soft? Feather-light?

Her eyelashes fluttered. She stared straight up. Softness rained down on her. Softness. Cold. *Snow*.

She knew snow was falling. That was the icy touch she felt on her skin. Her breath shuddered out. A white cloud appeared before her mouth. And pain pierced through her body.

Her hands flew down, touching her stomach. It was wet. Not wet like snow, though, more...soaked. Her dress stuck to her, and when she pulled at it, she felt the tear in the material. Her fingers lifted. She saw the red on her skin.

She looked down her body...and saw the red soaking her. Saw that the snow wasn't white around her, but was dark red. Her blood had flowed onto the snow.

Her head pounded. Throbbed over and over, and her blood-covered fingers rose to touch the left side of her head.

Swollen. Wet, too. From the snow? Yes, from the snow, but...blood. More blood.

She surged up. Dizziness nearly sent her tumbling back onto the snow, but she staggered and stayed on her feet—bare feet, frozen toes—as fear spiraled through her. "H-help..."

Her face hurt. Her cheekbone. Her lips were busted. Parched. "Help!" she cried again. She spun around, looking at the snow. How long had she been unconscious? There were no signs of footprints. Just the terrible circle of red where she'd sprawled in the snow. No tracks to show where she'd been.

Nothing around her but snow. So much snow in every direction. Trees heavy with the weight of the snow on their branches. Woods that waited in the distance. No person. No cars.

Fear settled deeper around her. One hand shoved against her bleeding stomach.

Run. Get away.

Her other hand stayed clutched to her head. She...she couldn't fall down again. Couldn't give in to the pain. She had to keep going.

Keep running.

She turned, spinning, and her blood spattered onto the snow. Where to go? Which direction? She had to escape.

Because he was coming for her.

She slogged through the snow, her blood dropping in her wake, but the snow fell and covered it. She kept going and going, hurrying desperately even when she had no strength. She couldn't feel her toes. Couldn't stop shaking. But she had to keep going. One foot in front of the other.

But her feet were sinking in the thicker snow.

She *had* to keep going. *Go, go, go.* Couldn't stop. If she stopped, she'd be dead. Or maybe she was already dead. Ice cold, through and through.

Is this what it feels like to die?

She headed forward. Straight ahead. No stopping. No hesitation.

Brakes screeched. Tires squealed. Her head whipped to the right. The darkness had grown. When had the night come? How long had she been walking? It had been lighter before, when she'd first woken. Light enough to see the blood.

But now darkness was everywhere. Darkness except...

Except for the two headlights that stared back at her. And there was no time to move. Only a split second to realize that she'd reached a road, that she'd stumbled right into the path of a vehicle.

Then it hit her.

Chapter Six

Melody's scream didn't wake him. Not like Victor had been able to sleep. When a ghost walked through the front door, you didn't sleep. Especially when that ghost was your fiancée. You grab tightly to her. You didn't let her go again.

But he wasn't holding her. He'd left her room. After she'd dropped the bombshell that she didn't know him—or herself—he'd left because he had work to do. People to call. People like Memphis. But the fast and furious chat with Memphis had only been the first of many phone conversations because he'd had a whole lot of plans to put into motion. And she'd looked exhausted. He hadn't wanted to push her, not yet. Even though he had so many questions.

How did you get to the estate? Where have you been? Who the fuck cut your stomach open?

But she was suddenly screaming, not sleeping, and he rushed into her room. He'd long since picked the lock. Not like he wanted to be away from her. And *maybe* he'd even opened the door after she went to sleep. The better to check on her. To make sure she hadn't disappeared on him again.

She was in bed. Thrashing against the covers. And her mouth opened as she prepared to scream again.

"Melody!" He ran to her side. His hand flew out. Covered her lips before another scream could pierce the night and bring the others running to her room.

Her eyes opened. She grabbed at him. Her nails raked his skin, and he realized that, oh, hell, yes, he'd made the wrong move. He'd scared her even more. Shit. "Baby, it's okay. It's me."

Instead of comforting her, that revelation just made her draw back her fist and aim it right at his face. He took the hit on the cheek. Not a slap. A punch.

Damn. He moved his hand. *"You're safe."* Fast words. *"You're with me. You're safe."*

She sat up in bed. The first thing he noticed? She was still wearing his shirt. The second thing? Her breath shuddered in and out. Her hand flew out and hit the lamp next to the bed. Illumination immediately flooded the room.

Terror was clear to see on her beautiful features.

"Bad dream?" Victor asked softly.

Her delicate shoulders shuddered. His shirt swallowed her. She hunched in on herself, as if waiting for a blow to come.

Fury coiled within him. Maybe it hadn't been a nightmare. "Bad...memory?" he guessed.

Her head whipped up. Tears gleamed in her eyes as she stared straight at him.

"What in the hell happened to you, baby?" He wanted to *destroy* someone for her.

Her lips parted.

A heavy fist thudded into the door. "Some of us are trying to get some freaking sleep!" Dario blasted.

She flinched.

"Don't move," Victor ordered her. He spun away from the bed and marched for her guest room door. Without a single hesitation—and maybe with utter deliberation, too, because the rules would be different this time—Victor yanked open that door.

Dario gaped at him. "What—" He blinked. "I...she was screaming?"

Yes, she had been. "And instead of checking on her, you decided to be an asshole and pound on her door?"

Dario closed his mouth. Then opened it again. Then he leaned to the side as he tried to look around Victor.

Because he knew exactly what Dario would see—a rumpled Melody, wearing *his* shirt—Victor let him look.

"What is going on here?" Dario asked, voice lower.

"Melody had a bad dream. Don't worry." Victor didn't think the prick had been worried, even for a second. "I've got her." He made sure the possessiveness in his voice was evident.

Dario rocked back a step. Suspicion clouded his pale, blue eyes. "Just what game are you running, man?"

The game where he would win. "Thanks for your concern. So nice that her *brother* came to look out for her."

Dario swallowed. "Thought we were getting a DNA test before we all believed she was Melody. A woman flashes one tiny scar at you, and suddenly, you're all in?"

When it came to Melody, he was always all in.

But he heard the rustle of the bedding behind him. Seriously, one order. He'd given one simple order to her. He'd told Melody to just stay where she was. And, yet, he could hear her padding toward him. Dammit.

"I'm taking the DNA test." Melody's voice. No longer fearful. Determined.

She edged to Victor's side.

Dario gave a low whistle.

She wore Victor's shirt. Nothing else. At least, nothing that he could see. Or that Dario could see. Her long legs were bare.

Victor thought he could also spy her nipples poking against the front of the shirt. She'd ditched her bra.

Did she have on panties? "Fuck," he breathed. He might just have to beat the shit out of Dario that night, after all. Because if the prick kept gaping at her...

"If the DNA test doesn't prove that I'm Melody Mage, I'll get out of your life." She nodded. "That's a promise."

Dario's gaze swept between them. Then dropped. Lingered a bit too long on Melody's legs.

Screw this. "Get your ass out of here, Dario." And with that, he slammed the door in her stepbrother's face. Locked it, too. Then he turned back, with his arms crossed over his chest.

Melody stared up at him. Beautiful. Tempting. With tears still clinging to her long eyelashes.

Once again, he wanted to *destroy*. To completely wreck whatever—whoever—had hurt her. But tears clung to her lashes, fear lingered like a perfume around her, and...Victor hauled her into his arms. "You're safe." Gruff.

She stiffened within his grasp.

Right. She didn't know him. Didn't remember a damn thing. As far as she was concerned, a stranger was hugging her.

He squeezed a little tighter. "You're safe," he repeated.

He felt her draw in a shuddering breath.

Slowly, he let her go. A hard task when all he wanted was to keep her close.

"Were you just trying to comfort me?" she asked as her head tilted to the side.

He had been. "Doesn't happen often." Actually, it pretty much happened never. As a rule, he didn't have close emotional attachments. There had never been room for those attachments in his life. Not with all the plans he'd long since had in place.

Melody was the exception to that rule. She was an attachment that he had never, ever been able to shake.

"Guess I'm special?" she mused even as she swiped away a tear from her cheek.

Oh, baby, you have no idea. Instead of saying that, he decided to get to the point. No more bullshitting allowed. "Where the hell were you?" For so many months.

"Why does it matter?" A shrug of one shoulder as she turned away from him. "Not like you looked for me. Not like anyone looked. I don't believe the story before about your PIs. You were just telling me what you thought I wanted to hear."

What? His hand flew out, curled around her shoulder and, at his touch, she spun to face him. The tears were still there, but, now, anger gleamed in her gaze, too. A bright rage shined in the green eyes that had haunted him for so long.

Like he hadn't woken up from plenty of his own nightmares over the last year. Nightmares where he woke up and he reached for her, but she wasn't there.

Nightmares where he heard her crying out for him. Begging for him. But he couldn't help her. He couldn't find her.

"I looked," he told her grimly. "I called the cops. I truly hired five different PI groups. You want to see the receipts for the fortune I paid them?" Money that had turned up nothing. "I freaking ripped the state apart. Ripped the world apart." There had been so many false leads that had wasted his time. "There was a video discovered of you getting on a private plane, one bound for Mexico."

Her brows rose. "Mexico?"

"Seemed like you left willingly." The cops had finally turned up that bit of video evidence. "Looked like you ran away. Left me behind." His back teeth had clenched. "I didn't buy that bullshit. I kept digging and digging. Found out that wasn't you going to Mexico. Just some weird-ass fake trail. Lost too much time searching for you there. Your phone was never recovered. It turned off after your father and I received those final texts from you."

She blinked quickly. "What texts?"

"The texts you sent." Except...*I don't think they were from Melody. I think they were from the sonofabitch who took my Melody from me.*

"Tell me what the texts said."

He already had told her what his said. *Don't look for me.* "Tell me what the fuck happened to you." There. Done. "Tell me *everything*," he demanded. "Because I damn well deserve to know."

Her lower lip trembled. "What were you to me?"

"Enemy," he said flatly.

She jerked.

"Lover," he said, softer.

She backed up a step.

"Which one do you think I was?" he asked.

She ran a shaking hand through her hair, shoving it back, and when she did...

He caught her wrist.

She stilled. "I think you might have been both."

He hauled her closer. Let go of her wrist. With one hand, he carefully tilted her head to the side. With the other, he brushed back the hair near her left temple. A faint line, twisted, unsteady, slid from her temple and disappeared into her dark hair.

Another scar. One that she hadn't possessed a year ago.

"There was swelling in my brain." Her voice was soft. Emotionless. "A fracture to my skull. I had to be placed in a medically induced coma for two weeks."

What. The. Hell. "Melody?" Victor's gut clenched even as ice encased his skin.

"Not sure if the head injury was from the car accident—"

Car accident?

"Or from the attack that came before that. The attack that left me bleeding and terrified in the snow. That was my nightmare tonight, by the way. I was back in the snow. Bleeding. So scared my whole body shook. And I ran and I was suddenly in front of the car and it hit me." Her lips pressed together. "That's all I could remember for so long, you see. Those terrible moments. For months, that's all I could remember. Nothing before that. Just the snow. The blood in the snow. My terror. Trying to escape. Then having the car slam into me as I screamed. I screamed for someone—and I can never remember who I called out for, who I begged for help."

A knife carved into his heart. Deeper and deeper with each word that she spoke.

"I kept thinking someone would come in my hospital room. Someone who was missing me. Someone who would know who I was. Someone who could identify me." A shake of her head. Her hair covered her scar once more as his hand slid away. "But that didn't happen. I left the hospital. I started over. And then...the flashes finally came. My doctors had told me that they might. As I healed, as time passed, the flashes could potentially start. Though they didn't know how strong they'd be."

"What flashes?" But he wanted to ask so much more. *What hospital? Where were you? Who drove the car that hit you? Why were you bleeding in the snow? Who the hell can I kill for you?*

"Flashes of my life before the snow and blood." A nod. "Flashes of glittering parties. Of Dario, riding on a horse near me. A big, black horse. Of you, glaring at me across a boardroom."

His hands fisted at his sides.

"Flashes of my father, marrying a much younger woman."

Yeah, Sebastian had done that a few times.

"At first, you were all total strangers to me. Faces with no names." A humorless laugh escaped her. "But then again, I was a woman with no name, too. Until I had more flashes. Flashes of this place. This life. People would look at me in the flashes—people I didn't know—and they'd call me Melody. The name would echo in my mind. I began to put the pieces together. The memories came more frequently. I learned who the people were in those memories. Dario Mage. Sebastian Mage. You." A swallow. "I realized I had a family. People who weren't coming to claim me." Her shoulders squared. "And I wanted to know why."

"First, I will *always* fucking claim you." Always. "Second, *I have been searching the whole time.*" He was still working to find out what had happened. His late-night call to Memphis Camden? It had been about updating the team on everything he knew so far. The Ice Breakers would find out how she'd gotten to the house. They would backtrack every step she'd taken to understand where she'd been. What had happened to her.

"I came here because I want to know who I am." A slow exhale from Melody. "And I also came back because..."

He found himself leaning toward her. He had missed her so much. When Melody had vanished, she'd carved out his heart. Left a monster in place of the man that he'd been.

"I came back because I want to find out which one of you assholes tried to kill me. And I don't care what hell I have to cause in this family, in this place, but I will do it." Grim determination as she stood in his shirt, barefoot, with dry tear tracks on her cheeks. "I will rip your lives apart until I find out the truth. Someone tried to kill me. To leave me dead in the snow. And I *will* find out who that bastard is."

SHE SHOULD HAVE BEEN DEAD. Dario Mage rushed back to his room. His hands were shaking with fury as he shoved open the door.

"Well?" Olivia sat in the middle of the bed, one of the delicate straps of her peach negligee falling down one soft shoulder. "What was all the screaming about?" She clutched a sheet to her chest.

"It was Melody." *She should have been dead.* Out of the will. Out of his life. He'd been so certain she was gone. Never in a million years had he expected her to show up *alive.*

"Why was she screaming?" Olivia rocked forward. Her green eyes—a shade lighter than Melody's—had widened.

"Fuck if I know. Bad dream, I think. Victor was with her." That sonofabitch Victor. Talk about someone who was always in the way. That prick should not have control of the company. He was a nobody. He'd come from nothing.

Now Victor had everything.

"Victor was with her?" She bounced a bit on the bed. "As in...fucking? The woman is back one night, and Victor has already moved in on her?"

"No." An adamant shake of his head. "I think he'd gone in to check on her."

"And how do you *know* that he was only checking on her?"

He took in the sight of Olivia. The tousled hair. The swollen lips. The pink stained cheeks. The red marks on her neck from the stubble that coated his face. "A woman looks a certain way after she's been fucked. Melody..." If it even was Melody. He wouldn't place a bet until the DNA test was in. Far too many scammers filled the world. "She looked terrified."

Olivia gave a mocking laugh. "Pretty sure that's exactly what a woman who'd just had sex with Victor would look like." She tossed aside the sheet and bounded from the bed. "Terrified." She hurried toward him with her hands outstretched. "Nothing has to change." She curled her fingers around his forearms. "The plan stays in place."

He'd had his plan in place for a very long time. He'd almost crossed the finish line, and now...this. "You knew Melody."

"Uh, yeah, we both did." Her head tilted to the right. Her blond hair—always carefully colored—trailed over her shoulder.

"Was she fucking Victor when she left?" Victor's reaction was just over the top. The way he'd carried her up the stairs...

But Olivia laughed. "No. Definitely not." Her hair flew with the negative shake of her head. "She couldn't stand him."

Right. Right. He expelled a breath.

"Victor is probably just covering his bases. He suspects she's a scammer, too, and he's not gonna let the woman out of his sight until he knows the truth about her." Her hands rubbed down his arms. "Now come back to bed. It's cold, and I want to crawl under the covers with you."

But he didn't move, not yet. "What if it is Melody? What happens then?"

She frowned at him. "What do you want to happen?"

Oh, that was easy. "I want her to disappear. And, this time, I want her to *stay gone*."

Chapter Seven

SHE CREPT DOWN THE STAIRCASE. AS SHE NEARED THE bottom, she could hear the tick-tick-tick of the grandfather clock that waited in the foyer. Melody had rushed by that clock earlier, when she'd first arrived at the estate. Not even truly sparing it a glance. Now, she peered at it, her gaze drawn to the big, swaying, golden pendulum. Ever so slowly, it rocked back and forth. Back and forth.

The house was quiet. It should be quiet, considering that it was nearly four a.m. After she'd finally gotten Victor to leave her room, she'd waited for silence to claim the house.

Had he believed her story? Hard to say for sure. Victor was an enemy she'd expected but...

He was my lover, too? Melody wasn't sure how to handle that revelation, and she certainly didn't know how the new truth fit into her plans.

At the bottom of the staircase, she paused for a moment, listening to make sure that she didn't hear anyone else moving around in the house. Then, still wearing Victor's shirt, she hurried toward the study. Not the den where everyone had been gathered before, but the study two doors down from the den. The room that waited just beyond double, gleaming doors. She reached for one of the door handles. Unlocked. Perfect. If the study had been locked, she would have needed to sneak in the kitchen and find something to help her pick the lock. And she doubted that she'd be a master lock picker like Victor.

She hurried inside and went straight for the mahogany desk.

She'd needed to get into Mage Mansion. The better to search for the truth. And she couldn't search if eyes were on her, so she'd had to wait and be sure everyone else was sleeping. She rushed forward, keeping the lights off. She grabbed for the first desk drawer of the left-hand side of the big desk.

"Are you intending to rob your father?"

Jeez—Melody bit back a yelp as she jumped.

And *he* turned on the lights.

Victor stood just inside the doorway. Victor, still without a shirt, clad in just his dress pants. No shoes or socks. And appearing far, far too awake. Seriously, did he ever sleep? And was he trying to give her a heart attack?

She blinked quickly then growled, "Lights off."

"I'll keep them on. And you didn't answer my question."

The stupid desk drawer was locked. "I'm not robbing anyone." She was also doing a piss-poor job of searching the premises, too. "I'm looking for clues."

He quirked a brow. "Are you now, Scooby Doo?"

Oh, someone wanted to be funny? While her heart was still threatening to leap out of her chest? "You try losing your whole life," she snapped at him, "and then judge me, okay? I'm looking for clues." Dammit, it *did* sound like she'd become Velma or Daphne and how the hell could she remember all the characters from a kids' cartoon so perfectly when her own life was etched in shadows? Talk about unfair, but her doctors had warned her that situation could occur. She'd woken knowing who the president was. Knowing that the Atlanta Braves were her favorite baseball team. But not knowing her own family. Or her name. "I'm not stealing. I'm searching Sebastian's desk because it's been an exceedingly hard year for me. And I need answers." She grabbed for the second drawer on the left. Yanked it open and—

Gun.

A black gun waited inside the drawer.

"What is it?" Tension thickened Victor's voice.

She reached for the gun and lifted it from the drawer.

"Fuck." He rushed forward. "Put it down, Melody. The gun *shouldn't* be there. Hatterson was supposed to remove all weapons."

Had she held a gun before? She had no clue. The weight felt alien to her. Surely it wasn't loaded, was it? "It's not loaded." Melody thought she sounded pretty confident.

"How the hell do you know? You just picked the damn thing up."

He was right in front of her.

"Sebastian isn't as...safe these days. That's why I ordered Hatterson to secure all weapons. The gun shouldn't have been in the drawer. *Put it down.*"

She stared at the weapon. "You think I'd shoot you?" Is that why he seemed so tense?

"You just told me an hour ago that you're back for vengeance. You don't know who the hell I really am. For all I know, you think I'm the bastard who hurt you."

Her gaze rose. Caught his.

"I'm not." Flat. "For the record, I'm not that person. I would *never* hurt you. So how about you don't get twitchy with the trigger, and you just put the gun back in the drawer? Then you can tell me why the hell you're doing your breaking-and-entering routine."

She had told him. It wasn't her fault if he hadn't listened to her. "I have to get answers."

He held her stare. "I will help you."

She wanted to believe him. Was it because she'd been alone for so long? Was she just desperate for someone else to stand beside her? Or was it more?

She began to lower the gun. As she lowered the weapon, Melody stepped back so she could put it in the drawer once more.

Victor reached out for her. "I can take—"

Glass shattered. The crack seemed so loud. Something wet flew toward her. Wet. Red.

It took a second too long for her to process what was happening. She still held the gun. Victor was reaching for her. But...his arm was bleeding. His blood had splattered onto the white shirt she wore.

She hadn't fired at him. She had *not* fired the gun.

Her head whipped toward the windows. The shattering glass had come from the window—

"Down!" Victor roared. But he didn't give her a chance to actually get down. He hurtled right at her and threw his body onto hers. He tackled her with a strong, heaving impact that took her to the floor. She was sure she'd crash hard into the hardwood floor, but he twisted his body, cushioned her head with his hands, and when they landed, she was surrounded by him. Protected by him.

The gun flew out of her fingers and clattered across the floor.

Cold air blew into the room. And then—

Bam. Bam. Bam. Bam.

Shots. Fired in quick succession. More shattering glass. She screamed. Had she even heard the crack of gunfire the first time? She didn't think she had. Or maybe—

"You're *not* hurt!" Victor's snarl.

He was telling her? Or was that a question?

"You're *not* hurt!" Victor snarled again. He heaved up. Glared at her. Began to pat her down.

She shoved at his hands. "I'm not hurt. *You* are." He was the one bleeding all over the place. Oh, God. Blood meant— "You were shot!"

He growled again. Then commanded, "Stay the fuck here."

Why? Where was he going? And shouldn't they both stay hidden from the shooter? "Victor!"

But instead of listening to her tell him that she thought the man may have a seriously flawed plan developing, he grabbed the gun she'd dropped and then he ran out of the study. Melody could hear voices rising and falling from other parts of the house. For a moment, she couldn't move at all.

Her heart raced. Her breath heaved out. And his blood was on her.

He'd been shot.

He'd thrown his body on her. Protected her. And now he was—what? Going to hunt the shooter?

An alarm was beeping somewhere. Maybe it had been beeping the whole time, perhaps since the first window had shattered, and she'd just become aware of the steady buzz because her thundering heart no longer echoed in her ears?

Melody didn't rise to her feet. She was too afraid that

the shooter might fire again if she presented a big target in front of the broken windows.

But Victor hadn't been afraid. He'd taken the gun. And he'd gone outside. Alone.

I can't let him face the threat alone.

Staying low, she crawled for the study's open door. Footsteps thundered on the stairs.

"What is happening?" Dario demanded. "Why the hell is the front door wide open?"

She'd finally made it out of the study. Melody rose, and she ran for the house's front door.

Dario jumped off the stairs and into her path. "What is happening?"

Breath still shuddering, she told him, "Someone just shot Victor."

FURY TWISTED and heaved inside of him. Victor barely felt the sting in his arm. The bullet had grazed him. The sonofabitch hadn't been aiming for Victor. His instincts told him that truth. The shot had been meant for Melody. But she'd stepped back. He'd reached out for her.

And the prick had shot him.

The snow swirled around Victor. Not as thick as it had been. It still fell, but in a lighter stream for the moment. He could see footsteps in the snow. The SOB had been feet away from the study's windows. Victor had been so locked and loaded on Melody that he hadn't even realized someone was outside. He'd never even looked toward the windows.

Can't be so careless. Have to always be on guard. She needs me.

His toes were fucking freezing already. His chest icy. But then again, he only wore pants. No shirt. No shoes. He gripped the gun in his hand, and he tried to follow the damn steps that the shooter had left in the snow. But with every step he took...

The snow decided it wanted to fall harder. Faster. The light stream suddenly changed on him. Wind blew and gusted, and he held the gun tighter as he surged forward. The sonofabitch was out there.

But the storm had picked up again. The footsteps were getting harder and harder to see.

His body shuddered as he fought the cold.

Dammit.

"Victor!" A scream. Her scream.

And he stopped chasing the footsteps that were already fading. In his rage, he'd left her in the house. Unprotected. He couldn't trust anyone else there with Melody's safety. Not even her father.

No one else.

He swung around. Lumbered through the snow, and there she was. Her faded, wool coat flapping behind her as she ran toward him. "Victor!"

She shouldn't be out there. Dammit, she didn't have on any shoes, either. His shirt. Her coat. Nothing else. The snow swirled around her as she struggled toward him. Light from the house poured down on her. The illumination made her a perfect target.

The shooter was still somewhere out there. In the snow. In the darkness. Armed. Waiting. "Go back!" Victor bellowed at Melody.

She didn't. If anything, she seemed to surge toward him with even more determination.

Dammit. He thundered toward her, plowing through

the snow. It slapped into his face and his head. Not soft snow. More like ice. Brittle. Hard.

She reached out for him.

Yeah, screw that.

He lifted her into his arms. His back was a damn target now, but there was nothing he could do about that fact. He had to get her into the house. Hadn't he told the woman to stay put? He distinctly remembered giving that flat order. A simple enough order to follow. You just stayed the hell inside when there was a shooter *and* a snowstorm happening in the darkness beyond your door.

But she hadn't stayed. And he hadn't found the shooter. And the rage within him twisted even more when he got back to the house and saw the front door hanging wide open and the eyes peering anxiously out at him.

Sonofabitch.

He stomped inside, still carrying Melody. Still holding the gun. He kicked the door shut.

"What in the hell is happening?" Dario demanded. He wore a black robe. Freaking slippers. His hair seemed a little damp.

"Why are you both running around outside?" Olivia followed up Dario's question. Also wearing a robe. Not black. Peach. Silky. And matching peach slippers.

"Did I hear fireworks?" Sebastian wanted to know. He hunched near the staircase. One hand gripped a black cane. His black pajamas were monogrammed with a big S, J, and M. Sebastian James Mage.

"No, sir." Hatterson hovered near Sebastian. No monogrammed pajamas for him. Instead, he wore sweatpants. A sweatshirt. Tennis shoes. "Don't think it was fireworks at all." He shared a hard look with Victor. "Saw the broken glass in the study." A pause. "Did you get him?"

No. "Lost his trail."

Melody struggled in his arms.

"Not the fuck now," he rasped at her.

"You've been *shot!*" Melody argued right back at him. "You're bleeding everywhere. So, yes, the fuck now. Put me down and let me help you!"

And there were lots of dramatic gasps. Hell. He put her down, but mostly so he could just bolt the front door. "Hatterson, we need to board up the windows in the study. You and Dario get material and secure the room, now."

"Are you *ordering* me around?" Dario sniffed. "Do I look like the hired help?"

"Yeah, I sure as hell am ordering you. Make yourself useful. Board up the damn windows. Yank some wood down from one of the bookshelves in that room if you need something sturdy. There are nails and hammers in the storage room."

Dario glared at him, but...nodded.

Hatterson inched closer to Victor. "I was a medic back in the day. Want me to look at that arm?"

Victor didn't care about his arm. Screw it. "Barely a graze. We need to get the study secure." He mentally ran through scenarios. Fears. "Correction, we need to get the whole house secured. We should make sure all the blinds and curtains are pulled. Every window covered. No one should be able to look inside." Because that was how the shooter had known when to fire. The lights had been on in the study, and Melody had made a perfect target.

He'd turned on those lights. He'd been right there when the bullets flew.

I could have lost her when I just got her back.

"You need to get that wound bandaged." Hatterson was adamant. The deep lines on his face seemed even thicker than normal. "And you need to warm up. Go into the den. The fire is going in there. We'll take care of everything else."

Tension held Victor in a tight grip. "Normally, there are at least two guards stationed at the entrance to this property. Why the hell aren't they on duty this weekend?" Something he'd noticed upon his arrival, but hadn't questioned, not then.

Hatterson glanced toward Sebastian.

"I gave them the weekend off," Sebastian's soft reply. His gaze lingered on Melody. He frowned. Leaned a bit harder on the cane. "Melody, when did you get back?"

And everyone tensed. Because...it was happening again. Sebastian, his memory coming and going as it would. Sometimes, he'd forget years. Sometimes, he'd forget days.

And sometimes, he'd remember everything perfectly.

"I've missed you," Sebastian told her. His words were sad.

Melody, her body shivering, and snow falling from her coat, stepped toward her father.

Sebastian smiled at her as he extended his left hand.

She stumbled for a moment but kept going. She took his hand. Squeezed. "I missed you, too."

Victor's blood dripped on the fancy entranceway's marble flooring. "We need to secure this house." He gripped the gun. "*Now.*" Because the shooter was still out there, and he hadn't succeeded in taking out his target.

Or...fuck...

Victor's suspicious gaze swept the small circle of people in the foyer.

Dario's hair is slightly damp. Hatterson is fully dressed. Why the hell is he fully dressed at four in the morning? And as for Sebastian...

76

Once upon a time, the man had been one hell of a shot. The best hunter that Victor had ever met.

Olivia clutched her silk robe tightly to her even as she watched everyone with a careful mask on her face.

Her gaze dipped toward Victor, only to immediately rush away.

His jaw tightened. The shooter could be outside...

Or the bastard could be standing right in the house with him. A shooter who, Victor was convinced, had been aiming at Melody.

He set the safety on the gun, then tucked it into the waistband of his pants. Victor stalked toward Melody as she leaned close to her father. Shivers racked her body.

Screw this shit.

He reached out, grabbed her, and lifted her over his shoulder.

There were lots of shocked exclamations.

Yeah, whatever. Did it look like he was in the mood for bullshit? *"Fucking secure the house."* He spun away, with one arm locked behind Melody's thighs as she dangled over his back. He was securing Melody. She came *first*.

He headed toward the den. The curtains had been drawn in that room earlier, he distinctly remembered that shit. So he strode inside, with her over his back and dripping snow, and his gaze immediately went toward the windows.

Still covered.

But even if they hadn't been, a line of bushes—dead now, but a tall hedge—would have blocked the glass of those windows. The fire crackled and churned in the fireplace, and he wondered just when Hatterson had started the flames.

When I was searching for the killer? What the hell, man?

The fire lit up the room. The big Christmas tree. The

antique couch and leather chairs. He marched toward the leather chair on the left because it was the closest one to the fireplace. And he plunked Melody down on that chair. "Stay here," he ordered before he rose to his full height. Automatically, he reached for the weapon. Gripped it in his right hand.

She grabbed his hand. Melody looked at the gun, then at him. She shivered again.

So did he. Dammit. He'd been a freaking ice cube outside. Feeling was starting to return to his toes, and they burned.

"You were shot."

"I was grazed. Big difference." He wanted to check the house. To search all the rooms. But... "Lock the door when I exit. Do not let anyone but me back inside."

"What?"

"Oh, you heard me, sweetheart. No one but me, got it? Because I don't trust *anyone* else here."

Her eyes had gone huge. "My father..."

"He isn't the man you knew." But then again, if she was telling the truth, Melody didn't know Sebastian Mage at all. "Look, he's just—he's not the same." Serious understatement. And when one of Sebastian's rages came on him... "I want you to lock the door. *Only let me inside, understand?*" Actually, he wanted her the hell out of that house. Until he could figure out what was happening...

Someone just tried to kill her. That's what is happening. And I will not allow Melody to be hurt.

"You don't even have on a shirt," she muttered.

"That's because you're wearing it," he returned.

"Oh." She looked down at the shirt. "Your blood is on it. That, uh, seems to happen pretty often with your shirts."

His fingers slid beneath her chin. He tilted her head

back up. "Promise you will lock the door after me. Drag the chair over to secure it if you have to, but do not let anyone but me inside, understand?"

"I'm supposed to trust you?" She swallowed. "You know I don't remember you."

"Yeah, got that." They'd deal with that problem. "But I was also standing right in front of you when the first shot was fired, and you know I didn't just try to kill you, so there's that."

"Th-the shot wasn't intended for me!"

He stared at her. Just stared. Then, "You stepped back. I reached for you. My arm was in the exact spot you'd just been in seconds before."

Her breath came harder. Faster.

"I think you have to realize, sweetheart..." Yeah, he kept dropping endearments. So what? "Not everyone is thrilled to have you home."

She wet her lips.

"But I sure as hell am." His mouth took hers. Quick. Hard. Possessively. "Lock the fucking door."

"*I fucking will.*"

He backed away. Stormed out. Yanked the door closed behind him. He stood there a moment, shivers racking his own body and then...

He heard the grating of a heavy chair being hauled toward the door. A savage smile curled his lips.

He turned away from the den.

Olivia waited a few feet away. She shifted from foot to foot. "Did, ah, did someone really shoot into the study?"

"No, the bullet holes in the wall are just for fun." He strode past her because he didn't have time to waste.

She caught his arm. Gripped the damn graze.

He hissed out a breath.

She let go.

"Why the hell does Dario have wet hair?" Victor demanded.

Olivia blinked. Several times. "He...ran outside after Melody. But I was worried, so I pulled him back. It must be wet from the snow."

Her hair wasn't wet.

She looked toward the closed den door. "Could have just been a hunter, you know." A low whisper. "A shot fired by mistake."

"You don't shoot five times by mistake."

She backed up a step.

"Was Dario in bed with you when you heard the first shot?"

A hesitation. A flicker of her lashes. Then, "Of course. Where else would he have been?"

"Oh, I don't know. Outside. Shooting a fucking gun."

"He *wasn't*. He has no reason to shoot his stepsister!"

His laughter was bitter. "Sure, he does. He has about a few million reasons to kill her." He hurried down the hallway.

Olivia scrambled after him. "Oh, really?" Loud. Too loud. "And what is *your* reason to want her back? To keep her alive? I figure you must stand to inherit plenty, too, if Melody stays dead."

She's not dead.

"So what's your reason to want her alive so badly?"

Oh, just the most basic reason...

I fucking love her.

His secret.

His dirty little secret.

Melody belongs to me. And no one will take her away again.

Chapter Eight

"The roads are impassable."

Hardly the news that Melody wanted to hear.

"The snowstorm hit much harder than anyone expected," Hatterson continued blithely as he puttered around the kitchen table. "The storm's force caught everyone by surprise. But, hopefully, now that the snowfall has finally stopped, the plows can get on the roads, and the guests may be able to leave by nightfall."

Nightfall was a very, very long time off.

"Here." Hatterson put a plate of pancakes in front of her. "Made your favorite for you. Blueberry pancakes. Syrup is on the side."

She stared down at the light, fluffy pancakes. Apparently, Hatterson truly was a jack of all trades. She'd thought he was Sebastian Mage's butler and guard, but the man certainly seemed skilled in the kitchen, too.

She hadn't gone back to sleep after the shooting. And the mad dash after Victor in the snow. She'd been chilled to the bone, and two very hot showers had finally resulted in her feeling semi-normal again. If she'd been that cold, how had Victor felt? He'd been out in the snow far longer than she had.

He'd checked and double-checked the house. Searched all the rooms. Made sure the windows were covered. The doors locked. The man had been shot—grazed—and he hadn't seemed to care about his injury.

He'd been pissed, though. She'd definitely picked up on that rage.

The others had eventually gone back to bed. Olivia and Dario were still sleeping. Melody didn't know where Sebastian was. *My father.* She just had such a hard time thinking of him that way. The people in the house were utter strangers to her.

She'd hoped that, once she crossed the threshold of the home, more memories would come to her.

That hadn't happened. Not yet.

"The pancakes are going to get cold," Hatterson muttered. He pulled up a chair beside her. "They are your favorite."

He'd said that before.

She didn't want to hurt his feelings, but eating was the last thing she felt like doing. If Victor was right and the shots had been meant for her, then someone had tried to kill her...her first night home. "I don't think I have much of an appetite, I'm sorry."

"Come on. I went to a lot of trouble. And you're skin and bones as it is." He sent her a frown. "Whatever you were doing the last year, there must not have been any damn good food where you were."

No, the hospital food hadn't been a culinary masterpiece. And after she'd finally gotten out of the hospital, there hadn't exactly been a lot of money. Not until she'd gotten her waitressing job. Gosh, she'd been a colossal failure as a waitress. So clumsy. Always spilling the trays.

At first.

By the end of the second week, she'd sailed through the diner with a heavy tray perched on three fingers. And the meals at Stan's Diner had actually been good. Breakfast and lunch. Though, she couldn't say that she'd ever tried the blueberry pancakes there. She'd never actually wanted to try them.

"Your father missed you, you know."

She didn't know. *Hello, story of my life.*

"Pick up the fork and the knife, Melody." A long sigh from Hatterson.

"He's...worse." Maybe if she ate some of the pancakes, Hatterson would keep talking. Hatterson could help her fill in some of the many blank spaces in her mind. "My father seems like he's just gotten worse over the last year." A safe enough statement to make.

"He tried lots of different medicines and therapies, but, yeah, he's worse. Don't think you should count on him getting a whole lot better." Another sigh. Sadder. "He has good days. Bad days. But don't we all?"

She cut into a blueberry pancake. Lifted it to her mouth.

Hatterson watched her with his dark brown eyes. "He missed you."

She put the pancake in her mouth. Almost immediately spit it out.

"There a problem?" Hatterson asked with raised brows.

She chewed, quickly, the taste of the blueberries flooding through her mouth. For some reason, revulsion filled her, but she didn't want to spit out the pancake right in front of Hatterson. Talk about rude. She choked down the bite of pancake, then she grabbed the glass of milk—

"What in the hell are you eating?" Victor demanded as he stormed into the kitchen. He frowned at the pancakes. "Are those blueberries? Melody, you hate blueberries."

That would be why she had needed to choke down her lone bite. She hated blueberries. Check. Her accusing eyes swept toward Hatterson. What kind of game was he playing?

"Oh, did I say they were your favorite?" He rose, all falsely apologetic. "My mistake. But then, shouldn't you *know* which foods you like? And which ones you've hated since you were three years old?" Disgust twisted his lips. "That DNA test can't come fast enough. You might look the part but—"

"She doesn't have her damn memory, Hatterson," Victor snarled. "Back off. *Now*."

Hatterson blinked.

So did Melody because...what, he was just going to tell everyone? So much for keeping that secret, but, then again, her best laid plans were currently going to shit. She was also exceedingly terrified because, deep down, she suspected Victor was right. The gunshots had been meant for her.

She was in over her head. She needed help.

Her gaze crept back to Victor. Big, bold, dangerous Victor. He'd rushed out to confront the gunman in the darkness. He'd protected her.

Yeah, okay, she needed *him*.

But would he help her?

"What do you mean she doesn't have her memory?" Hatterson's sharp voice drew her gaze. His bushy brows beetled. "What kind of bullshit is that?"

"It's the kind of bullshit that's my life," Melody replied.

The jerk had deliberately fed her pancakes filled with blueberries that she hated. How lovely. What a kind soul he must be. "And obviously, you suspected something, or you wouldn't be serving me up this particular breakfast treat. Want to tell me why you decided I needed testing?" How had she tipped him off so that he'd felt the need to serve her the blueberries?

"You failed the test," he told her bluntly.

Yes, obviously. Because she was walking around blindly and hoping like hell she would trust the right person. *Victor, be the right person. Please, I need you.* Because there was no one else she could rely on.

"I saw you come down the stairs last night." Hatterson stood near the table, bobbing his head a bit. "Like a thief in the night. Tiptoeing. Sneaking into the study. I knew you were up to no good. Then shots were fired. You appear and hours later there is gunfire? Oh, hell, no. That's too much trouble. I knew something was off." His hands were on his hips. "And you just proved my point right here. My Melody would never eat blueberries. She's hated them ever since she got violently ill after eating them when she was a kid."

"Violently ill, huh?" Her hand went to her stomach. "Thanks so much for telling me that." Should she be expecting some projectile vomiting? What a fun visit she was having at Mage Mansion.

"What's this bullshit about not remembering?" Hatterson's thin lips tensed. "This isn't some soap opera. You don't get to call amnesia for shits and giggles. Either you are the real Melody, or you aren't. My money says you are *not*. You're not her. Something about your face is just a little off, and it's not just because you're thinner. It's *different*."

She jumped to her feet. "It's called having your

cheekbone broken, asshole. And your nose. The docs did the best job they could, but no, I'm not perfect. I'll never be exactly like she was before."

She. Crap. Talking about herself in the third person again. Sometimes, she did that because Melody Mage just seemed like a different person. Someone she didn't know.

The silence in the kitchen was deafening.

"Well?" Hatterson finally challenged as he tossed a glare over at Victor. "Aren't you going to say something? Or maybe you want to throw her ass out into the snow for me?"

"Let me be very clear." Victor moved to stand beside Melody. "No one is throwing her anywhere. She *is* Melody."

"I heard you last night! We all did!" Hatterson pointed his index finger at Victor. "You wanted her DNA checked! You didn't believe her, either, then she pranced out and did the little strip tease. So she has a scar on her shoulder? Big damn deal!"

Victor's arm brushed Melody's. "It's not your job to test her. Not in any way."

"I *raised* her." Brittle. His hand curled into a fist before falling to his side. "Who taught her to ride her first bike? *Me.* Who was there at all of her volleyball games? *Me.* When her father was too damn busy, when he was out of the country on his trips, or going off with wife number three...who took care of the bully who was making her life hell? *Me.* Who taught her self-defense? *Me.* It was always *me.* Who got her to love scary movies because it's better to be the villain than the victim? *Me.* Who taught her—" Hatterson stopped.

Her head tilted as she stared at him.

"I raised Melody Mage." Softer. Sadder. Tears glistened in his eyes. "I mourned Melody Mage." He grabbed for the plate of pancakes that had been placed in front of her. Hurried steps took him to the garbage. He tossed the pancakes inside. "I won't be fooled. Melody wouldn't just vanish. Not for a whole year." His back was to her. His wide shoulders tensed.

A memory stirred in her mind.

Better to be the villain...

"*Candyman*," she whispered.

He whirled toward her.

"*Candyman* is my favorite scary movie." And why? Simple. "He won't be a victim again."

Hatterson's gaze searched hers.

"Trish Yates was the bitch who made my life hell in ninth grade." The name was just there. A vague flash of a girl with curly hair, braces, and a mean grin.

How on earth could she suddenly remember Trish Yates, but she could not remember so much more? Why something so insignificant? Dammit...*why?*

Oh, sure, she'd talked to doctors about her condition as she tried to understand what was happening. Plenty of them. They'd told her brain injuries could be unpredictable. Especially the sort of severe trauma she'd faced. One doctor had called her a miracle.

Bull.

She didn't feel like anyone's miracle.

But...

The docs had been clear that she couldn't force her memories. Flashes would come. And the truth was that they'd warned her—the flashes might be all she'd ever get.

Hope crept across Hatterson's face, only to be almost immediately wiped away. "What's my favorite color?" Hatterson asked.

She didn't know. It wasn't like she could snap her

fingers and random facts just hit. Trish and *Candyman*—they'd just been there in her mind, no prompting. Just—there.

Hatterson took a surging step toward her. "My favorite food? What is it?"

She had no clue.

Another step. "What did you give me for my last birthday?" Gritted from between clenched teeth.

Victor stepped between them as he faced off with Hatterson. "Pretty sure that's where her *not remembering* would come in, Hatterson. Now stop being a jackass."

"Oh, sure, she can toss out that *Candyman* bullshit and that crap about Trish—gossip that she could pick up anywhere. Hell, I think Melody even posted on social media about her favorite movie when she met the *Candyman* actor in real life that time, but this woman can't tell any personal information about me—"

"Because I don't remember you." And she was sorry if that hurt. But it just was.

Victor glanced over his shoulder at her.

"I don't remember either of you. Not really. I've had images. Like quick snapshots that come and go in my head, but hardly anything more. I'm sorry that I can remember Trish and her curly, blond hair and mean eyes, but I don't remember your favorite color or your favorite food, Hatterson. I can remember the President, I can remember how to do multiplication and how to set a dinner table for twelve, but I can't remember if I ever had any pets. I can't remember any birthdays I celebrated." She could hear her own frustration. "I don't know why or how that I know some things and not others. It just is that way." She squared her shoulders. "Hamilton, Ontario. That's where I woke up in the hospital."

Victor raised one brow. "Canada?"

"Yeah. Yeah, Canada." She raked back her hair, and her fingers slid along the scar she worked so hard to keep hidden near her temple. "Don't ask me how I got there because... you know, I can't remember."

"Hatterson." Victor didn't look at the other man. "Get the hell out of here, now."

"Oh, right, I'm just supposed to do what you—"

"I own the damn house. I pay your salary. Get the hell out or you're fired."

Wait, he owned the house? But...but she'd thought it belonged to Sebastian—

"And don't you say a single word to *anyone* else about what you just learned here, understand me?" Victor fired at Hatterson. "In case you missed it, someone tried to kill her hours ago. Melody's life is on the line."

Hatterson angled his body so he could see around Victor and lock his stare on her. That stare of his lingered a moment before it darted toward her left temple.

She smoothed the hair into place. Made sure it covered her scar.

"Of course, *boss*." A deliberate emphasis. "Wouldn't want to do anything to piss you off." Hatterson spun on his heel and stomped for the door.

"Oh, trust me, I'm plenty pissed." Victor's curt response.

Hatterson hauled the door shut behind him.

Victor slowly turned to face her.

She felt frozen in place, and she should absolutely say something but...

"You had to know everyone was going to realize you were...different."

Different. Yes, how about she was a blank slate? One

who didn't even know what kind of pancakes she liked. *Future reference note—stay the heck away from blueberries.* "Are the roads really blocked or was Hatterson playing mind games with me on that bit, too?"

"They're blocked. But only for the time being. You won't be here another night."

"Where will I be?" Because she'd really wanted to search the estate, and she'd had zero success with that plan.

"You're coming home. With me."

He acted like that was a foregone conclusion. "And you're really convinced that I'm not some fraud? Don't you want to wait for the DNA test, too, before you go inviting me into your home? Or are you just all in because I have the scar on my throat?"

He closed in on her. Stopped when their bodies were nearly brushing. "Not your throat." His hand rose, and, through the shirt she wore—a black blouse—he touched the scar that slid along her right shoulder. The exact spot, without being able to see the scar. "It's right here, and it slants toward your collar bone."

Warmth spread through her. That tempting, tormenting warmth she felt each time he touched her.

His hand dropped. Curled around her waist. Rose up. One inch. Two. "And your birthmark is right here. In the shape of a crescent moon."

Uh, yeah, actually, she did have a faint birthmark right there. But he could have seen it when she took off her sweater to prove—

"I know the birthmark is there because I've touched it a dozen times. Kissed it plenty." His hands slid down, down as he bent before her.

His fingers slid between her thighs.

What is happening right now? Anyone could come in the kitchen. "Victor..."

"You have two freckles here. You also have a birthmark behind your left knee. I think that one looks like a heart."

She was far too conscious of each hard beat of her heart. "You seem to know my body pretty well."

"I like to think of myself as an expert."

Right. "Because we were lovers." Clearly. No denying the obvious there. He seemed to have every inch of her body memorized which was kinda scary. "Okay, so you know my body." And since he knew her body so well. "You saw things that prove I'm Melody—"

He rose before her. Towered over her. "We were far more than just lovers. You and I weren't some sort of casual hookup. You weren't having hate-sex with me for fun because I was taking over your father's company."

His expression had changed. Gone predatory. And... Calculating.

"What were we?" Melody asked, voice soft, even as she heard footsteps coming toward them.

"You were going to marry me."

No, impossible.

"You *are* my fiancée, Melody. And believe me when I say, I always will protect *and avenge* what is mine."

Chapter Nine

He'd scared her.

He probably could have handled the scene in the kitchen differently. No need to just straight up drop the bombshell that she was his fiancée. Or, you know what?

Screw it. There was every single freaking need. She'd been *shot* at by some bastard in the darkness. Victor had just gotten her back, and someone had already wanted to take Melody away from him again. Not happening. When they left the mansion—and they would be leaving ASAP, he'd already made arrangements to get her the hell out of there— she would be staying with him. Staying as in *living* in his house. Staying under his careful watch. Staying *alive* while he tried to figure out who the hell had taken her from him and why someone was still trying to kill her.

"I don't want a DNA test." Sebastian sat in his chair in the den. The lights of the Christmas tree gleamed beside him. His gaze was on the fire, not Victor.

"Pretty sure that's gonna be necessary. Dario is already chomping at the bit for the test. And with the team of lawyers at Mage Industries—hell, you know that you can't just accept her with no questions asked." Victor remained standing, his body tense. He didn't want to be in that room. He wanted to be with Melody.

She had gone back upstairs, supposedly to rest.

But the truth was that she'd practically *run* up those stairs after he dropped his engagement bombshell.

Yes, he really had more explaining to do.

Except he'd been *summoned* to the den for a meeting with Sebastian. Sebastian's nurse had been the one to get him. Tracy Ryder had knocked on the kitchen door even as Melody had gaped up at him with a mixture of disbelief and shock on her face.

Clearly, Melody had a hard time believing she'd ever wanted to marry him.

Right, sweetheart, sometimes, I can't believe you said yes, too. But she'd taken his ring. She'd said she loved him. The life he wanted had been right there, within his grasp.

Then some sonofabitch had snatched that life away. Had snatched Melody away.

You will pay.

The nurse's interruption had given Melody time to flee, and Victor had headed in to face off with Sebastian.

Tracy Ryder, private nurse. A nurse practitioner. Age thirty-eight. Divorced. She'd been a live-in caregiver for Sebastian since March. "He's having another good day," she'd informed Victor, with a curious glance toward Melody as they stood in the farmhouse-style kitchen, "and he's asking to speak with you, Victor." A delicate clearing of her throat. "Says it is urgent."

Like there weren't plenty of *urgent* issues facing them all.

So now Victor stood in the den, when he wanted to be upstairs. No, correction, he wanted to be a million miles away from that place. Curled up with Melody. Holding her tight. Telling the rest of the world to fuck off.

When you got a second chance, you did not screw it up. You fought like hell for it.

Sebastian huffed and shifted uncomfortably in his leather chair. "A DNA test is a waste of time. Why can't I just accept her? You have."

Yes, he had. But then again, he knew every inch of her body. Every birthmark. Knew every mole and freckle because Melody was his obsession. But he cleared his throat and replied, "Legally, we'll need more to convince the others."

"Then we'll run a fingerprint check. Get her prints. Get one of your FBI buddies to run a match. See what the hell turns up. A fingerprint check will be faster, won't it? Faster than DNA, I mean."

Probably, if it could be a simple matter of matching prints. It wouldn't be, though. Because of one obvious problem. "Her prints aren't in any database." They didn't have a point of comparison.

"Oh, I have prints." Sebastian narrowed his eyes. "When she was sixteen, Melody was dating that troublemaker, Brant McKee. Asshole had been raised with a silver spoon shoved down his throat, but he thought he was some kind of badass. Picked Melody up one night in a car he'd stolen. Didn't tell her that fact, though. Fool just got off on riding around town with her in the front seat with him. They were both busted. Taken in by the sheriff. Fingerprinted."

This story was news to him, and Tracy had been right. Sebastian was definitely having one of his good days. His mind seemed razor sharp. "Let me guess. You made the charges vanish."

Sebastian grunted. "McKee's father did. Then he sent the dumbass boy to military school. Served him right." An exhale. "The sheriff at the time was a total prick, though. He never uploaded her prints anywhere, but he kept the file on her. Even blackmailed me a time or two."

Uh, come again?

"Had to pay him twenty grand, but the details never went public. In fact, her prints—and that old file—are in the safe in my study." He waved vaguely. "You know the combination." Bitterness came and went in his eyes. "You know everything, don't you?"

"Apparently not. I wasn't aware of Melody's brush with the law." He also didn't understand why Sebastian hadn't just destroyed the file long ago. Especially if it was an original and he was worried about Melody's past sins coming back to haunt him.

Sebastian's jaw hardened. "You think you're gonna take her away from me."

I think I'm gonna take her away from anyone who wants to hurt her. And some days, on Sebastian's not so good days, the older man would rage about Melody. About how she was just like her mother. About how...

He would make them both pay.

Except Melody's mother was long dead. The dead couldn't pay any price. That pain was purely for the living.

"Open the safe," Sebastian directed. "Get the file. Take her and the old file to your FBI buddies and get them to compare prints. If it's a match, we don't need any DNA test. The truth will already be proven."

Victor considered the matter. "We can do both, you know. Fingerprints and DNA."

"*No DNA test.*"

This was interesting. Sebastian was certainly adamant. "Why are you so against the DNA test?"

Sebastian swallowed. "There was always a chance...that she wasn't mine."

Fuck.

"The fingerprints will tell us." Sebastian nodded. "The fingerprints are all we need to know if she's Melody."

Sebastian had just been damn honest with him. Time for Victor to be honest, too. "You were right before." Flat. "I'm taking her away today."

"Why the hell would you do that? Even if it turned out that she didn't have my blood, Melody is *my* daughter. She was always my daughter." Sebastian lunged from his chair, only to immediately falter. Before he could fall down, Victor was there. He lowered the older man back into the seat.

"I'm taking her away because someone wants to hurt her. I'm not letting that happen." Victor stared into Sebastian's eyes. "No matter what I have to do, it won't happen."

"I want to talk to her." A shuddering breath. "Now while I'm...me."

Victor nodded. "I'll go get her." He swung away.

Only to have Sebastian's hand fly out and curl around his wrist. Sebastian's grip was surprisingly strong. "It *is* Melody."

Victor looked at the fingers holding his wrist. "I think it's her, yes."

"She came home?" Hope. Unmistakable.

The same wild, stubborn hope that Victor had held onto for the last year. "She came home."

❄

FIANCÉE. *Fiancée. Fiancée.* She was supposed to be Victor's fiancée? For the last year, when she'd thought that she was utterly and completely alone, Victor had been out there...a man she was going to marry?

Nerves had her practically bouncing in the room. The guest room. She'd fled back up there as quickly as she could. To clear her head. To think. And now—

A knock on the door. Her head whipped toward the door. Not the connecting door. The door that led to the hallway. She hurried toward it, yanked it open, and blurted, "Are we really—" *Getting married?*

But those words didn't come out. Because Victor wasn't standing on the threshold of her guest room. A woman was. The one who stuck so closely to Dario's side. Long blond hair. Gleaming, pale green eyes.

"Hi, Melody," she said. She quirked a brow. "What? Seriously? No warm greeting at all for your best friend in the entire world?"

Olivia Hatcher was supposed to be Melody's best friend. She'd picked that up from searching through images on social media. And now she believed that Olivia was sleeping with Dario. Considering they were constantly touching one another when they were together, they certainly seemed to be heavily involved. How long had that relationship been going on?

"Uh, hello?" Olivia prompted when Melody just stared at her. "I get that it's been a big twenty-four hours but, hey, how about a hug, at least? Didn't get one last night, what with your dramatic return home and all of that." Olivia pulled Melody into a big hug. Squeezed her tightly. "I swear, you ever pull this shit again, and I will kill you."

Melody stiffened.

Olivia eased back. Grimaced. "Probably shouldn't have

said that, what with the shooting and all, right? Terrible taste. But, it is me."

What was that supposed to mean?

"Are you gonna invite me in? Or do I just get to stand in the doorway forever?"

Melody backed up. "Come in."

"Gee, thanks. Your enthusiasm is overwhelming." Olivia crossed the threshold. She paused to shut the door, then asked, "Are you still pissed at me?"

Melody had no idea. She crossed her arms over her shoulders.

"Figured you were, and that was why you didn't tell me that you were splitting town." Olivia wore designer jeans. A soft, gray sweater. Probably cashmere. The other woman adored cashmere.

Wait, how do I know that?

Excitement hummed in Melody's blood.

"Seriously, how long can one woman hold a grudge?" Olivia's hand slid over the top of the dresser. Diamonds glittered from several fingers. "God, you hated this room. Can't believe you're willingly staying in here. I mean, when your parents were getting divorced, this is where your mother slept. She used to call it her prison cell. Or at least, that's what you told me." She shot a sympathetic look at Melody. "So tragic the way she died. Skiing accident. All that blunt force trauma when she collided with the tree." A shudder slid over her body. "The closed casket at the funeral was terrible. I remember shaking with fear because she'd been so incredibly beautiful, but in death, we couldn't even see her to say goodbye."

Melody just stared at her.

"I'm not being tactful, am I? Bringing up your dead

mother. You probably don't want to talk about her now. But, then again, you never talk about her."

She didn't think that Olivia wanted to be tactful. In fact, Melody wasn't sure what game the other woman was playing. But it definitely *felt* like a game. Like Olivia was saying things to deliberately provoke a reaction from Melody. Except Melody didn't have a reaction to give her.

I knew that my mother was dead. I read the newspaper reports. Dead in a skiing accident. Her lover—the skiing instructor—was the one who found her body.

"Anyway..." A long exhale from Olivia. "I did get a bit nervous when you first vanished. What with that stalker situation you had going on..." Another shudder eased down her body.

Now Melody snapped to attention. "Stalker?"

"Yes, you know." Olivia rolled one hand in a vague wave. "You told me that he was following you on your runs."

No, she did not know.

"You said that you'd turn around, and you'd swear some guy in a hoodie was tailing you on the jogging trail. I mean, come on. A hoodie? How stereotypical is that? I told you it was probably just another jogger but you—you swore you *felt* eyes on you." Olivia bit her lower lip. Her head dipped down. "I laughed it off. Told you it was your imagination. Then you vanished for a whole year. Some nights, I worried that maybe—maybe he really had been there. And thought I shouldn't have laughed." Her hands twisted in front of her before she slowly lifted her head. "I'm not laughing now."

No. She wasn't. "You're my best friend."

Olivia nodded. "I hope so. I didn't realize quite how boring life was..." She walked toward Melody. Extended her hands.

Melody lifted her own hands. Olivia immediately clasped them in a tight grip.

"I didn't realize how boring life was, until you weren't there." Olivia blinked away tears. "I had no one to hit the bars with. I had to dance on tables by myself." A wan grin. "And that is just sad."

Melody searched Olivia's eyes. Then she decided to play a game of her own. "I'm engaged to Victor."

Olivia exploded into a fit of laughter. "The hell you are." More laughter. "You can't stand him." She didn't just grasp Melody's hands. She drew her in for another crushing hug. "See, this is why I missed you. You are *hilarious*."

No, she wasn't.

Her best friend had just told her that she wasn't engaged to Victor.

The door opened. A hard squeak. No knock from the visitor. Just the door instantly swinging open as if the visitor owned the place.

Surprise, surprise, Victor was the one standing there. He frowned at them.

Olivia stepped back but didn't completely let Melody go. "Melody just told me the most hilarious story," she began.

Oh, uh, Victor was not going to find this funny.

"She said you two were engaged." More laughter pealed from Olivia. "Can you imagine? The two of you would *kill* each other if you were married."

Victor's jaw hardened. "Melody, your father is asking to see you." A brief pause. "It's one of his good times."

She wasn't exactly sure what a "good time" meant, but she nodded anyway. "Olivia, if you'll excuse me?"

Olivia squeezed her hand. "I'm glad you're back. Things weren't the same without you." Her gaze searched

Melody's. "You get the urge to vanish again, how about you come and talk to me first? It wasn't cool to make me worry and wonder about you for a year. Friends don't ditch friends."

They did if they had no choice. If they were running through the snow, leaving blood in their wake, and a car slammed into them. But Melody didn't say any of that. She just forced herself to smile. "Absolutely. I'll come to you first." Did the words sound as hollow as they felt?

But Olivia seemed satisfied. She nodded. Let Melody go. Ambled for the door. Her gaze raked over Victor. "Try to be nice to her, would you? We both know she probably went running before because of you. You take away everything a woman wants, and what else is she supposed to do?"

With that parting shot, she left the room.

Melody could hear Olivia's steps padding softly away.

She squared her shoulders and hurried for the door. "I've been wanting to talk with Sebastian—"

He didn't move out of her way. If anything, Victor blocked the doorway more. "We had just become engaged before you vanished. As in, moments before."

She raised her brows. She also bit back the response of... *That seems convenient.*

"We had told no one. After you left..." A slow shake of his head. "I didn't tell your friends or your family. Didn't tell the cops."

"Why not?"

"Because I was already a suspect. And part of me wondered—hell." He ran a hand through his hair. "I wondered if you'd changed your mind. Fled to get away from me."

She wished she could remember him. "Did I love you?"

The hand he'd raised fell back to his side. "Your dad's good bouts don't last long. Especially in the middle of the day. He always seems to get weakest then. Probably because he tires out. A nap usually helps."

What exactly was wrong with her father? A form of dementia? "Victor..."

"We should hurry downstairs. And we're getting out of here *today*. I called the local sheriff. Let Jamal Wroth know about the shooting. He's coming to investigate as soon as he can, but the guy was spouting off about hunters." Disgust and disbelief tightened his hard features. "Hunters, my ass. That was someone deliberately stalking close to the house. Someone taking a shot *into* the house. Multiple shots. It was deliberate, and I want you out of here. I want you safe."

She wet her lips. "And I'll be safe with you?"

He didn't blink. "Yes."

She wanted to believe that. And he *had* been with her when the shots were fired. That meant Victor wasn't the bad guy, right? But...as for the others in the house...

One of them could have fired the gun. Then circled back inside. Isn't that possible? Couldn't the shooter be right here with me? Or maybe not...maybe it would have taken too much time to circle back inside. She didn't know. She had no idea what the layout of the property and all of the rooms were really like.

Victor turned away. "Your father is waiting."

Her stomach clenched.

Melody opened the door to the den. She eased inside, and surprise, surprise, Victor followed right on her heels. But he didn't speak. Just took up a position near the wall on the left. Crossed his arms over his chest. Waited.

Her breath rustled out as she closed in on her father. What was she supposed to call him? Dad? Sebastian? Father? Or—

Sebastian's head turned toward her. A warm smile curled his lips. His eyes—dark, not green like hers—seemed to shine. He remained in the tall, leather chair, but he reached out for her with his right hand. "I'm so glad you're home, Melody."

Her lower lip trembled. Her steps were suddenly hurrying toward him. She caught his hand and gripped it tightly. Desperately.

"I missed you," he told her.

The hand she held only trembled a little bit. "I missed you, too." The words poured from her, and they *felt* true. As she stood staring down at him, sadness pulled at her. *My father. He's my father, and I want to remember him. I lost a year. An entire year without him.*

"You look so much like your mother," he told her. His face softened.

Melody had seen pictures of her mother throughout the house. And before she'd come here, she'd looked up her mother online. Her mother had been a failed Hollywood actress who'd married business mogul, Sebastian Mage. She'd supposedly charmed everyone that she'd met.

But she'd been unhappy, always looking for excitement.

"Your mother." He sighed. "I—"

"*Sebastian.*" Victor's sharp voice. "Melody is home. Focus on Melody."

Sebastian nodded. He swallowed. "I missed you," he said again as he stared up at her. Tears glinted in his eyes.

Melody found herself dropping to her knees in front of

him so they could be on eye level. "I'm sorry I wasn't here." Absolute truth. Her father was sick, she could see it. They'd lost so much time.

He leaned toward her. "It's my fault," he said.

Chill bumps rose on her arms.

"I was supposed to get you back." A tear slid down his cheek.

Those chill bumps got worse.

"I was supposed to pay," he added, voice roughening.

Her heart beat faster. So much faster.

"*Sebastian.*" Victor surged toward them.

"But I didn't." Another teardrop. Sebastian's hand had turned so that he held Melody in a hard grip. A grip that nearly crushed her fingers. "Forgive me?"

Her mouth hung open. She didn't know what to say or do, and what did he mean, he was "supposed to get her back"—back from where? And what hadn't he paid? Like...a ransom? Was he talking about a ransom for her?

Victor touched her shoulder. "Melody."

She ignored him. "Who were you supposed to pay?"

A furrow appeared between Sebastian's eyes.

"Who were you supposed to pay?" Melody repeated. "Who took me?"

Sebastian shook his head. The lines on his face appeared deeper. Harsher.

"Please." Melody was begging and didn't care that she sounded so desperate. She was desperate. "Please, who took me? Who were you going to pay? How much were you supposed to pay?" And... "*Why didn't you pay?*"

Sebastian blinked. Several times. His head tilted to the side as he studied her. Then a slow smile curved his lips. "Melody."

A shiver slid over her.

"You look so much like your mother," he told her. Then nodded. "I'm so sorry I killed her."

She jerked her hand from his grip. Wrenched back. She would have fallen, but Victor caught her and steadied her.

Her father smiled at her. "And I'm sorry, but I think I killed you, too."

She had to get the hell out of that place.

Her father hummed. Turned his head. Stared into the flickering flames that twisted inside of the fireplace. She could not speak. Terror had stolen her voice. Every part of her wanted to run out of that room.

But she wanted answers. Deserved them. Melody cleared her throat. "Father."

His head swiveled back to her. "Melody!" A delighted smile. His hand extended toward her. "I've missed you."

Chapter Ten

She didn't trust him.

The blades of the helicopter swirled as it lowered to land. Snow kicked up, flying in the air around Victor as he stood near the landing pad with Melody at his side. He had a backpack slung over one shoulder and rage festering in his heart.

Someone tried to kill Melody.

Someone would pay.

He'd cleared the landing space for the helicopter a bit earlier, with help from Hatterson. Hatterson had grumbled the whole time, as if Victor gave a shit about his grumbles.

The estate's grounds had been searched. No trace of the shooter. Or the gun that had been used in the attack. Roads *were* being cleared nearby, and the sheriff had sworn he'd come out to the estate as soon as possible in order to do his own investigation...

But Victor still intended to get Melody the hell out of that place.

After her chat with her father, Melody seemed even

more skittish. Who the hell could blame her? Her father's memory came and went, and when he got confused...

The man tended to confess to murder.

The helicopter touched down flawlessly.

Melody's shoulder bumped into Victor's arm. She'd been waiting beside him, watching the chopper lower, and the snow still swirled around them both.

His head turned toward her. He found her eyes on him.

There was fear in her gaze.

He wanted to take her hand. Or put his arm around her shoulder and pull her close. *Don't be scared, baby. I'm going to protect you. I swear it.* But he didn't touch her, and he didn't say those words because she didn't remember him. And his touch was more likely to scare her than reassure her.

She doesn't know me at all. Something that gutted him. Because he'd been lucky as hell to have her fall for him the first time. Despite all the odds against him. How in the ever-loving-fuck was he ever supposed to get Melody to love him again?

He wasn't freaking lovable. He knew that shit. He was cold. Domineering. Arrogant. Twisted. Vengeful.

And, when it came to Melody...

Possessive. Obsessive.

Hardly a prince charming type. And even now, all he wanted to do—all he *was* doing—was spiriting her away from everyone else. So he could protect her? Yeah, sure, absolutely. But also because...

I need her. I have to get her alone. If we are away from the others, I might have a chance...

Her hair flew around her face, and he automatically lifted a hand to tuck the heavy locks back behind her ear.

She sucked in a sharp breath and immediately backed away.

Dammit.

But her gaze never wavered.

The blades on the chopper slowed. The snow that had been flurrying around them fell back to the ground.

"Tell me I'll be safe with you," she said.

"You will be safe with me." A vow. Should he offer to be a perfect gentleman? Nah. *Screw that shit. I dreamed about her for a year. The woman is lucky she's not currently handcuffed to my side.* Honestly, that was an option that he was considering. Because she would not vanish again.

The chopper had stilled. Victor angled toward the helicopter. The door on the left opened. A figure emerged, hurrying toward him. A man, tall, with broad shoulders covered by a thick, black sweater. Dark hair and eyes. Those eyes immediately met Victor's.

Backup—and an escape plan—had arrived in the form of Hunter McQueen.

Hunter was a fairly new acquaintance of Victor's, someone he'd met when he'd been desperately searching for Melody. A former Ranger, Hunter now worked part-time with the Ice Breakers. Part-time when the guy wasn't running security for one seriously secretive bastard named Declan Flynn.

During their short acquaintance, Victor had discovered that Hunter had quite a few admirable skills. And the ability to fly a chopper and land it under basically any conditions? Definitely admirable. And useful, particularly at that moment.

"Well, well…" Hunter closed in on them. "Someone is back in the land of the living." A low whistle escaped him as he surveyed Melody. "Got to say, you look pretty good for a ghost."

She hunched into her brown coat.

Was she trying to figure out if she was supposed to know Hunter or not? Hell, how on earth had she thought her ruse would work? It had been immediately obvious to everyone that there was something very different about her. The woman had been like a lamb prancing straight into a den of sharp-toothed lions.

"This is Hunter McQueen," Victor explained, voice curt. "Hunter, stop staring at her so fucking hard. Fly us the hell out of here, and then we'll talk, cool?"

Hunter's lips curled into a half-smile. "Do you realize there are about three people standing up at the house glaring at us right now? If you think I'm staring hard, then you really don't want to get a look at them."

But he did turn to look at them. He glared right back at them. Dario. Olivia. Hatterson.

"And..." Hunter's voice pulled Victor's focus back to him. "I'm pretty sure that I saw a sheriff's car heading this way when I was overhead." He rocked forward onto the balls of his feet. "Roads are being cleared as fast as possible. You could just, you know, wait. Drive out after what I'm sure will be a super friendly chat with the sheriff."

Super friendly, his ass. It wasn't a damn social call. Jamal Wroth had a job to do. "I told you already." And he had. He'd spoken to both Memphis Camden and Hunter earlier. Hunter was just being a dick. "Someone *shot* at her. We're getting out. Now." He could fly the chopper himself, but, honestly, Hunter was a better pilot. Still, if the guy didn't get his ass moving in the next thirty seconds, Victor would be taking the pilot's seat.

Hunter stepped to the side and motioned with one hand. "Your carriage awaits."

Oh, yeah, total dick. But also a smart, savvy, and dangerous guy. One who had been digging hard as hell with the Ice Breakers to try and help Victor find Melody.

And now I have her. Only getting Melody back had just opened up even more of a mystery.

"I'm not getting in the carriage." Melody's voice. Very flat. Very definite.

Very expected. He'd had to practically drag her outside with him. And he might have needed to lie a bit in order to get her out there. Perhaps he'd said that *he* had to return to town. And that he wanted to talk more with her.

Both true points, actually. He did have to return to town. And he wanted to talk with her. He just wanted her *in town* with him as they talked. Thus, the chopper trip.

The woman was determined to stay at the nightmare of a house where she'd been *shot at* so that she could continue her investigation. Nah, fuck that. "Did you bring the handcuffs?" he asked Hunter.

Sighing, Hunter hauled the cuffs from his pocket. "I did, but I'm pretty sure what you have planned is called kidnapping so...let's rethink it, shall we?"

Melody instantly backed up a step. More fear flashed in her eyes. "What in the hell?"

"Easy." Victor kept his voice low. Calming. Or at least, he hoped it sounded calming. "Everything is all right."

"Everything is *not* all right. It hasn't been all right for a very long time." Another step back. More like a leap back, away from him and away from Hunter. "You want to go somewhere? Then fine. You go. You get into the helicopter and fly off. I came out just to see you off. You never said I was part of your departure deal."

"I'm going nowhere without you." Okay, that probably hadn't sounded so calm. Asking for the cuffs had been a mistake, he could see that now. But...

If she runs, I will grab her and put her in that chopper, and if I have to do it, I will cuff her to me. Savage and dark and damn well not thoughts of a prince charming. Fuck it. He'd always been cast in the role of the villain and not the hero, anyway. "Melody..."

"Uh, yeah, sport, how about you let me have a try?" Hunter cleared his throat. "Ma'am, an attempt was recently made on your life. I'm just here to transport you to safety."

Behind Hunter, the right door of the chopper opened. Closed. Another male strode forward. Gray jacket. Jeans. A gun holstered on his hip.

"Who is he?" Melody demanded. "And why is he armed?"

Victor had a gun tucked beneath his coat. He figured Hunter was armed, too. But she'd just noticed the weapon on the new guy because when he moved, his arm had slipped back to reveal the holster.

"That's John Henry Cook." Hunter motioned toward the man.

John Henry looked like a linebacker. Victor figured that he'd probably been cramped as hell in the front of the chopper.

"He's going to be taking over the security detail for your father, per Victor's instructions," Hunter added.

Her head whipped back to Victor. "What instructions?"

"The instructions I gave when I arranged for the chopper to come get *us*." A deliberate emphasis. As far as the security detail bit, that had been necessary. He had no idea why Sebastian had ordered the normal guards away from the property, and, frankly, no one should have followed the man's commands. Until those individuals could be brought back, John Henry would be Sebastian's shadow. As if Victor would just fly away and leave Sebastian on his own. Not in the man's current condition. "A shooter is close. Call me crazy, but I don't exactly trust the people in that house." He jerked his thumb over his shoulder. He was sure the little crowd still watched them. "Do you?"

A small shake of her head.

"While no attempts have been made to injure your father, I thought it would be a good idea to bring in outside protection for him." Thus, John Henry. A guard he'd used for private security work in the past. "John Henry will stay close to your father. He'll make sure that Sebastian is safe. He'll also keep an eye on everyone and report back to me. Though, I'm sure the others will be cutting out of here as soon as the roads are passable." Dario had actually tried to hitch a ride on the chopper.

Victor had refused him that ride.

"Will my father be leaving when the roads are passable?" Her head had turned toward the house. A shiver skated over her.

It was damn cold out there. Another reason to move this scene along and get her sweet ass in the chopper. It was cold and...*I don't like her being out in the open.* He moved his body a bit closer to her. The better to shield Melody. "Your father doesn't leave the estate. He hasn't, not in months. His nurse stays with him. His doctors come to check on him. Hatterson is at his beck and call." Her father's condition was far worse than she realized.

She also didn't know...

Months ago, before things had gotten so bad, her father

had made a decision about his treatment. *The end is coming. Time is short.*

Not something Victor wanted to tell her right then.

"I'm staying here." Her voice was definite. "You said the sheriff was going to search the property. I want to talk with him."

The urge to carry her into the chopper was just growing stronger and stronger. But he could try a bit of careful manipulation, first. After all, he did know her end game. As for his own end game? Simple. It was her. "You want answers about your disappearance. That means you need to come back to Richmond with me." The estate was about fifty miles from the city, nestled off the back roads. "You can talk to the lead detectives there. The one who ran the investigation into your disappearance." A piss-poor investigation that had turned up jack shit.

"I thought the Feds handled missing persons' cases," Melody murmured.

Victor had gotten anyone he could to look into her disappearance, including plenty of FBI agents who'd worked off the books. She'd never officially been declared as missing or as a kidnap victim, but that shit was changing. *She was taken away. Nearly killed.* But he tried to keep his rage in check as he worked to convince her that she needed to get on the damn chopper. "Once we're in Richmond, you can go back to the last place where I saw you—the Mage Industries building. Or you can go to your house. I have the keys. I have the new security code." Should he mention he'd *bought* the place? Again, probably not something to tell her right then and there. The rest of her family had wanted to sell her house. Dario had made that request again and again. He'd been making it when she reappeared the previous night.

After her disappearance, payments hadn't been made on her home. She'd always wanted to own the place on her own, without her father's money. She'd worked hard to get the home, and when she'd vanished and the house notes had come due...

I stepped in.

Something the others didn't know. Dario probably thought Sebastian held the title to her place. Wrong.

"You really don't remember anything?" Hunter asked.

Her head whipped toward him. Then back to Victor. "You *told* him?" she snapped.

Yeah, he had. "Guilty. But since Hunter has been helping me find you, he needed to know. He's with the Ice Breakers."

Her lashes flickered. Her stare cut from him.

"You've heard of them," Victor noted.

Once more, her gaze darted his way. "I...considered contacting them when I read about some of their cases in the news. Thought they could help me."

Hunter took a slow, gliding step toward her. "We *can* help you. Step one in that helping process is to get you on the chopper." He shoved the handcuffs back into his pocket. "Willingly, ma'am."

Aw, Hunter was being cute.

Willingly or not, her sweet ass is getting on the chopper. He was actually about to lift her up and carry—

"And what about John Henry?" Melody asked.

John Henry hadn't spoken the whole time. Mostly because the big, blond guy basically never spoke. Chatter wasn't his friend.

"Is he going to rush inside and tell everyone that I can't remember a thing?" Melody wanted to know.

Hunter snorted out a laugh at her question.

She glowered at him. "I wasn't making a joke."

"I know," Hunter assured her. "That's what makes it funny. For future reference, John Henry never rushes to tell anyone anything."

John Henry shook his head.

"John Henry doesn't share secrets," Victor informed her. They had wasted enough time out there. She was cold and scared, and he was getting her away from that place. Done. "But the truth is gonna come out, and it's gonna come out fast. You can't keep acting like you remember people when you don't. You'll slip up. You probably already slipped up with Olivia, the same way you did with me."

She gasped. Looked insulted. "How did I slip up with you? What gave me away?"

Enough. Time to get airborne. He surged toward her. He lowered his head near hers, because these words were for her alone. "You forgot that I fucked you until you screamed," he rasped against her ear. "You forgot I was your lover. That you belonged to me." And instead, she'd treated him like a stranger.

Her hands rose and pressed to his chest.

He eased back, just a little. Just enough so that he was staring down at her. For those watching—Hunter and John Henry who were right there and for the people spying from the house—it would look as if they were about to kiss.

He would love to kiss her.

Her lips pressed together, then she whispered, "Olivia said we weren't engaged."

"Olivia didn't know about the engagement."

Her gaze searched his. "You aren't lying to me?"

His back teeth ground together. "No. And I'm not lying when I say...either get in the chopper willingly, or I will carry your ass onto the bird. One way or another, I'm getting you to safety."

Pink stained her cheeks, and he didn't think the pink came from the sting of cold in the air. "You're a bossy bastard, aren't you?"

Hunter snorted. "Maybe she's starting to remember you!"

Such an ass.

"Victor…" Melody began, voice husky.

Every part of him tightened. Yearned. He'd missed hearing her say his name. He'd missed everything about her.

"You could try asking nicely," she advised.

Sure. He could go that route. Why the hell not? "Melody, will you *please* get your gorgeous ass in the helicopter?"

She hesitated.

Shocker, asking nicely had clearly not been the way to go—

"If I do go with you, then you'll take me to the scene of my abduction? You'll take me to the detective? Take me wherever I want to go?"

"Yes." He'd be with her every step of the way.

"Thank you for the kind invitation of the helicopter ride." Very formal. Very…Melody-like, though she probably didn't get that. "I find that I would like to take you up on that offer." She turned and crept toward the chopper.

John Henry opened a door for her. As she climbed in, Victor extended his palm toward Hunter. He waited, with his palm open.

"Seriously?" Hunter asked.

Did it look like he was joking?

Hunter passed him the handcuffs. "You're one crazy asshole. She'll go ballistic if you cuff her."

If she tried to leave him, he would be cuffing her. Until he found out what threat she faced, he could not let her go.

Who the hell am I lying to? No matter what, I don't intend to let her go.

He reached for his backpack. Unzipped it and dropped the handcuffs inside. They fell right next to the manila file, the file he'd taken from Sebastian's safe before he went upstairs to tell Melody that her father wanted a meeting. A quick scan had shown him that Melody's fingerprints were in the file, but so was an entire sheriff's report. Pages and pages that he hadn't read. Not yet.

But he would.

For now, he rezipped the backpack. He climbed into the chopper with her. Got a seat up front, the one vacated by John Henry. In moments, he, Hunter, and Melody were in the air. A sea of white waited below them as the chopper headed away from the mansion. Snow everywhere the eye could see.

The clear area where they'd landed gave way to trees. Thick brush. Too many places for someone to hide. The shooter didn't just have to be someone inside the house, Victor understood that. The shooter could have been some asshole who'd followed Melody out to the estate.

And if that was the case, then maybe the SOB had gotten trapped while fleeing. Maybe they'd see a vehicle stalled somewhere along the way. Maybe they'd see...

A truck. Slammed into the side of an old cedar tree.

Well, sonofabitch.

Chapter Eleven

Hunter could truly land a chopper nearly any place.

So when Victor spotted the wreckage, Hunter lowered the helicopter toward the snow-covered road. The helicopter hovered. Sent snow billowing and the black of the asphalt was revealed.

Down, down the chopper went. And the battered Ford pickup remained lodged against the old cedar tree, the front of the vehicle smashed to hell and back.

The blades slowed when the chopper landed. Victor jerked off his headset and reached for the door. "Radio the sheriff," he ordered Hunter. Then he was out the door. He'd pulled his weapon, and he rushed right to the vehicle.

The thud of footsteps told him that someone was hurrying behind him. He turned, threw out his left arm, and caught Melody as she barreled forward. "Fuck, no."

"Fuck, yes!" Melody tossed back instantly. "That person needs help!"

"That person..." Victor gritted out, "could be the asshole

who shot at you last night! The vehicle is too close to the Mage property." Not really Mage land, not anymore. *I own it all.* "Get back in the chopper!"

"How about I just get behind you?" Melody returned without missing a beat. "You have the gun. You can keep us safe. Let's just *go*."

Dammit. He pushed her behind him. And advanced. Glass crunched under his shoes as he neared the driver's side of the truck. He raised his weapon. Peered inside.

More broken glass. A crushed console. Deflated air bag. Red on the airbag. Blood.

But...

No driver.

He spun around.

Melody stood inches away. The helicopter waited. Hunter waited.

But where in the hell is the truck's driver?

"You don't have a Christmas tree." Melody stood in Victor's den, and her hands twisted in front of her body. Those words hadn't been the ones that she'd intended to say. She'd planned to go with something like...

When is the sheriff going to tell you who owned that wrecked and abandoned truck?

Where is the driver?

Are you really my fiancé?

And did you truly fuck me so hard that you'd make me scream for you?

Um, ahem. All good questions. Or, at least, she'd thought they were good. After finding the abandoned truck in the woods, Victor had done a fast search for the driver. He'd searched on foot, then from above in the chopper.

There'd been no sign of the missing driver.

Hunter had radioed the sheriff. Jamal Wroth had promised a full search. The sheriff had also promised to follow up with any discoveries that he made about the driver and the shooting at the Mage estate.

Victor and the sheriff had seemed awfully chummy when they spoke. She supposed that was a good thing. Wasn't it?

They'd traveled back to the heart of Richmond. Victor had assured Melody that her bag would be transferred from the Mage house. He'd brought along a backpack, nothing else. Well, the gun, but nothing other than the backpack and the gun.

"I don't have a Christmas tree in here because I didn't exactly feel like decorating," he told her, and she realized that her question had hung in the air for several uncomfortable moments before he'd finally replied. "Celebrating wasn't big on my to-do list." He sprawled on the black couch and watched her with a predatory gaze.

Predatory as in...*he's looking at me as if he could eat me alive.*

She stopped twisting her hands and instead crossed her arms over her chest. "What was on your to-do list?" She knew what was on her list. *Going to the estate. Getting inside. Finding out who left me for dead in the snow. And, hopefully, unlocking my past.*

"My to-do list. Right." The fingers of his right hand tapped against the cushions near him. "Teaming up with the Ice Breakers. Finding you. Finding the bastard who took you." A slight pause. "Making him pay."

He sounded so lethal when he added that final bit. She

got the feeling that when he said "making him pay"—well, Victor wasn't just talking about jail time.

She crept away from him and headed toward the fireplace. No fire crackled. The room felt cold. No decorations at all. No signs of warmth. A big, beautiful fireplace. A big, beautiful home, one situated in West Franklin. Historic, probably built in the early 1900s.

And how do I know that? Again, random facts that flittered through her head. But she could just look at the design and architecture and *know* that it dates to the early 1900s.

Corner lot. Gated entry. Big, heavy, wrought-iron gates that were paired with a tall, brick wall. Security cameras had been perched at all sorts of angles and in all sorts of positions around the house. The fireplaces appeared to be original—she'd caught sight of several fireplaces in the different rooms they'd passed. Arched entranceways dominated in the house. Wide windows. Ceilings that stretched up so very high.

Gorgeous architecture. Really. The beauty of the place made her want to sigh. But...there was just nothing personal there. Nothing that made the house feel like a home.

And being inside, well, she would have never even suspected it was the holiday season. Not a single wreath. No Christmas tree. No presents.

So cold.

"You were in Canada."

Melody nodded. "Told you that already. Hamilton, Ontario." At first. But then she'd started inching her way down.

"How the hell did you get back in the US if you didn't even remember who you were? Not like you had a passport on you. I've got your passport locked up in my safe."

Now that news surprised her. "You do?"

A nod.

She wet her lips. "I snuck in. For the right price, getting a fake ID really isn't that hard." A roll of one shoulder as she ambled away from the fireplace. "I got a job waitressing. Saved my cash. Tried to come up with a plan once a few bits and pieces started coming back to me."

"What was the first thing you remembered?"

"Snow. Blood. Fear." She licked her lips. "A car coming at me." The nightmare that replayed so many times when she tried to sleep.

But there were some things you could never escape.

Hunter had vanished after the chopper landed. She had suspicions about where he'd gone. And her first suspicion... "I'm assuming Hunter is accessing my hospital records from my time up north?"

"Of course."

Of course. "Won't he need my permission to do that? Shouldn't I sign a release or something?"

A soft rumble of laughter escaped him. "We have ways to work around that. Don't worry."

Too late. She worried all the time. "Every single thing I'm telling you is the truth. I woke up in a hospital bed. I remembered nothing about my past. It was that way for a while. Then the pieces started sliding back to me."

He rose from the couch. A slow, graceful lift of power. He began to close in on her.

She didn't retreat. It was his house. Where could she go? And wasn't she tired of running? "When I realized I was Melody, I thought about staying away."

He stopped, mid-stalk. "What?"

"I researched her—I mean, I researched *me*. And each time I considered coming here, to Richmond, I would get terrified. Like my body knew something my mind didn't want to face. I could have stayed away. I could have just started over. A new life."

He shook his head. Resumed his stalk.

A wall was behind her, one painted a dark gray. He stopped right in front of her. His hands rose, but he didn't touch her. Instead, his palms flattened on the wall. "I would have found you."

Maybe.

"I would never have stopped looking for you."

Her heart beat faster. Wasn't that what she wanted? So very badly? To know that she'd mattered enough to someone that the person was *looking* for her? "How did you know I wasn't dead?"

A muscle flexed along his jaw. "Some days, I feared you were." There was pain in his voice. A dark, savage rage. "But I was going to search until I found you, whether that was you...living, breathing, beautiful..." One hand left the wall and curled under her chin. "Or you cold and..." He stopped. His nostrils flared. "I wasn't giving up until I found your body. I had to search. You were there one minute, gone the next, and sometimes, I felt like I had lost my mind when I lost you."

She ached for him.

"You don't remember us."

"No." So far, she'd remembered nothing personal about him. Couldn't recall any of their time together.

"You stare at me, and you see a stranger."

"Not...exactly."

His eyes narrowed. Such dark, dark eyes. "What the hell does that mean?"

"It means, I stare at you, and I get terrified." The same way she used to get terrified when she thought of returning to Richmond. *Like my body knows something my mind doesn't want to face.*

Victor backed away as if he'd been burned. "*What?*"

"When I saw you at the estate for the first time, it was like an electric shock went through me. My first instinct was to run."

Victor shook his head. "I would chase you. You *can't* leave me again."

"I'm not running." She wet her lips. His dark gaze followed the movement. The darkness in his eyes seemed to heat. "Because I'm afraid, but at the same time...I-I feel this pull to you that I don't understand."

A mocking smile curved his lips. "We always had that pull. You wanted to hate me."

She had?

"But you wanted to fuck me more than you hated me."

"You are not reassuring me." Quite the opposite.

"I want you to kiss me."

She sucked in a breath. "You said you'd help me solve the mystery of what happened to me."

"I did say that, and I will. But in order to do that, you have to remember everything. Good and bad. All the stuff in between."

"And kissing you is supposed to do that? Help me remember, I mean? Spoiler alert, we kissed already. I *didn't* remember anything. I'm not Sleeping Beauty, and your kiss is not going to wake me up." But she did want his mouth on hers. She wanted to see what it would be like if she just let go completely and gave in to the strange attraction she felt for him. An attraction that scared her just as much as it turned her on.

"Ah, brutal honesty." He put a hand over his heart. "Got a rusty knife that you want to jab into me a few times? Or are you happy enough telling me that you felt nothing when I kissed you?"

"I never said I felt nothing."

His hand dropped. The mocking smile of his had turned sly. "I know."

Tricky bastard.

He quirked one eyebrow. "So what *did* you feel when I had my lips against yours?"

Desire. A dark and twisting need that had slithered through her and tempted her to give in to her hunger. To kiss him ferociously. To not care about anything else.

"I am the best lover that you ever had," Victor said.

Her eyes widened. "You are one cocky bastard."

"True." A shrug. "You're the one who told me I was the best. The most amazing. The man who utterly rocked your world and ruined you for everyone else."

Her breath left in a quick rush. "I did *not* say that."

A shrug. "How do you know? You don't remember."

Anger stirred. "You're playing with me."

"Kiss me back and find out. I mean really kiss me. Don't be afraid. Don't hold onto your control. Let yourself go and see what you feel."

Her gaze had fallen to his mouth. "And if I feel nothing? What happens then? You gonna kick me out of your fancy house? Leave me on my own to figure out what in the hell happened to me?" She'd been on her own for the last year. She could be on her own again.

"No." Flat. "I will stay with you whether your body ignites or if you don't feel a damn thing. I gave you my word that I would protect you, and I mean that."

Melody deliberately widened her eyes. "My body ignites, huh? You honestly think you're that amazing?" Talk about an ego.

"I think we were that amazing together. Half the time I couldn't wait to even get you home. I'd fuck you in the back of the limo. I'd fuck you in a stairwell. If I'd had my way, I would have fucked you twenty-four, seven."

She rubbed her sweaty palms on the front of her thighs. "I have no idea how I am supposed to respond to that."

Another shrug. "Kiss me and let's see if you respond."

He kept tempting her. No, he kept pushing her. And this wasn't going to end well. She wasn't the type to be swept away by passion. That much, she did know about herself. "I've actually gone on a few dates over the last year." Why did she feel compelled to admit that truth to him?

His jaw hardened. His gaze went even darker. Not a cold dark. Hot. Burning obsidian. "Did you fuck someone else, Melody?"

He sounded possessive. Jealous. Dangerous. "I said I went on dates."

"That's not an answer to my question." His hands fisted at his sides.

"It's been a whole year since Melody vanished." Crap. She'd done it again. Talked about herself in the third person. When would she stop doing that? When would she stop feeling as if she was a fake pretending to be the other woman? "A year since I have been gone," she rushed to correct. "I'm really supposed to believe that you stayed faithful the whole year?" No way. "Come on," she scoffed. "I was gone. You got over me. You found someone else, and I am sure you, ah, fucked the person." And just why was her heart suddenly aching? Why was she feeling her own rage starting to build in her body? Talk about making zero sense.

But she ached. And she was pissed.

Victor shook his head. "No."

No to which part? To the getting over her? Or fucking someone else? Both?

"There has been no one else. At least not for me. How could there be? I knew you were out there. I just had to find you." He swung away.

She sprang forward and curled her hand around his shoulder. "I said I went on a few dates. Two of them, actually." He was rock hard beneath her touch. "I kissed Lucas on the second date." A kiss that had left her confused because Lucas Paul had seemed like such a nice guy. An engineer that she'd met while working at the diner, Lucas had been fast to tell jokes. He'd had a warm smile. Been outdoorsy. Fun. The whole vibe had been there for him. But when they'd kissed...

Maybe something is wrong with me. Because she'd kissed Lucas, and it had been nice, but, just that. Nice. No giant sparks. No deep connection. It hadn't seemed right to keep seeing him when she didn't even know who she was.

She'd only gone out with Lucas because she'd been so lonely.

But...

It felt wrong.

"Glad you didn't fuck him." Rasped. "But you should know, sweetheart, I don't like hearing about you kissing another man. Makes me want to drive my fist into the prick's face. I was here, fucking lost without you, and you were out there, you were dating—"

She pulled him toward her. Rose up on her toes and pressed her mouth to his.

Maybe I won't feel anything intense. Maybe...

His hands clamped around her waist. "You're gonna do this *right*," Victor gritted against her lips. And then he was lifting her up. Carrying her easily and her back soon pressed to the wall as he pinned her there and held her effortlessly. "Let me in," he whispered. "Open your mouth for me."

Her lips parted. Her hands remained clamped around his arms. And she let him in.

Maybe I will feel nothing...

One of his legs slid between hers as he held her.

His tongue thrust into her mouth.

She kissed him back, her tongue sliding against his. And...

Lust exploded within her. A savage need that tore past the cold darkness that had held her in its greedy grip for so long. Hunger, desire pulsed in her blood. Her mouth opened wider. A moan rose in her throat, and she kissed him with more intensity. More passion. More... everything.

His hold was strong and sure. His body hard and powerful against her. He kissed her deeply. Slowly. Savoring and taking, and it was like he *knew* everything about her. How to make her shudder and gasp and...

He does know. He knows my body better than I do.

He lifted her higher, and her legs wrapped around his waist. She didn't mean to do that. Or, hell, maybe she did. She just wanted to get closer to him. A wildfire had ignited, and Melody wanted to be as close to the flames as she could.

She was so freaking tired of the cold and the dark.

He growled, and she loved the savage sound.

But his mouth tore from hers.

"No! Victor!"

He kissed her neck. Open-mouthed, hot kisses. His tongue licked over her. His teeth bit lightly.

Her eyes closed as another moan broke from her. Harder this time.

His mouth kept moving. To the side of her neck. He licked and sucked and...

She was wet. She knew it. Getting wet and she was rocking against him. Riding the big, hard cock she could feel shoving at the front of his pants. She dug her nails into his arms and wanted him so badly that she was ready to rip off his clothes and have sex with him right then and there. *Yes, yes, Victor. Now.*

Her eyes flew open. Her breath heaved in and out. Her nipples ached, her panties were getting wet, and it was all from a kiss.

His kiss.

A kiss that had just nearly obliterated her. Her legs unlocked from his waist. She pushed at his arms as she tried to lower herself down.

He growled again. His grip became even tighter, and, at first, she thought he wasn't going to let her go. But...

He lowered her until her boots touched the floor. He didn't release the hold he had on her waist, and he continued to pin her between his body and the wall. His eyes glittered as they met hers. "Still feel nothing?"

If she said that she felt nothing, they'd both know she was lying. *He* had to feel the tight nipples that had been stabbing against his chest. And she'd been rubbing her body against his like some kind of cat in heat. Even now, she wanted to grab him and haul him back to her. Press her mouth to his and just *give in.* Let the passion take over so that she could stop worrying and fearing and get lost to pleasure for just a little while.

Oh, so tempting.

"I think you feel plenty, don't you?" Rough. Deep. Rumbling.

She *yearned.*

"I want to fuck you, Melody."

Yes, she'd gotten that clue with the giant dick that thrust against her.

"I want your nails raking down my back. I want your pussy against my mouth."

Oh. Okay. It was *way* hot in there.

"I want to be so deep in you that I own you."

That was scary. Intense. Too much. It was—

"Because you own me." Even rougher. Harder. "You have for years. And, hell, no, I didn't fuck someone else while you were gone. No one else compares to you. It's you or nothing. Do you get that? When I say I was searching, I was never going to give up. I was always going to hunt for you because you are mine."

She wet her lips, and she tasted him. His hands around her waist seemed to brand her. Fear and need twisted inside of her.

And then a bell rang. It echoed in the house.

But he didn't let her go. Victor stared at her with his dark eyes and his granite-carved face. He looked at her as if he truly wanted to devour her.

"You didn't answer me," he muttered.

What had the question been? She was really gonna need a refresher on that one.

"Still feel nothing?" A taunt.

Her chin lifted. She could handle his taunt. "I feel like I want to rip your clothes off."

His eyes widened.

"But I also feel like I should run as far from you as I can." Utter truth. "*Why?* Why am I afraid? What is it that makes me want you and fear you at the same time?"

A muscle jerked along his clenched jaw. "I would never hurt you."

The bell chimed again.

This time, he let her go.

Before he backed away, Victor told her, "But I will kill anyone who ever tries to take you from me again." He turned to exit the room.

She stood there, frozen.

Someone was at the front door. They had to leave the den and yet... "I didn't remember."

"I think we've established that." He kept walking.

"No, I mean..." She surged after him. Caught herself before she grabbed him. "Sleeping Beauty didn't wake up with a kiss. I told you, it wouldn't happen." But hadn't she still stupidly hoped for something? Some wild flash of them kissing in the past? Of them...having sex?

Or even just talking. Laughing. Being a couple. Being *normal*.

Just a memory of them.

Victor glanced over his shoulder. "Maybe you need more than a kiss."

Longing swept through her because his gaze was full of such dark, dark desire.

"You ever think of that?" His deep voice demanded. "Maybe what you need..."

The doorbell rang again.

Her shoulders stiffened. "I don't think you can fuck my memories back into place for me. But thanks for the generous offer."

"Maybe not." Then the man actually winked at her. Hard-faced, intense, scary, dangerous Victor *winked*. "But don't you believe it would be fun to try?"

Her jaw dropped right before he walked away.

And, damn him...yes, yes, she did think it would be fun

to try. She thought it would be outstanding to try. Toe-curling. Body-melting.

She hurried after him, rushing across the foyer just as he was opening the front door. Hunter waited on the other side of the door. He gripped a black duffel bag in his hand.

Raising the bag, he asked, "Who's ready to get fingerprinted?"

Chapter Twelve

"I THOUGHT I'D BE GOING TO THE POLICE STATION TO BE fingerprinted." Melody frowned as she peered down at the small black box on Victor's kitchen countertop.

The fingers of her left hand were currently pressed to the surface of that box, a green screen.

"Aw, you figured you'd do the old ink and stamping routine, huh?" Hunter carefully guided her fingers. He'd already taken scans of her other hand. "Got to move with the times. Digital scans are one hell of a lot faster. The device is transportable, and I happened to know an agency in town that had one readily available." He released her hand. "I've been trained on the scanner before. My, uh, boss Declan Flynn actually helped to create the tech. And when I say the results are fast, I mean it."

Victor hadn't said a word during the screening. He'd mostly been trying to get his ass back under control. When he'd had Melody pinned between him and the wall, he'd nearly gone feral. To have her back—back in his arms, her mouth beneath his, her body rubbing against him as she moaned in desire—talk about a dream come true.

Hell, yes, he'd gone over the edge. He'd wanted to strip her. Take her right there.

Had he thought that kissing her might stir her memories? Honestly, no. Things just would not be that easy. He got that. Nothing in his life had ever been easy.

As for fucking her...

Yes. Absolutely. I want to fuck her until neither of us can move.

But did he think fucking her would stir her memories?

No. It would feel helluva good, though, and he could one hundred percent make her understand that he could give her more pleasure than anyone else ever would. He knew exactly what she liked. What drove her wild. What made her shudder and quake and beg for more.

She dated some asshole this past year? While he'd been ripping the world apart, she'd been—

"You gonna give me her old fingerprint cards? And I am assuming those are the old ink and paper version?" Hunter thrust back his shoulders. "I'll take them to my contact. Get the old material scanned and get your comparison points ASAP with this new scan."

Without a word, Victor reached for the backpack he'd slung onto the barstool earlier. He pulled out the manila file. Carefully leafed through the report and only handed Hunter the fingerprints. He would be reading that full report later. Something about the report bothered him. *Why the hell did you hold onto it for so long, Sebastian?*

"Am I going to do a DNA test, too?" Melody asked.

"Not with me, you're not." Hunter's quick reply. "But I'm sure Victor can snap his fingers and get that done for you. Pretty much when Victor says jump, I'm realizing everyone rushes to do his bidding. He and Declan are a hell of a lot alike in that regard. Most folks seem scared as hell of them, and fear tends to be one powerful motivator."

Declan Flynn was a tech billionaire. He was also known as one of the most dangerous and secretive individuals in the world. Describing Declan as Hunter's boss, though, that was not exactly true. Sure, Hunter did still provide security work for the tech mogul, but from what Victor had uncovered, the two men were best friends, closer to brothers than anything else. Hunter carried all of Declan's dark secrets. In return, the story went that, once upon a time, Declan had saved Hunter's life.

"Why are people afraid of Victor?" Melody asked.

"Because he's a tough, unforgiving sonofabitch." An instant response from Hunter. "Traits I always look for in new friends." He packed up his scanner. "All done. I'll get back with you both as soon as I have the results, but I figure the way Victor is dead set on keeping you close, we can assume those results will come back as a positive match."

"She's my Melody." Did the possessive *my* slide out? Yes, it did. Because she might not be wearing his ring any longer, but she was his.

Hunter grunted. "Figured that was the way of it. I contacted Memphis and let him know about the development with the abandoned pickup truck. Do I need to take care of guards for her or are you already on top of things?"

"Already have guards scheduled to start tomorrow. They'll be her shadow whenever she isn't by my side."

Melody's mouth dropped open, only to hurriedly shut. "By your side? Look, it's not as if I'm going to move into your house."

Wasn't she?

"You're going to help me, and I appreciate your help.

The help that you are *both* giving me," she hurried to say as her gaze swept over to Hunter, then back to Victor. "But I'm not expecting you to upend your life for me."

What did she think his life had been like for the last year? Upended didn't even come close to describing things.

But her lush lips firmed. "I'm not going to wreck your life."

Cute. Again, his life had been utterly wrecked when she left.

How can I get her to marry me? Preferably within the next twenty-four hours. Because when he called her *his* Melody, he'd love the legal ties to prove that point.

Except, yeah, getting her to marry him was like a pipe dream right now.

Then again, becoming a billionaire had been a pipe dream for a poor kid who'd grown up in an Alabama trailer park. A kid who'd lost his dad to a factory accident at six and then been dumped by his mom on an extended relative less than six months later. He'd grown up on hand-me-downs and hand-outs. But he'd worked his ass off, made deals with more than a few devils over the years, and he'd clawed his way to the ownership of Mage Industries.

He didn't give up on his dreams.

Not ever.

No matter what he had to do in order to achieve those dreams.

"And, uh, can someone please tell me just *who* is Memphis? And why did we update him about the pickup truck?"

Victor and Hunter shared a long look. It was Victor who responded. "You know I'm working with the Ice Breakers."

"Yes." She motioned toward Hunter. "Got that."

"Memphis Camden is an integral part of the team," Hunter explained. "Guy has been training me pretty much from day one. Former bounty hunter, tough as nails bastard. Never gives up. Freaking pit bull. The only thing he loves more than danger is his wife and family. You should see the guy with his baby girl. Talk about obsessed." A faint laugh. One that slowly faded. "Memphis is doing the back-end work on this case. While he's pulling strings behind the scenes, I'm front and center on field work. You are not alone, Melody."

A soft sigh escaped her. Relief? *Baby, I will never let you be alone again.*

"The team is fully engaged on your case. We're gonna find answers for you."

Regarding those answers—they could take time. While they found the truth, he couldn't allow her to be unprotected. He'd lose the last bit of his mind if that was the case. "The person who took you hasn't been caught, Melody." Was his voice level? Victor figured it mostly was. A little rough around the edges, but, then again, he was rough around the edges. Always would be. "And considering you were shot at so very recently, do you seriously want to stay alone, or would you prefer to stay in my house with state-of-the-art security and with extra guards who will keep an eye on you so that you can stay safe and protected?" Victor crossed his arms over his chest and waited for her reply.

"Okay, right." Melody cleared her throat. "When you put it that way...I'll go with the state-of-the-art security option, thanks very much."

He'd thought so.

"But I'm not sleeping with you," she added in a quick rush.

Hunter whistled. "This so does not feel like a me conversation."

It wasn't.

"I don't care how good of a kisser you are," Melody continued determinedly to Victor even as her cheeks pinkened. "I'm not jumping into bed with you."

Why not? You've been there plenty of times before.

"Out of curiosity..." Hunter ambled closer toward the kitchen door, his bag gripped in his left hand. "Am I going to be getting my handcuffs back anytime soon?"

"Nope." Victor's immediate reply. He slung the backpack over one shoulder.

Melody sucked in a breath. "You are *not* cuffing me."

"Ahem. You know what? Keep the cuffs," Hunter offered. "Consider them an early Christmas gift." He headed down the hallway. "Jeez, this place could sure as hell use some Christmas spirit." His voice drifted back to them. "And I thought my rental was bad."

Victor held Melody's gaze a moment longer.

"You are not cuffing me," she said flatly.

"Oh, come on, baby. Not like it would be the first time."

She gasped.

He followed Hunter. The guy had almost reached the front door. Hunter's hand reached out for the doorknob, but he turned back. "You know I'm staying close, if you need me."

Check, he knew Hunter wasn't leaving town anytime soon. "Thanks." He dropped the backpack onto the foyer floor, setting it next to the small entranceway table.

Hunter nodded. His stare swept beyond Victor, to Melody. "I'm glad you're back," he told her. "Not all the cases I've been working end this way. Usually, I'm watching families try to pick up the pieces after they've buried the dead."

"I'm not ready to be buried yet." Her clear voice.

"I can see that." With his left hand, Hunter waved to indicate the foyer. The whole house. "Since you're not, why don't you try bringing some life back into this place? Sure as hell could use it." Then he slipped away.

Victor locked the door behind him.

"Am I going to get a DNA test?"

He stared at the shut door. "Your father doesn't want one." A careful response. "The fingerprint check will be faster." A pause, then he turned to face her. "There is a guest room at the top of the stairs. You can take it. Rest for a while." He didn't mention that he'd be taking the room right next to it. Normally, he used the master bedroom that was downstairs.

Not while Melody was in his house. While she was there, he wanted to be closer. So he could be at her side faster if she needed him.

"It's not even night yet."

"You didn't exactly sleep much last night. When you did sleep, you woke up screaming." And there was something about her late-night scream that they hadn't discussed. Something that he hadn't mentioned to her yet.

The whole reason he'd gone running so fast...

She'd screamed his name.

"I don't want to sleep. I want to hunt." Her shoulders rolled back. "You told me that you'd take me to the scene of the abduction."

They technically *had* gone to the abduction scene. Or, rather, to Mage Industries. The chopper had landed on the helipad located on the roof. But he'd rushed her through the building, only wanting to get her to the security of his home.

A tightness had been in his chest the whole time, and that tightness had only eased once he had her over the threshold at his house.

She's back. She's safe. I can protect her.

"You said I'd talk with the detective who was in charge of my case."

Ah, yes. Detective Angus Clinton. Talk about a pain in the ass. She could talk with him, but, based on previous experience, the conversation would hardly be what Victor would call enlightening.

"And I want to see my home. I want to go back there because maybe something in *my* home will click my memory. Nothing here is." She turned in the foyer, her gaze sliding over the walls. "I mean, I look in here, and it all feels wrong. So empty." She pointed to the staircase. Or, rather, to the staircase's curving bannister. "I feel like fresh garland should be wrapped around the bannister. Garland and red bows. The scent of pine should be in the air, and...in the den—the den we were just in—everything should have been different. A Christmas tree should have been nestled there, with its lights blinking and a pile of presents underneath it."

He stiffened.

"The ornaments on the tree should have been some crazy, happy mismatch." Her hand fell. "All colors and shapes. Bright. Joyful. There should be Christmas music playing in the house. And...fresh baked cookies. I should smell freshly baked cookies."

His chest burned. "Anything else?"

A sad shake of her head. "No. Sorry." Her eyes squeezed closed. "Sorry," Melody repeated.

She didn't have a damn thing to be sorry for.

"I get it," Melody continued doggedly. "You aren't big

on Christmas. I don't even know why I just rambled like that. Crazy, huh?"

No, not at all. He closed the distance between them. "You're right. I'm not big on Christmas. Honestly, I fucking hate the holiday." His hand reached out and curled under her chin. "I never really celebrated."

She jerked at his touch, and her eyes flew open. "Y-you..."

I don't want you afraid of me. That has to stop.

"You said your favorite word again." She smiled at him. Like he didn't recognize a forced smile when he saw one.

"Your real smiles show the dimple in your right cheek." Something else that couldn't be faked. Something else that said she was the real deal. His Melody. "You only have a dimple in the right cheek. You used to complain about that. Said you didn't know why you were mismatched."

Her lashes fluttered.

"You aren't mismatched. You're perfect." His thumb brushed over her lower lip. "And you *are* remembering."

A faint furrow appeared between her brows. "Uh, I don't think so. You're not big on Christmas, you just said that yourself. Not like you'd have this whole place decked out. So there's no reason for me to be standing here and thinking that everything is wrong."

It wasn't wrong. Not anymore. "You love Christmas."

"I—" She glanced around again. Then back at him.

"I told you I never really celebrated. Not on my own." And he could see the foyer as she did because it had been that way. Another time. Because of her. "Growing up, I was the relative no one wanted. My dad..." Victor hesitated, just a moment, then finished, "My dad died when I was six."

"I'm so sorry."

"My mom—ah, she turned to drugs after that. I got passed around to distant family members, then did the foster home routine." No emotion entered his voice. He didn't like talking about his past.

"Victor..." Melody shook her head. "That must have been so difficult for you. I'm so very sorry." She inched forward, and her hands even lifted, as if she'd reach out to comfort him. But Melody stopped. Her eyes widened as she seemed to catch herself. Then, again, she said, "I'm so sorry."

Not your fault. Nothing was ever your fault. "Eventually, I wound up basically living on my own when I was sixteen." *Don't think about what led to that moment. She doesn't need to know.* Because she didn't need to fear him.

Victor cleared his throat. "There were never any big, family holidays for me. Never presents. Christmas trees. People singing. None of that shit." Just a poor kid with thread-bare clothes staring at the lives other people had. Being envious as hell. "When we were together, you asked me why I didn't celebrate. I told you all this before." He'd told her more about the secrets of his past than he had ever told anyone. "I opened up about my past and shared more with you than I ever had before." Because, yes, he was a secretive bastard. *And there are some secrets that I even kept from you, sweetheart.* Why? Because he'd been afraid the full truth would send her running, and he couldn't have that. He needed her too much.

He still needed her, and he was still keeping secrets. "I told you...I said the whole magic and miracles bit wasn't for me. Then I came home and..." Again, he could see the foyer as it had been. "You'd decorated. *You.* You didn't hire some crew like your father always did at his estate and at Mage Industries. You'd spent hours decorating and transforming the house. I came in, and Christmas music was playing." He could still hear it. The lyrics that had haunted him for so long. *"I'll be home for Christmas..."*

But she hadn't been home. She'd been gone. Everything he'd wanted, ripped away. And he'd been right. Magic and miracles didn't happen to him.

His nostrils flared. "You even baked cookies. I could smell them."

"Chocolate chip," she whispered. Then her eyes widened. "I—" A smile. A huge one that swept over her face. It made her dimple flash, and it made the green of her eyes sparkle as the shadows slipped away. "I know—the same way I knew Olivia liked cashmere." She did a little bounce. Joy. "You—you like chocolate chip cookies. I remember that! I remember that about you!" She threw her arms around him and held tight.

His eyes squeezed shut for just a moment.

And, for just a moment, it was the same. The exact same...

He'd come home last December. He'd known she was inside. He'd given her the key ages ago. The better for her to come to him whenever she wanted. And that night, he'd walked in to the scent of freshly baked cookies. To the smell of fresh pine in the air. To the sound of Christmas music.

Decorations everywhere. His Melody, standing nervously in the foyer, a little flour on her cheek because she'd made the cookies from scratch.

She smiled at him, and it had been like every dream that he'd pretended not to have. A home. A real one. A real holiday. With someone who loved him.

She'd rushed to him. Thrown her arms around him. *"Please don't be mad."* Her voice whispered through his mind. *"If you hate the decorations, I'll take them down. I just wanted to do something nice for you. Because you deserve some magic, too."*

His arms had locked around her.

Just as they locked around her now.

And he'd known that he was damn well holding magic.

Only for that magic to be ripped away.

Never. Again.

"I'm sorry!" Melody pushed back.

His grip tightened as she peered up at him.

"Probably shouldn't have, um, jumped you like that."

"You can jump me any day of the week." She always had an open invitation.

"I just...I hadn't gotten any big memories of you." Her smile had vanished. "I guess I still don't have them. I just know that you like chocolate chip cookies."

He stared at her. Could not look away.

"Victor?"

"You decorated. You made the house feel like a home for the first time. Any personal touches here came from you, and when you were gone, I boxed everything up." He'd even boxed up the pictures of her because looking at her image had hurt too much as more and more time passed.

He'd been told to move on. Everyone had said he needed to move the hell on.

But how do you move on when you feel like you were buried in the ground?

Where I feared you were?

He'd boxed away everything at his house, but he hadn't changed anything at her place. And maybe that was what she needed to see. A home that she'd truly known.

Something that was hers. "Come with me," he told her. He let go of her waist, only to immediately grab her hand. His fingers threaded with hers.

"Where are we going?"

"To find your memories."

Chapter Thirteen

VICTOR BRAKED AND PARKED HIS CAR IN THE SPOT THAT waited in front of the house. Her gaze automatically turned to the left. Hanover Avenue, so close to Lombardy Park. They'd passed the park just moments ago, and she'd seen the kids running and swinging on the playground. At first, she'd smiled, because the families seemed so happy. But as they'd driven away from the park in Victor's black BMW, she'd found herself tensing more and more with every passing moment until...

They'd reached her home. He'd told her it was in "The Fan"—something she already knew through her own research. She'd actually driven by the home several times before. When she'd first come to Richmond—before she'd even gone to the Mage Mansion, hell, before she'd even checked into her temporary spot at the cheap motel—she'd driven by her home. She'd even thought about sneaking up and peering in the windows.

She didn't have to sneak now, though. Victor had the key.

He killed the car's engine and exited. Breaking from her

stupor and cursing the nerves that filled her, Melody shoved open her door.

But Victor was already there. He reached for her hand. His fingers curled around hers as if it was the most natural thing in the world. The sun peeked through the lingering clouds as they walked up the sidewalk. Snow lingered—snow and ice—and he caught her when her boots slipped on the sidewalk.

"Steady," he murmured.

She didn't feel steady. The streets had been cleared, but snow still clung to surfaces all around them. The air held a vicious bite, and the wind stung against her cheeks.

But she ignored the cold and stared at the home before her. Her home. The place Melody had bought and lived in for the last three years. The exterior bricks had been painted a dark gray, but the front door was a bold red.

"Your favorite color," he said. "Red."

They climbed up the steps, and, automatically, her free hand reached for the black railing. Snow completely covered the bushes near the stoop but, in her mind, she could almost see them...green, bursting with flowers in the summer.

Is that a memory? Or just something I want to be true?

He unlocked the door. "Ladies first."

Right. And she shouldn't be hesitating. She shouldn't be so nervous. But she was. She edged across the threshold and into her home.

Wooden floors.

"Those are the original floors." He shut the door behind them. "I know because you told me. Architecture is one of your things. You've got ten-foot ceilings, bay windows..."

Her gaze lifted to the ceiling and lingered on the chandelier. Then she crept forward, moving toward the white banister that waited in the entranceway. Her hand pulled from his as she reached out to touch the wood. A large, gold and white rug covered the hardwood floor.

The house smelled fresh. Lemony. She turned her head and darted to the left, going into the den. Inside, white bookshelves were lined with dozens of titles. Romances. Thrillers. And bold, big abstract artwork covered two of the walls.

Victor had followed her into the den. He pointed to the closest piece of artwork. One with bright red and blue splotches. "You told me that was your Jackson Pollack period."

She spun toward him. "*I* painted those?"

"Um. Yep. You explained to me once that you've never been good at painting between the lines, but you could do anything you wanted with abstracts."

She glanced back at the paintings. Then she crept toward the soft, white couches. Two of them. Facing each other. With a fireplace in the middle. A red throw had been tossed over the side of one couch.

Unease prickled at her nape. "Is someone living here?" Then, worried and angry, she hurried from the den. Practically ran down the small hallway and into the kitchen. White cabinets. Marble countertops. An oven mitt on the counter. "Is someone *here*?" she demanded, voice more agitated because someone else had to be living there. There was no dust. She'd been gone a year, but the place was spotless. The oven mitt was positioned on the counter as if someone had been baking recently, and the throw had been tossed to the side as if someone had just finished snuggling beneath it and—

"I have a cleaning team come in every two weeks."

She'd been preparing to rush from the kitchen. Maybe

from the whole house. *Someone else is here. This isn't my home any longer.* Yet now Melody felt rooted to the spot.

"No one else is here. It's your home. Everything is just as you left it." Victor's lips pressed together. "Okay. That's not exactly true. I had the Christmas decorations taken down. And I, um, I moved all the wrapped presents you had to my place. I just wanted to keep them safe for you. I didn't open anything."

She shook her head, not understanding. "You—you had someone coming to clean? You left it all the same?" For an entire year? Her chest began to ache.

"When the cops finally did search your home, they left a damn mess." His mouth tightened. "At first, I had the cleaning crew come in to get things back in shape. Not like I could have you coming home and finding things that way."

He sounds so certain that I would be back. That ache in her chest grew stronger.

"But after the first big cleaning, then...then I realized you could come back any day. I wanted it ready for you. Always ready for when you came home."

Her eyes widened. And it hit her. Really hit her. It one hundred percent sank in. Something that she had not fully realized until this moment. "My God."

"Your bedroom is upstairs."

She didn't go upstairs. She did not move from that spot. "You loved her."

His dark eyes narrowed. "You *are* her."

"And she...*I* loved you?" A stark question.

"Told you, you were going to marry me." A half smile. One that was somehow sad. Questioning? "You think you would have agreed to marry someone you didn't love?"

Her chest didn't ache. It *burned*. And then she was rushing away. Running down the hallway. Up the staircase.

Her feet thudded on the wooden steps and when she reached the landing, she spun to the right. The door was open. As if the room was waiting for her.

Then again, he'd had the whole house ready and waiting for her. *For an entire year*.

She ran inside the bedroom and stopped dead.

A fluffy, white robe on the edge of the bed. Monster slippers near the nightstand. Like, actual monster slippers. Silly and big and blue and her lips trembled when she looked at them. Monster slippers did not fit at all with the image she'd gotten of Melody Mage from the online posts.

But those slippers...

This room...

It does fit. It feels right.

More books. A wall of framed pictures. Not of people, though. The pictures were of different places. So many places. Pulled to those framed photos, she lurched closer to them. Behind her, she heard the sound of Victor entering the bedroom.

The Eiffel Tower. The Grand Canyon. The Statue of Liberty. Giant, cascading waterfalls. A dark cloud-covered top of a dormant volcano. Amazing places. Beautiful. Magical. And—

A black and white picture of her and Victor rested in the middle of the wall. She blinked. Stepped closer to that picture. Even lifted her hand as if she'd touch it. In the image, they seemed to be on a lake. Canoeing? Kayaking? They weren't kissing. Not hugging. Not even touching. It looked like a selfie shot that she'd taken because she was in the front and part of her arm was extended. Victor perched behind her, and she could see him gripping a paddle. She was grinning, from ear to ear.

He was smiling, too, and his gaze was completely on her.

She realized that she'd stopped breathing. Her breath left her in a fast whoosh as she whirled toward him.

His gaze was on her. Not the wall. He wasn't smiling. But now she knew exactly what he looked like when his face was lit with warmth. When Victor was really happy.

"You tipped the canoe over five seconds after you snapped that pic. We came out of that lake soaking wet." A shake of his head. "You were laughing your gorgeous ass off. See, that's who you really are. Don't believe the BS that's splashed online. The stories that circulate about you being spoiled. A trust fund brat. That's not you. I realized that truth about ten minutes after we first met. You were nothing like what I expected you to be. And you changed everything for me." He looked over her head at the photos. "You went on backpacking trips to most of those places in the photos. You liked to camp outside when you hiked. You'd be covered in mud and sleeping on the ground, and you'd act like it was better than the Ritz. You were never some cold-blooded ice queen. You were warm and beautiful, and you lit up the world around you. When you were gone, without that light, everything was too dark." His hands fisted at his sides. "I was too dark."

She wanted to lunge at him. Grab him and hold on tight. That had been real joy on her face in that photo. On his face. You couldn't fake that emotion.

For the last year, Victor had been looking for her. Victor had never given up. Someone had been searching for her. Someone had been missing her.

Someone had been loving her.

"One year." He took a step back. Then he began to prowl the confines of her room. Skimming his fingers over the spines of books. Touching a faded quilt that sat near what she strongly suspected had been her favorite reading chair. How could it not be? Oversized, tucked in the corner, with a lamp perched nearby and a footstool just waiting beside it. "I held onto hope for a solid year," he told her. "Even as fear grew in my heart, and I understood that...you were probably gone. Dead."

I'm not. I'm right here.

"When you reached the estate, when you walked in, I'd finally given voice to the fear that haunted me. I said you were dead." His gaze lingered on her bed. Four-poster. With a canopy. An antique that had gleaming wood, as if it were carefully polished. Probably was. Victor probably made sure it stayed polished. Without looking back at her, he said, "I knew I was obsessed, you see. Keeping this place exactly as you left it. Keeping it ready in case you walked in the door..."

I did just walk in the door.

"I bought the house, Melody."

Her lips parted. She didn't know what to say.

"You were gone. No one was paying the mortgage. You'd saved up, and you'd worked so hard to get this home on your own. Sebastian never gave you a dime for it, and, honestly, when you vanished, I don't think he even remembered the place half the time. His condition—hell, baby, it took so much away from him."

A lump rose in her throat.

"I bought the property because when you came back, I needed your home to be ready." He looked down, as if seeming to just realize his hands had fisted. "At the Mage estate, Dario was saying it was time to sell your house. He wanted you out of the will. He wanted everyone to move on."

"I-I heard..." Like those words hadn't felt like knives sinking into her.

His head whipped up. His shoulders squared. "You need to know...I was going to do it."

She blinked quickly, hating that stupid tears wanted to fill her eyes.

"I wasn't going to stop looking for you, don't mistake me on that point. I would *never* have stopped looking. Never. But I knew I couldn't keep this place like a shrine for you much longer." A vague wave of his hand. "Hell, I get that I'm obsessed. Even the cops thought I was. Though they had no clue just how deep that obsession truly runs when it comes to you." A muscle jerked along his jaw. "Sometimes, I'd come here just to fucking be closer to you. At first, the home still smelled like you." He wrenched around. Lurched to the dresser. Picked up a bottle of perfume. "Champagne and vanilla. With just a hint of honeysuckle. Your signature scent. You didn't blow cash on a lot, but you always had to wear this perfume." He set the perfume back down. A little too hard. It clinked when the glass hit the wood of the dresser's top.

She should say something. Do something.

A slow exhale blew from him. Victor rolled back his shoulders. "I'm not rational when it comes to you. You need to understand that. I want to grab you and hold you and take you away from every threat in the world." His gaze pinned her. So, so dark and possessive. "I do want to handcuff you to me. I wasn't joking or just threatening with that shit before. I have to know that you're safe. I have to make sure you're tied to me. I want to fly you to Vegas. Marry you. Spend the rest of my life with you." Now he began to stalk back to her. "I want to tie you to me in every possible way because I cannot lose you again."

She could not move.

Victor closed the space between them with hard, deliberate steps.

"I am not an easy man, Melody."

She wet her lips. "Yes, I got that impression."

The faint lines near his mouth deepened. "Once, you loved me despite that fact. The rest of the world thought I was a cold-blooded, dangerous bastard. But you still loved me."

Her boots pressed harder into the floor as she found herself leaning toward him. Drawn, no, pulled, to him.

"I will get you to love me again. No matter what it takes. I did it before. I can do it again." An absolute vow. "Though I am probably fucking scaring you to death with my obsession—"

"I thought I didn't matter to anyone," Melody cut through his words. "Days passed. Weeks. Months. No one came for me. I didn't think anyone looked." It had been like the whole world forgot her.

"I looked. You will always matter to me."

She believed him. Something seemed to break apart inside of her. She could almost hear the shattering. Maybe it was the ice around her heart. The ice that had trapped her for so long. Because she'd been locked away. In so much pain and all alone. So sure that no one had cared. That she'd been forgotten.

As she forgot everyone and everything.

But this man—this man had never forgotten.

She surged toward him. Her hands grabbed his shoulders. She pulled him down and his mouth locked onto hers. And it was the same—the very same way it had been the last time they kissed. Desire blasted through her blood. A white-hot need and burning lust that obliterated the cold.

Her tongue slipped into his mouth. Tasted him, and when he growled for her, the rough, primitive sound just made her want him all the more.

Right then. Right there.

His fingers curled around her waist. But he didn't haul her even closer, as she wanted him to do. Instead, his grip tightened, and his head wrenched up as he took that sexy mouth of his away from her. "What are you doing?" he rasped.

She'd thought it was obvious. "Fuck is your favorite word," she reminded him.

His eyes narrowed.

"So fuck me right now, Victor. Fuck *me—*"

He lifted her up and carried her to the bed.

Chapter Fourteen

"ARE YOU LISTENING TO ME? THE BITCH IS *BACK*. SHE waltzed back in here like nothing had ever happened!" The words rushed out. "And Victor flew her to Richmond in a chopper. The bastard took a freaking bullet for her and then just flew out of here." A quick expulsion of air. "The sheriff and his deputies are searching the estate now. Bullets were fired into the study. They almost hit her. One *did* hit Victor." Grazed him. Hadn't slowed down the bastard at all.

"The shooter is long gone."

So confident. And...

No surprise. There was zero surprise or reaction to all the news. "You already know all of this." Well, hell.

"The shooter was mine. Extra eyes that I wanted on the estate."

Why would extra eyes need to be on the estate? "Why?" Then, almost fearful, "Don't you trust me?"

"I trust you completely. It's the assholes around you who are problems." A pause. "You trust me, too, don't you?"

Maybe.

"My watcher reported when she arrived. I told him to take her out before she caused trouble."

"Well, your watcher missed her. Whoever he was, he's a colossal screwup. I'd get rid of him." Because now, evidence could be left behind. Maybe evidence that was currently hidden by the snow, but snow always melted. "They found a smashed-up truck not far from the estate. I was…worried." *I thought that maybe you'd been out there. That you'd come to the estate. Seen her, freaked the hell out, and taken that shot yourself.*

"You don't need to worry."

Bullshit. "Her coming back is a major problem. It's going to wreck us."

Silence. Then, "If she knew who I was, wouldn't I have been locked away long ago?"

Yes, yes. Okay. *Breathe.* "What are we supposed to do now?"

"Not we. *Me.* I started this. I'll finish it."

Don't ask. Don't ask. You don't want the gory details. Don't… "How are you going to finish it?"

"This time, I'll personally make sure that Melody Mage is dead. Not comatose in some hospital. *Dead.* That good enough for you?"

"Yes. Yes, that's good enough. Just…don't tell me what you do. I don't want to hear about knives or pain or blood or —just do it, would you? *Fast.* Victor took her back to town. She's there. *Get rid of her.* You and whatever watcher-slash-goon you have who missed the damn shot before—just get rid of her. Permanently this time, okay? No loose ends." Though that was not going to be easy. "Victor is going to stay close to her. He will be a problem." He was always a problem.

Silence. "Maybe I'll get rid of them both."

A quick and eager nod. That plan had serious potential. "Do it."

Chapter Fifteen

FUCK ME.

Hell. Yes.

Victor's hands were too rough as he lifted her up and took her to the bed. His mouth too wild and hard as he took her lips. Tasted her. Took and took and took.

But he couldn't seem to pull back.

Melody's hands stroked over him. She was moaning and rubbing against him, and she wanted him to fuck her.

Not a dream. Not some desperate fantasy. The real deal. She was back. His Melody.

And he was going to fuck her until she screamed his name.

He lowered her onto the bed. Heaved up long enough to wrench off her top. Her breath came in quick pants as she grabbed his shirt, too. She yanked, and buttons went flying.

Her eyes widened. "I am so—"

He kissed her again. Drove his tongue past her lips and tasted the sweetness that he craved. He wanted to rip away her jeans and her panties and plunge as deep into her as he could possibly go. He wanted her nails raking down his body as she bucked against him.

Slow down. Slow. Down.

A refrain in the back of his mind. But he couldn't slow down. His hands were practically shaking with need because this was Melody. Finally. Back.

His.

Her fingers slid over his sides. Across his back. "I want you inside me," she whispered against his mouth.

Like there was any other place in the entire world he'd rather be.

But his lips claimed hers once more, and he kissed her just a little longer because he'd missed the softness of her mouth. Craved her so badly.

Missed her touch.

Her sighs and her moans.

Missed every single thing about her.

He eased away. Stared at the white bra she wore. Saw the curve of her breasts. *Fuck, fuck, fuck.* Victor backed away. Her legs dangled over the edge of the bed. He hauled off her boots and socks, and his hands went to her waist. His fingers tangled with hers as she helped him to unsnap her jeans. Unzip them.

Then he was hauling those jeans down her legs. The jeans and her panties, and she was left clad only in the bra. For a minute, he just drank her in.

She pushed up onto her elbows. "Uh, Victor?"

"I missed you."

"I missed you, too."

His gaze flew to meet hers. No, she couldn't have missed him. Not when she didn't even remember him.

"I was walking around and feeling like my heart was missing. I think I might know why. I think I gave it to you, didn't I?"

And he could remember words that she'd spoken to him so long ago. The best words that he'd ever heard.

I love you.

When he'd been at his darkest, those words had tortured him. They'd also given him the strength to keep searching for her. To believe that she would come back. Melody had to return.

I have her back now. Back. Safe. Alive. The next step? To kill the bastard who took her from me.

His gaze slowly drifted over her body. Those perfect breasts. The bra would be going. He wanted her nipples in his mouth. She always went wild when he played with her nipples. And he knew just how to play. Knew how to give her so much pleasure that she shattered beneath him.

On down his stare went and...

The scar on her stomach. Such a long slice. A reminder of the hell she'd faced.

I won't just kill the bastard who took you. I will make him suffer. He will beg for your forgiveness.

"Victor?"

His gaze rose once more.

"You look..." Melody bit her lower lip.

"How do I look?" His hands curled around her legs. He pulled her closer to the edge of the bed as he stood beside the mattress. Her bed was raised, higher than normal, and it put her at the perfect height for what he wanted.

"Angry." A pause. "Scary."

"You should never be afraid of me." Because his rage would never be for her. He only wanted to give her pleasure. And he would.

His hands rose to caress her inner thighs. Then, slowly,

deliberately, he pushed her legs apart. A rough sigh escaped him. "Oh, baby, I have missed you."

Then he feasted as his mouth lowered to claim the heaven between her thighs. His mouth took her. Soft at first, then harder as the frenzy of need within him drowned out everything else.

She'd gasped at the first lash of his tongue. Her hips tried to back away, but his hands whipped up and locked around her waist. He brought her even closer to his mouth as he licked and he sucked and he tasted her again and again. Mercilessly. Using his tongue and his lips in just the way that he knew she wanted.

He sucked her clit. Licked her over and over. Heard her gasps and felt her fingers sink into the thickness of his hair.

He'd missed her taste. Her sexy scent. Missed the softness of her body and the way she trembled before she came for him.

The way she was trembling *right then*—

"Victor!" Her hips jerked. Her thighs trembled. "*Victor!*"

He'd missed that scream of pleasure. And when she came, he lapped up her orgasm. Worked his tongue over her. Into her. Again and again.

Her heaving breaths shuddered in and out. Slowly, so slowly, his head lifted.

She still wore her bra. Problematic.

He stood. Stared at her as she sprawled on the bed—*her* bed. With her hair on the bedding behind her. Dark hair. White bedding.

I missed you.

If she ever left again...

No. He stopped the thought. It would not happen.

He reached out. Pulled down the left strap of her bra.

Then the right. He tugged down the material so that he could see those pert, perfect breasts. Her nipples were tight, and his fingers skimmed over them. First one, then the other.

His fingers. Followed by his mouth. He sucked and he tasted, and she hissed out a breath. "My nipples feel so sensitive."

They'd always gotten extra sensitive, right after she came for him.

His dick was thick and hard, so eager for her. He kept licking her nipples. Sucking. Kissing.

Take her. Thrust into her. Make her come around your cock.

Not yet. Not...

Yet.

He kissed a path down her body. His lips were extra careful when he touched the scar on her stomach. *I will make him pay. Pain for pain. I swear it.*

Her fingers curled around his shoulders. "Victor?"

His head rose.

Pink stained her cheeks. Her lips were red. Swollen from his mouth. Her eyes bright with passion. She stared at him with lust. With need.

Melody. His Melody.

He pulled from her, but only so he could yank open the front of his pants. His shirt still hung open. He should probably toss it away.

Screw it.

He kicked out of his shoes. Ditched his pants and his boxers. His heavy, thick cock thrust forward, and she was reaching for him.

She was wet. Ready. He'd made sure of it. He guided his cock to the entrance of her body as her legs dangled over the edge of the bed. No condom. He wanted her, skin to skin, but...

Fuck. Don't be selfish with her. Don't.

"Condom," he gritted.

"I..." A lick of her tongue over her lips. "I don't exactly have one on me."

The head of his dick had dipped into her.

Heaven.

Torment.

Perfection.

"I had a full check at the hospital. No diseases. No, um, nothing like that." Husky, trembling words as her hips arched against him and tempted him to thrust into her. To go deep. Exactly where he wanted to be. "I got one of those birth control shots. I-I haven't been with anyone. I told you that."

He hadn't touched another woman since her. "I'm clear. You have nothing to fear from me." He would never risk hurting her in any way.

Never.

Her long lashes lifted so that her incredible green eyes were on him. "Then what are you waiting for?"

His control shredded. He sank into the hot, tight paradise that was Melody, his Melody, and there was no holding back. No stopping. He pounded deep and hard into her even as she wrapped her legs around his waist. Her hips arched up against him. She met him, wild, heaving thrust for thrust. Her breasts bounced. Her lips parted. Her eyes never left his.

He sank into her. Withdrew. Drove into her as far as he could go.

Her moans urged him on.

Her hands gripped the bedding. Twisted. Knotted.

His fingers slid between her legs. Rubbed her clit even as he pounded and pounded into her.

She came again for him. Pleasure swept into her bright gaze, and she gasped out his name as her body heaved and shook, and he was hauling her off the bed. Up against him. Her legs locked tightly around him. Her hands flew out to curl around his shoulders. He lifted her up and down. He turned, pinned her to the wall, and drove into her even as her inner muscles contracted greedily around him.

Her mouth went to his throat. She licked. She sucked. She bit…

Fuck me, she bit in just the spot she knows I like. In just the way I like.

Melody. *His* Melody.

Her nails raked over him.

He exploded within her.

DRUMS WERE POUNDING. A thunderous echo.

Wait. Not drums.

Her heartbeat. Pounding and pounding and seeming to echo in her ears. She was trapped between the hard wall and Victor's equally hard body. Her legs were curled tightly around his waist, and he'd just come inside of her.

Fair, she'd come at least twice for him.

She pressed a kiss to his neck.

He growled.

Her fingers fluttered over his broad shoulders. At the end, Melody was sure her short nails had been digging into his shoulders. Maybe his back, too. And potentially his ass. Now, though, they fluttered nervously, uncertainly.

Holy crap. I just had sex with Victor Alexander.

And she'd loved every second of it.

"Two things." Her voice came out extra husky. She cleared her throat. "One, I was literally on top of a perfectly good bed before you moved me."

He was getting bigger inside of her. She could feel the swelling. *Already?* Talk about impressive. Testing, she squeezed her inner muscles around him.

He growled again, a deeper, even rougher sound than before. A sound that she liked. Call her primitive, but his growls turned her on. Actually, almost everything about him turned her on.

He pulled back, almost taking his cock out of her, leaving just the broad head and—

He sank into her again.

She sucked in a breath. "Do that again." Because it had felt so, so good. Sending off aftershocks of pleasure.

He did it again. Only his dick was bigger, harder, and it felt even better.

Her legs tightened around him. "Again."

He did. Again. Again. He withdrew, then sank into her. She lifted her body, twisted and heaved as she fought to get closer to him. As the need within her spiraled and grew. A need that had flared to life and now, she felt starved, as if she'd been desperate for this—for him—for the last year. Now her body ached and longed, and she wanted him driving into her. Sinking into her. Pumping into her. Sending them both into oblivion.

"The bed was good," he rasped as his lips skimmed her jaw. "But you always love it when I pin you against the wall."

Yes, yes, she did love it. She thought it was *fantastic*. Because he was so strong and he held her easily, and his hips rocked in just the right way. Melody tightened her inner muscles around him in a hard clamp, and the orgasm was just —*there*. Surging through her body. Rippling across every nerve and cell. She couldn't even cry out this time. Her breath was gone, and all that she could do was hold on. Take the pleasure.

He pumped into her. He kissed her neck. Licked her. And then she felt the hard, long jet of his release inside of her.

"You said...two things."

Melody turned at Victor's voice. She'd showered. She'd *had* to shower because her thighs had been sticky. She'd been wet and, ah, cleaning up had been necessary.

Victor had gotten into the shower with her. She'd tried to stop him, worried about the graze he'd gotten from the gunshot getting wet, but, in typical Victor fashion, he'd just said, "Fuck it."

He'd washed her off, shared the soap, like it was some normal task they'd done together a million times.

Maybe it had been.

When she'd gotten out of the shower, she'd felt his eyes on her as she dressed. There were plenty of items to choose from for dressing. Not like before, when she'd had maybe four good outfits from her thrifting. Oh, no, now, she had a closet full of clothes—her clothes. Things that were a little loose, but she made them work. Boots that had her sighing in absolute joy because she loved them so much. They were lined and soft and *amazing*.

But Victor's words had just drawn her attention away from the amazing boots. Two things? What two things?

"What are you talking about?" Her body ached. In good ways.

"When I had you against the wall..."

Her gaze automatically darted to said wall. Oh, but that had been incredible.

"You said, there were two things you wanted to tell me. One was that I'd dragged you off a perfectly good bed. And, you know, guilty. Did that. Spoiler, will do it again." He'd put his clothes on again. Though the shirt was seriously missing some buttons. Her bad.

"What was the other thing, Melody?"

She smoothed her hands over the front of the designer jeans she now wore. A red sweater completed her outfit. "The other thing was that you hadn't exaggerated. I thought you had. I was wrong."

He leaned against one of the wooden posts on her bed. "Exaggerated?"

She could give credit where it was due. "I strongly suspect you are the best lover that I've ever had."

"Oh, sweetheart." The faint smile that had curled his lips vanished. "I was trying *not* to fuck you again."

He had been? Why?

"At least, not fuck you again here. Right now. But I was planning to strip you and fuck you all night long once we got back to my place."

Good to know that he was a man with a plan. She wet her lips.

His gaze burned. "But you keep saying things like that, and my good intentions will not last."

"Do you have lots of good intentions?"

His head cocked. "Honestly, where you are concerned... not really."

Someone was very blunt. "Bad intentions, then?" Breathy.

"Very, very bad."

She *yearned*. "Victor, I—"

Something pounded against her front door. Hard. Heavy thuds. Again and again. Thuds that she could hear even though they were upstairs because they were so loud. As if someone was trying to break down her front door. Her eyes widened. "What is that?" No, correction, "Who is that?"

A sigh escaped him. "Got a feeling I know." Not looking the least bit rushed, he walked from her bedroom.

For a stunned moment, Melody didn't move. Then, shaking from her stupor, she hurried after him. "Victor!"

He was already on the stairs.

Gripping the banister tightly, she followed.

The fierce pounding came again. Only this time, it was also followed by a shout. "Police!" Melody caught the bellow quite clearly. "Open the damn door!"

Again, no hurry from Victor even as dread curled around Melody. He took his time once he reached the main floor. Even stopped to glance through her peephole. "Well, you did want this opportunity," Victor told her as he spared a look over his shoulder at her. "You're about to get your chance to chat with the detective who was lead on your case. Detective Angus Clinton."

Melody had stopped steps behind him.

His head swung forward. Victor hauled open the door.

Melody crept to his side. The better to see the cop.

A tall, broad-shouldered redhead stood on her small stoop. Curly hair. Pale skin. Sharp, golden eyes.

"Detective Angus Clinton," Victor said. "Let me guess...

you asked one of her neighbors to call you if there was ever any sign of Melody showing up here?"

The detective grunted. Then his gaze jumped to her. Narrowed. He did not look pleased to see her. Quite the opposite, in fact, and he snapped, "Melody Mage. Finally decided to return home again, did you?"

She didn't know what to say. She was fighting to remember her home.

Another grunt. "Glad you're back, and by the way, your ass is under arrest." Then he hauled out handcuffs.

Her mouth dropped open. Why in the world was everyone trying to cuff her?

"Take a step toward her," Victor dared as he immediately positioned his body in front of hers. "And I can assure you that it will be the worst mistake you ever make."

Chapter Sixteen

SHE DIDN'T THINK THAT SHE'D EVER BEEN INSIDE A police station before. Or, particularly, inside an interrogation room before. But then again, she couldn't remember shit so...

Melody cradled the stale cup of coffee between her hands. She was in an actual interrogation room. One with a one-way viewing mirror on the wall. How *Law & Order* crazy was that? She was sitting at a little rickety table, Victor stood in front of the mirror, and the detective—Detective Angus Clinton—sat across from her, a cold scowl on his face.

"I didn't fake my disappearance," Melody told him. She'd told him this several times.

His scowl just deepened.

"I told you..." She had. All the bits and pieces that she had—she'd *told him*. After she'd made it to the station with Victor, a trip they'd made driving on a few sketchy roads with too much sludge and ice. "I woke up in a hospital. Most of my memory is still gone. I gave you the name of the hospital where I was treated. I gave you the names of my doctors. I signed paperwork, releases so that you could get all of my medical information." One hand lifted to make a shooing gesture toward him. "Don't you have people who can check all of this out? I didn't do anything wrong." *Hello, I'm the victim.* "I thought you were working my case to help me. Didn't realize you were looking to lock me up."

"You said you woke up in a Canadian hospital. And you admitted you used a fake ID to get back in the country." Angus glowered at her.

"No one is locking Melody up." Victor spoke with utter certainty. "We are here as a courtesy, nothing more."

The well-dressed woman who sat at Melody's side cleared her throat. "I think we should all take a few deep breaths." That would be her attorney talking. The lawyer who resembled a supermodel had come running as soon as Victor called her, despite the dangerous roads. *Amaya Abba.* Chief counsel at Mage Industries. "My client is cooperating."

From what she'd gathered, Amaya was more Victor's attorney than hers. Or maybe Amaya just worked for Mage Industries. But the woman had magically appeared at the station just as Angus began his interrogation proceedings, and Melody was certainly grateful for her presence. Not like she wanted to wind up behind bars.

Melody hadn't even realized that was a possibility, not until Angus had begun making his threats.

"My client is confused and clearly traumatized, yet here she is." Amaya sent her a sympathetic smile before she focused back on the detective. "She's patiently answering your questions. Being a good citizen. Giving you as much information as she can so that the evil perpetrator who attacked her can be brought to justice."

Melody didn't know if she'd really been *patiently* doing anything.

Victor had swiftly updated Amaya on Melody's, um, situation. He had also stopped Angus from cuffing Melody.

Since they'd been in the interrogation, Angus had gone on and on about her misusing police resources. He'd groused out something about a false abduction.

The abduction was real. Everything about that nightmare was real. And she didn't like the scowl on Angus's face. The man seemed pissed that she was alive. Call her crazy, but she didn't think cops were supposed to respond that way when they found a missing victim.

"I've got uniforms checking into the hospital story," Angus groused.

"Good for you," Melody muttered.

His eyes narrowed. "You just got home? That's the story you want to stick with? You seriously expect me to believe you simply sashayed back into town after being dead to the world for a year?"

"I didn't sashay." *Jerk.* "I scrimped and saved my money, and I followed the trickle of memories that I had back to Richmond."

"Uh, huh. Followed on a fake ID."

"Not like I woke up with my driver's license and passport on me in that hospital. If I had, then I would have known exactly who I was. I would have known where my home was. *Months* passed with me knowing nothing. I thought I would stay like that. Having no one. Nothing."

A low rumble came from Victor.

Her chin lifted. "Then I started to get flashes. Bits and pieces. I'm in Richmond because I want to know what happened. I want to put all of those broken pieces back together. I almost *died*. I think I deserve to know what happened to me." She leaned forward. She also ignored the light hand that Amaya tapped against her shoulder. She was getting that the other woman wanted her to stop talking, but Melody couldn't. Not yet. "I had hoped that you could help me," she told the detective. "I wanted to see the files you had on me. I wanted to see what suspects you had in my disappearance."

"Oh, I can absolutely share that intel with you." Angus pointed toward Victor. "Suspect number one."

"Victor didn't do anything to hurt me," she scoffed without even glancing his way. "He wouldn't."

"Exactly the same shit you told me before," Angus muttered back. He gave a disgusted shake of his head. "Still singing that same old tune, are you?"

His words caught her off guard. "What? Why would I tell you that? And when would we have talked?"

The tension in the room seemed really, really thick.

Victor took a step away from the mirror. "When in the hell did you talk to Melody?"

But Angus wasn't looking at Victor. His stare was only on her. "You really don't know, do you?"

"Give the man a cookie." She snapped her teeth together. "This isn't some game or some joke. It's my life. I was attacked. Bleeding in the snow. Someone took me. Someone hurt me. I'd like to know who the hell that person was, and I'd prefer for you to *arrest* that individual, not threaten to cuff me." Okay, those words had come out fast and angry. She should probably take a breath. Or maybe a sip of stale coffee. Do something to calm herself down a bit.

"Huh." Angus sucked in the side of his left cheek. "Huh."

She sipped the stale coffee. Almost immediately spat it

out again. That was truly the stuff of nightmares. Melody pushed the coffee cup away.

"Detective, you never told me that you knew Melody." Victor stalked across the small room. "You never told me about any conversation you'd had with her."

"I didn't? Odd, isn't it, how people can leave out details?" Angus shuffled the manila files in front of him. "And it's those little details that matter a great deal."

"How did you know Melody?" Victor questioned, voice harsh.

Angus glanced at Victor.

So did she.

Oh, yeah, he definitely looked pissed. "Victor, it's okay." It probably wasn't, but she didn't want the man taking a swing at a cop. If he did that, then Victor would be the one winding up in jail. She'd prefer for them to both get out of there without an arrest, if possible. Was that too much to ask? Melody didn't really think so.

"It's not okay," Victor gritted back. "This detective grilled me again and again while you were gone. Like he just said, I was suspect number one. I wanted his help to find you. At first, he refused to even consider the fact that you'd been taken. Thought you'd left on your own. So much fucking *time* was lost because I was the only one who knew you were missing from day one. Everyone else—including this prick—thought that you'd just walked away."

It was probably not the best idea ever to call the detective a prick. To think it, sure, but to say it? The animosity between the two men was clear. Super, super clear to see.

"The first forty-eight hours after a disappearance are vitally important." Victor's voice thickened with fury. "Evidence is strongest. You can find physical evidence faster—you can preserve it. Use it. That's also the best time to get leads because any witnesses still have fresh memories." His jaw clenched. "The more time that passes, the less likely you are to find the missing person alive."

A shiver skirted down her spine.

"Yet here you are," Angus murmured. "Alive."

Her gaze whipped toward him. He was staring straight at her again. His intense gaze made her feel uncomfortable. She shifted a bit in her chair. "You need to mark Victor off your suspect list. He didn't do anything to hurt me."

"Yes, he did." Angus seemed certain. "I think you and I need to talk, Ms. Mage, and we need to have that talk alone."

Amaya laughed. Hard. "That is adorable." More laughter. She even wagged her finger toward the detective. "Here I am, representing my client, proudly using all of the wonderful years of schooling that my parents worked so diligently to pay for...and you think I'm just going to walk away from my job so that you can privately grill a victim?"

Angus flushed. "I'm not grilling her. I'm simply going to remind her of a few facts, seeing as how her memory is impaired."

"Then remind her," Amaya invited. "By all means. Just do so with me present." Her smile taunted him.

Angus's flush deepened. But his head turned toward Victor. "Not sure you want what I'm about to say to be common knowledge."

"What the hell are you driving at?" Victor's face darkened.

"You should ask the lawyer to step outside."

"Amaya..." Victor directed, "don't move."

"Wasn't planning on it."

A dull ache began behind Melody's left eye. Dammit. Not another headache. Not now. They came and went far too often. She had no idea if she'd suffered from bad headaches before her attack or not, but she certainly faced them a lot now. A fun side effect of her head injury. "I don't understand what's happening here." There was a lot she didn't get. "How did you even know I was at my house?" she asked the detective.

"Neighbor contacted me. Mrs. Belle Finley. Told her to text me if she saw anything unusual at your place. You just waltzing in the front door right after a snowstorm? That struck her as unusual."

Yes, she could see how it might be unusual, given the last year. "Why do you want to talk to me alone?" Something that was obviously not going to happen. "Whatever you have to say, say it in front of Victor and Amaya."

The detective didn't say anything.

Impatience ate at her. "Then at least tell me the names of the other suspects in my disappearance. Who did you think could be involved?"

"How do you know she's the real deal?" Angus suddenly asked. His fingertips tapped across the top of the manila files.

She figured the question was supposed to be directed at Victor.

"You running a DNA test?" Angus pushed. "Checking dental records?"

Melody automatically rubbed her jaw. She hadn't thought about the dental records.

Victor's phone rang. A quick, low peal.

"I know she's the real deal." Absolute certainty in Victor's voice. He pulled out his phone and glanced at the screen. "But a fingerprint check will back up her claims. If you'll give me a minute..." He put the phone to his ear.

"Oh, sure," Angus huffed. "Take your call right now. Not like we are in the middle of anything important. Ignore me. Ignore my suspicions. If you're just gonna chat with your friends, you can take that shit outside, you know—"

"A match. Yes, that's what I expected," Victor said into his phone. "But I'm a little tied up with the local detective at the moment, so I'll have to call you back, Hunter. What's happening? Oh, the usual. Detective Angus Clinton threatened to arrest Melody, and now he's busy spouting off about how I'm the number one suspect in her disappearance. It's the same song he's sung about me for months now."

Angus's brows beetled. He leaned forward, shoving his upper body halfway across the table as he got close to Melody. "I came to you before," he said quickly. "Tried to warn you because I was working another case with ties to him. Told you that he was a liar."

Victor wasn't talking any longer.

She found herself trapped by the detective's angry glare. "What has Victor lied about?"

"I knew after I talked to you that day...I knew right then and there that you were personally involved with him."

She'd just had insanely powerful sex with Victor. Yes, they'd been personally involved before, and they were again.

Faint lines ran from the edges of Angus's eyes. "For whatever reason, you two were trying to keep that shit quiet."

Delicately, Melody cleared her throat. "Probably for our own privacy."

"Bull. You blasted everything you said and did on social media. Privacy wasn't big for you."

Yes, she'd seen the old posts. Those posts had helped her to piece together parts of her past.

"He was sleeping with you a year ago but keeping the relationship secret."

She could feel Amaya staring at her.

Victor, too.

"He keeps lots of secrets." Angus nodded. "You know, in all my time with him, Victor never told me that you two were hooking up. No matter how many times I pushed, he wouldn't confess. Don't you think that's odd?"

Maybe. Maybe not. *Maybe he didn't want to be an even bigger suspect.* She wasn't sure what reaction Angus expected, but Melody wasn't going to do or say anything to incriminate Victor. "I trust him."

"Fuck." Angus slumped back against his chair. "That's the exact same shit you told me a year ago."

Why would she have needed to say those words?

"When I came to you then...told you I was looking at a very old case...when I asked for your help and I informed you that I suspected Victor Alexander just might be one very dangerous man. A potential killer."

Her lips parted.

"You stared me in the eyes and said that you trusted him. That I had to be mistaken." Angus's fingers tapped across the files once more. "And then you vanished. Disappeared seemingly without a trace. Damn convenient timing, don't you think?"

Her head swung toward Victor.

"We are done." Amaya clapped her hands and rose to her feet. "Such a great chat. Detective Clinton, if you have any additional questions for Melody or for Victor, please

direct them *my* way. And by that, I mean, don't you dare consider talking to either one of them without me present. That shit will not fly. Now, we are leaving. I'm trudging back through the snow, and we will not be returning to this lovely interrogation room any time soon." A brisk nod. "Good night."

Because it was night. As they'd been climbing up the slippery steps to the station, the sky had already been darkening. Hours had passed since their arrival.

Amaya's fingers slid over Melody's shoulder once again. "Come on. We are leaving."

The detective had just accused Victor of being a murderer, and she was supposed to walk out of the door?

Why hadn't Victor said anything? Defended himself? Would it kill the man to tell the cop that he hadn't murdered anyone? "This is bullshit."

"Uh, Melody." A loud throat clearing from Amaya. "We are not talking with the detective any longer, remember?" She pulled on her arm. No more soft taps. "Let's go."

Melody rose to her feet. She tossed a glare toward Victor. "Why aren't you telling the detective that he's wrong?"

"Because he can't," Angus replied.

Her glare jumped to him. "Then fine, I can do it." Her hands slapped down on the table. The coffee cup jumped. Sloshed. "You are *wrong*. Victor has not killed anyone. Victor is not the bad guy."

"You have no memory. How can you know that? How can you be so certain of him?" His lips twisted. "You don't even remember me, do you? You have no memory whatsoever of our previous interaction."

A scream of fury wanted to erupt, but she held it back.

How was everyone else in the room so calm? So what if she didn't remember the damn detective? "Victor looked for me. He never stopped. He didn't hurt me. He's a good man."

"You truly don't know him." Now that was *pity* in Angus's eyes. "Or maybe...maybe you still love him. Despite everything, and that emotion is making you blind."

"You haven't given me one shred of evidence to think that Victor has done something wrong. Know what? I get why he didn't tell you about our relationship. You are way too eager to lock people up—and by people, I mean him and me. Too bad, though, because you're going to have to forget that plan. You aren't going to do anything to hurt him. Victor is a good person." How many times would she need to say that? And why was she wasting her breath? "I thought talking to you would help me, but it's just pissing me off. Let's go." An announcement to, well, Victor and Amaya.

"I was trying to get you to go," Amaya mumbled back. "You're the one who wanted to break out into an emotional monologue with the cop, despite your lawyer's advice to stay quiet."

Victor was staying quiet enough for them both.

But he strode for the door. Opened it. Waited for her.

She marched toward him. "Why the hell didn't you tell him to fuck off? It's so not—"

"Colton Crane," Angus dramatically dropped the name.

She paused and looked over her shoulder at the detective. "Is that name supposed to mean something to me?" Did they need to cover the whole definition of amnesia or what? *I can't remember shit.*

"Not to you, no. It's supposed to mean something to

your boyfriend." His smile was chilling. Taunting. "After all, that's the name of the man he nearly beat to death when Victor was just sixteen years old."

Chapter Seventeen

"Colton Crane." A nod from the detective. Melody did not like the smug look on his face. She also didn't like the growing knots in her stomach. "He's the whole reason I first started looking into Victor's life. Looking past that shiny veneer and all the money and fancy business titles he has now. Once upon a time, he was quite a different person. A criminal. A thug. Had one very interesting rap sheet as a teen that was—"

"My juvenile records were expunged," Victor said. His voice was flat. Arctic. When she angled a bit to look at him, no emotion showed on his face. He'd just been accused of assault—attempted murder?—yet he was as cold as ice as he added, "Charges when I was a minor don't really enter into the equation, and, if we're going to talk about all the business titles I have, let's not forget that I'm a lawyer, too. Amaya tends to be one hell of a lot more tactful than I am—"

"Thanks for noticing," Amaya broke in to say. "Always good to know when one is appreciated."

"So I called her in for the interrogation scene," Victor

continued doggedly. "But maybe you don't want tact, detective. Maybe you want a direct confrontation." He turned and faced off with the other man. "Be warned. You don't want to walk down this path with me right now. I'll have your job faster than you can blink. I played nicely with you for the last year because I thought you or one of your contacts might turn up something to help with my search for Melody. But you provided jack and shit. I have her back now. That means I do not need you any longer. Not in any form. Play time—my *nice* time—is over."

Yet the detective did not back down. "Did you nearly beat Colton Crane to death? Because I've seen the pictures." A low whistle. "His attacker certainly seemed to be filled with a whole lot of rage."

"Victor?" Melody prompted when he just stared at Angus. "We should go." The sooner, the better. She wanted to run out of that police station and never look back.

Victor glanced her way.

"We should go," she said again. A faint plea had entered her voice.

"It might be wiser for you to leave on your own," Angus advised her. "Don't trust the wrong person. Not having a memory makes you very, very vulnerable. You don't want to be prey again."

Like she needed to be reminded that not being prey was the goal. "Appreciate the concern, but being prey isn't on my to-do list, thanks."

"Are you *threatening* her?" Victor demanded. Now emotion was in his voice. Unfortunately, that emotion was rage.

Amaya pushed back her chair. The legs screeched over the floor. "I think my tact is needed. Definitely needed." Her high heels clicked over the floor. "There are no threats.

There are just concerned individuals, on both sides." She flashed a sunny smile. "Since my client—actually, *clients*, plural, since I represent both Melody and Victor—have done nothing wrong, they will be leaving. Unless, of course, I missed some charge that you were leveling against them?"

"Her fake ID—"

"If Melody's memory hadn't been impaired by her tragic attack, then she would have easily been able to contact the embassy or even contact her *family* and get proper ID. Do you really want to charge *Melody Mage,* the victim in this tragedy, when you know I can get any good judge to see things my way? When I can absolutely crucify your unfeeling self in the Press?" She waited a beat. Blinked. "No? Good. By the way, that's me being *tactful.* Now, I think we're done here." She motioned toward the door. "Let's end this scene."

Gladly. Melody gave up waiting on Victor. She grabbed the man's arm and heaved him forward. The better to get him away from the detective. "Come on." They'd been there for *hours.* Going over the same details. How many times did a woman have to say that she had no memory?

And how many times did the detective have to grill a victim?

Though he'd certainly been sitting heavily on that little bombshell about Victor's past. Was it true? Had Victor really beaten a man so badly that the guy had almost died?

Victor let her pull him forward. She kept right on tugging him down the narrow hallway. Amaya's heels click, click, clicked behind them. And then...

Outside.

Cold, biting night air. No more snowfall, but the temperature was still far, far too icy. When Melody breathed, a puff of fog drifted in front of her mouth.

"That was miserable," Amaya announced as she paused on the top step near them. She'd bundled back into her designer coat. Her hands shoved into its deep pockets. "The detective was clearly planning for some sort of ambush in there, and I don't like walking into a scene unprepared." She edged closer to Melody. "My God." A puff of frozen air drifted near her face. "I can't believe you're back." She shook her head, sending her dark hair sliding against her jaw. "And I can't believe that dick detective threatened to arrest you when you're clearly the victim." Her focus shifted to a silent Victor. "You know he was trying to push you into an attack."

"I didn't attack him."

"Right. Because you were being *nice*." A shiver worked over her body, and Amaya pulled her coat even closer. "I'm going home. I'm defrosting. We *will* all talk again soon, yes? And no one will get arrested or get hauled to a police station again in the immediate future? Promise me?"

"I'll do my best," Victor said.

"That's not the passionate promise I was looking for." She inclined her head toward Melody. "You keep him out of trouble?"

Did she know the lawyer? Had they been friends before? Amaya wasn't trying to hug her or say anything personal to her so...maybe not?

"I'm not getting a promise from you, either," Amaya huffed into the silence. "You two are not being dream clients right now." Another shiver. "Whatever. I did my due diligence. I'm going home and wrapping some presents for my kids. Please, *please* don't antagonize the cops. I would like to have a merry holiday with my family."

With that, she cautiously made her way down the steps

and toward a black Range Rover parked near the front of the police station.

Melody shivered as she watched Amaya walk away. At her shiver, Victor cursed. He shouldered out of his coat and draped it over her shoulders. It was warm. Huge, but warm, and she hunched into it. *I'm wearing two coats.* Granted, one was too thin but...now he had nothing.

"Come on, baby," he said, "we're going home." He'd driven them to the station in his BMW. One that he'd parked around the side of the station when they'd arrived.

They made it to the bottom of the steps. Amaya was already in her vehicle. Her lights flashed as she pulled away.

Victor turned to the side of the police station. His BMW waited about twenty feet away and—

"What the fuck?" Victor snarled. He let her go and surged forward.

She hurried forward, too, and saw what had caused his flare of anger. The BMW's two passenger side tires were completely flat. The vehicle sank down, twisted to the side.

The BMW was the only car left on the side of the station. She figured it had to be nearing midnight. The streetlamp near the BMW kept flickering, on and off, on and off...

And she heard a faint rustle from the surrounding darkness.

Instantly, her head whipped to the left. Then to the right. More buildings. But they were all closed. Shuttered for the night.

"Slashed," Victor said as he bent near one of the tires.

Okay, that was bad.

Victor rose, quickly. "Melody, I want you going back inside. *Now.*"

"Not without you." They'd both go back inside the

police station. She held out her hand toward him. "Come on Victor, let's—*Victor!*"

A man jumped from the darkness. Jumped to stand between her and Victor, and he gripped a knife in his hand. The same knife he'd used to slash the tires? Even as she screamed, he was coming at her, slashing at her. The blade sliced toward her chest, and she leapt back. Her boots lost purchase on the icy ground, and they slipped from beneath her. She slammed down on her ass, and that timely fall saved her from getting cut with the knife.

"*Melody!*" A roar. But not one that came from Victor.

She looked over her shoulder. That roar had come from Detective Angus Clinton. He'd followed them. He yanked out his weapon.

Frantic, her head swung back toward her attacker. Only as she watched, Victor launched his body at the attacker, and they both slammed into the cement near her.

There was a thud. A grunt. Then Victor rose. The attacker groaned but didn't get up.

"You sonofabitch," Victor snarled. "*You don't hurt her.*"

She scrambled back, her hands freezing as they slapped against the icy cement.

Victor flipped over the attacker. The man's big, black coat had fallen open.

Oh, God.

The knife was in the guy's chest. Lodged in him. For a moment, she thought he was dead.

"Victor," she whispered.

Then the attacker lunged up. A wild scream broke from him as he yanked the knife out of his chest. Blood dripped onto the ground, and he twisted the knife in his gloved grip as he drove it at Victor.

"*Victor!*" Not a whisper this time. A scream.

Victor knocked the knife out of the attacker's hand. It clattered to the ground. Then Victor drew back his fist and slammed it into the other man's face, a face covered by a ski mask. Victor hit him once, twice, again. *Again.*

A hand clamped around Melody's shoulder.

She jumped.

But it was just the detective. "You okay?" he demanded.

She nodded over and over, jerky movements as fear poured through her veins.

"Get behind me." A sharp order.

She scrambled up. Moved behind the detective with the gun and heard him yell, "Police! Freeze!"

Only Victor didn't freeze. He kept right on punching the assailant. Over and over, even though the man in the mask didn't appear to be fighting back.

"I said for you to freeze!" Angus shouted. "Victor, move away from him, now!"

Victor's hand flew once more.

A thudding impact.

"Victor!" Melody cried out.

His head whipped toward her. His hand froze in mid-air.

"He was trying to stab me," Melody said quickly, not sure what all Angus had seen. "The car's tires were slashed. Victor told me to go inside, and this guy came at me with a knife." An attack right beside the police station? You had to be bold as hell to pull off a stunt like that.

Except...

I think he was waiting for me. The slashing tires had been deliberate. And the attacker hadn't gone for Victor. He'd come straight at her.

Victor's hand fell. He stepped to the side. The man in the black ski mask immediately fell.

"Get over here!" Angus barked at Victor. "Move away from the perp!"

Where had the knife gone? It had fallen before, but she didn't know where it was any longer.

Victor didn't move away. "Melody?"

"I'm okay." Her teeth chattered. From the cold and from straight-up terror.

"Move away," Angus snarled.

The man on the ground lunged upward. He gripped the knife in his hand—The same knife? A second one?—and he swung it out toward Victor.

"Drop it! *Drop—*" Angus fired his gun.

Chapter Eighteen

The bastard yelled when the bullet tore into his shoulder. The knife clattered from his fingers and fell, and then the prick—he *ran*. He turned, and he lunged away from Victor. Away from the station. He plunged into the darkness.

Oh, the hell, no.

Victor chased after him. That sonofabitch had just tried to attack Melody. No way did he get to just escape into the night.

And Victor wasn't the only one giving chase. He could hear the pounding footsteps behind him. Angus. Melody. Angus was bellowing for the perp to stop.

Spoiler alert, he wasn't stopping. If anything, he just ran faster. Victor looked down. Beneath the street lamps, he could see spots of blood on patches of snow that still lingered on the pavement.

"Dammit, *stop!*" Angus's order. "Don't make me shoot you, too!"

What the fuck?

Victor glanced over his shoulder, then slowed because

the freaking detective was running at him with his gun *aimed*. What in the hell?

Huffing, puffing, Angus barreled toward him. "You're not...cop. Stop...giving chase!"

Oh, yeah, screw that.

But when he whirled again, the perp—shit, the perp had vanished.

Victor stilled. *You don't get to escape. Oh, hell, no.*

"Where is he?" Angus demanded. "Where did the sonofabitch go?"

They'd lost illumination from the street lamps and had slipped into a dark alley.

"Victor?" Melody's careful voice. His head whipped toward her.

"Victor, you're okay?"

No, he was seething with rage, and he damn well should have made certain the punk didn't escape. But what mattered most right then... "*You're* okay." She was safe. She hadn't been stabbed.

Melody nodded.

He yanked out his phone. He hit the button for the flashlight and shone it on the ground. And sure enough, the trail was clear for them to see. *Blood. Wet, dark drops that have to be blood.*

"Stay the hell back," Angus thundered. "I've got this!" He pulled out a flashlight, directed it at the ground, and rushed after the blood drops.

But, no, Victor did not stay the hell back. He did clamp his hand around Melody's wrist, though. Because he wasn't about to run off and leave her alone. For all he knew, this was some divide-and-conquer bullshit, and he wasn't going to let her stay unprotected. Where he went, she went.

They gave chase together, and, up ahead, the alley

emptied out into another street. A busier road that he could see just in the distance. Maybe about twenty, thirty feet away. Except...

The blood trail led to a dumpster. It didn't head toward the street.

"We've got you, asshole!" Angus snarled as he paused near the dumpster. "Come out, with your hands up! *Now!*"

The man in the mask came out, and his hands were up, all right. Up, and holding what looked like a broken computer that he'd hauled from the dumpster. The attacker threw the old tech at Angus and then took off for the alley's exit.

The computer drove into Angus's shoulder. He cursed. Tried to get off a shot. Fired—

The bullet missed the fleeing target.

Snarling, Victor raced forward, still holding tightly to Melody.

"Victor, wait," she began.

"*Stop!*" Angus roared.

The perp didn't stop. He ran out of the alley and straight into the street, even as he looked back. Looked back, not forward.

So he didn't see the van that rushed forward and slammed right into his body. The thudding impact was loud. Bones snapped. The guy in the black ski mask screamed, a terrified, pain-filled cry that echoed, as he went airborne for a timeless moment. Then his body slammed onto the pavement. The scream stopped.

Shit. Victor let go of Melody. "*Stay. Here.*"

Her horrified eyes were on the scene. The twisted body of the perp. The blood. Blood that had seemed to go... everywhere.

"Dammit! Dammit!" Angus yanked out his phone. Victor could hear him calling for help.

Victor ran for the road. The attacker had landed about five feet from the van, his body was twisted. Legs broken. One arm outstretched. He still had on the ski mask.

"Move away from him!" Angus shouted. "He could have another weapon!"

Another weapon wasn't gonna help the bastard. Victor didn't think anything could help him. He grabbed for the ski mask and ripped it off the jerk's head. The headlights from the van lit up the scene. *So much blood.* The ski mask was wet with it. But when he pulled it off the attacker's head...

Too young.

Some young punk. Barely looked twenty-one. Shaggy, brown hair. A pathetic excuse for a beard. Just scruff. And... wide, scared eyes.

"H-help..."

The kid's lips were busted. Bleeding. His entire body was busted and bleeding, and, hell, he was not gonna make it. You didn't need to be a doctor to figure out that shit.

"I didn't see him!" A door slammed. The driver's side door of the van. "He just ran out! *OhGod, OhGod*...is he all right?"

No, he was not. The perp's breath heaved in and out. And his body shuddered.

"Get the hell back, Victor!" Angus's shout again.

"*Is he all right?*" A desperate cry from the driver.

Blood covered the kid's chest. From the knife wound Victor had given him? Yeah, sure, but also from the stunning impact of the van's front end slamming into him. The kid couldn't breathe right. He was just wheezing. And the blood—*everywhere*.

Melody dropped to her knees beside the perp.

Angus cursed.

The driver staggered closer. "I didn't see him! I swear, I didn't! He just ran out! Didn't stop..."

Victor put his hands on the biggest wound he saw. A gushing wound on the kid's chest.

"Look at me," Melody told the kid. "Look at me. *Focus on me.* You're going to be okay, do you hear me?"

Ah, no, he was not. Blood immediately soaked Victor's fingers. Angus had called for help, he knew that. Just how long would it take for that help to arrive? They were so close to the police station. *It should be fast, right?* And why the hell weren't other cops already nearby? Surely someone had heard the gunshots. "Tell the EMTs to fucking hurry!" Victor snarled to Angus because this kid could not die without giving him answers.

"Hurry!" Angus immediately blasted into his phone. "We've got a perp down. He's...shit. *Hurry.*"

"Breathe," Melody urged the kid. "You just have to breathe. We're going to get you to a hospital." Her hands were shaking as she tried to apply pressure to some of his wounds, too.

The kid's eyes began to sag closed.

"It was an accident!" A yell from the driver. "He just ran out! You all saw that, right? He *ran out!*"

The kid's body jerked. More blood pumped between Victor's fingers.

Melody shuddered. "Don't die. *Don't.*"

Sweetheart, that ship is sailing. But maybe he could get answers first. Because he knew the attack near the station had been targeted. The SOB had been waiting for him and Melody. The kid's eyes had almost closed completely. *No.* "Dammit, look at me!" Victor snapped. "Who are you? Why the hell did you attack her?"

The kid's busted lips parted. Was he going to answer? Blood trickled from his forehead. From his nose.

"Don't move him!" Angus loomed over them. "He could have spinal injuries."

Could have? Uh, try definitely did have. The kid's body was twisted as hell, but the gushing blood was a current priority because Victor feared the perp was about to bleed out. *Far, far too much blood.* But, no, he was trying not to move the kid. Maybe they'd get a miracle. If the ambulance and the EMTs could just arrive, and they could get the kid to the hospital before—

His eyes closed.

"No!" A sob broke from Melody.

"*Why her?*" Victor demanded.

There were tattoos on the kid's neck. Disappearing down to his chest.

Blood was everywhere. And the kid wasn't speaking. Was barely breathing.

Or...

Not breathing at all. Time trickled past.

Other hands appeared. Some tried to push Victor away. Some grabbed for the kid. The kid who hadn't spoken. The kid who'd tried to kill Melody right in front of him. That hadn't been a robbery. The knife had flown straight for her, and if she hadn't slipped on the icy ground...

Dammit, dammit! He'd sworn to keep her safe, and she'd almost been killed right in front of him.

"EMT! Coming through, coming through!"

Victor and Melody were hauled back even as others crowded around the injured perp. Victor didn't know how long he'd been trying to stop that terrible blood flow. He rose to his feet. Stared at his hands.

So much blood.

"The perp never made it to the hospital."

They were back in the station. Same damn interrogation room. Victor would have preferred never to see that room again. He also would have preferred for the kid to have survived. He wouldn't get answers from a dead body.

Angus heaved out a breath. Lines of weariness bracketed his mouth. "Perp probably thought it would be an easy mugging. Saw the BMW. Planned his attack."

"No." Just that. Victor didn't say more.

He stood beside Melody as she sat in the chair at the little table. She hadn't spoken much. Hell, she'd just watched a man die in front of her. *She'd* nearly died. And, of course, all of those fun events had happened *after* the detective revealed that Victor had nearly killed a man at the tender age of sixteen.

Yeah, I'm guilty. Did the crime. Would do it all over again if I had to do it. Because the sonofabitch had deserved it.

Was he a vengeful bastard?

Only...always.

"What do you mean, 'no'?" Angus sighed. "Look, I knew that guy, okay? He was one of our frequent flyers at the station." A rough exhale. "Benny Turner. A twenty-year-old kid. His rap sheet stretched for days. Hell, Benny had been in trouble since he was thirteen. His mom died. His dad ran off. His grandparents kicked him out because they couldn't control him. He bounced around more foster homes than I can count."

Victor stiffened.

"Kid got involved with gangs. Then got hooked on

drugs. The guy was always looking for a quick score. Pretty sure he was in holding earlier this week." His voice thickened. "Like I said, he was a frequent flyer here. Kid was in and out of this place all the time. Revolving damn door with him. Such a fucking wasted life." Angus rolled back his shoulders.

"Why didn't he just stop?" Melody's soft voice.

Victor slanted a glance her way. She'd been far too quiet. He had the feeling she was holding onto her control by a thread. Seeing that accident—shit. *Same thing happened to you, didn't it, baby?* No wonder she was so pale. So tense.

The van had plowed into Benny Turner. He'd gone flying, only to land, broken, near the vehicle.

Tear tracks had dried on Melody's cheeks.

"He should have stopped," Angus muttered, drawing Victor's attention back. "The ME will perform a full exam. My money says the kid was sky high."

"No." Again, that was all Victor said.

Angus glared at him. "That really all you've got to say? Don't you want to elaborate?"

He'd made arrangements for the limo to pick him up—him and Melody. He'd already changed clothes. His driver-slash-guard had brought in fresh clothing for him. The blood-stained items had been taken in as evidence.

He'd planned to keep guards on Melody. But they'd only been back in town for such a short time. He'd thought she was safe with him, that they wouldn't need the guards until the next morning and yet...

I was fucking wrong. "Benny had a target." *Bounced around more foster homes than I can count.* Like that shit wasn't too familiar. The cop might as well have been talking about Victor's life. "He slashed our tires so we couldn't escape. He waited for us to come out of the station." Which begged the question...how had Benny known they were there? "And he didn't attack me first, even though I was the bigger threat. My back was turned while I was looking at the car. He had the perfect opportunity to stab me in the back."

Melody sucked in a sharp breath.

"But he didn't. He went after his goal." He looked directly at Melody. "You, sweetheart."

When the blade had sliced at her, he'd known that he was too far away. That he couldn't get to the attacker in time. The blade had gone straight toward her.

Then she'd fallen.

Luckiest fucking fall of her life.

"He had a target." Victor knew this with certainty. "Someone wanted him to take out Melody."

Angus shuffled forward. "Uh, yeah, I get that it's been a stressful night, but that's one big-ass conclusion," Angus told him.

"And like I told *you* during our marathon interrogation session, some asshole with a gun tried to shoot Melody at her father's estate. That's two attempts now. *Two*." He was not going for attack number three. "The person who took Melody from me—that bastard knows she's returned. That person wants her eliminated." He rolled back his shoulders. "We need to find out if that kid happened to own a blue pickup truck."

"Benny didn't own shit." A pause. Then, musing, "But he was a real pro when it came to boosting. And he always liked trucks."

Could Benny have been the shooter at the Mage estate? If the kid had lived, they could have gotten so many answers.

If the kid had lived…shit, dead at twenty. So young.

"Dammit." A long sigh from Angus. "Benny, why the hell didn't you just stop?"

He hadn't stopped, though, and now he was just a body in the morgue.

Chapter Nineteen

The limo door clicked shut. Warmth filled the interior. Warmth and heavy silence.

The driver headed around to the front of the vehicle. A few moments later, the limo pulled away from the police station.

Melody didn't speak. Victor's hands curled into fists. She had to be terrified. After all that she'd seen—

"Are you okay?" she asked him.

She was worried about him? Screw that. Why the hell would she worry about him? She'd been the target of the attack. And then to see that van slam into the kid...*It was like a scene straight from your nightmares, wasn't it, sweetheart?*

"Victor?" Her hand reached out to touch his clenched fist. "Are you all right?"

He'd nearly let her get killed. Right in front of him.

They were alone in the back of the limo. The privacy screen separated them from the driver. Jenner knew to take them home.

"I couldn't get that kid to talk." Victor could still feel the pump of Benny's blood against his fingers. "I needed to know why."

Her fingers squeezed his. "You think the *why*—you think it's me."

He stared into her eyes. "Don't you?"

"Yes."

"Me, too." A whisper.

The limo turned to the right. Rain was falling lightly. Rain, not snow. The roads would turn into black ice soon with the frigid temps.

The van had no chance to stop. The roads were too slick. And the kid just raced right out into the street, without looking. Too afraid of what was behind him.

Victor had been behind him.

"I don't understand why any of this is happening," she murmured.

He damn well didn't, either. A soft, faint glow of light illuminated the back of the limo. The bluish glow came from the floor. Soft, instrumental Christmas music played from the speakers.

It's Christmas. Doesn't really feel that way. All I can think is...

I almost lost her, just when I got her back.

The last Christmas had been the worst one of his life. Even worse than when he'd been a kid and his dad had died in that accident at the factory. Everything in his world had changed with his father's death. His mom had crawled into a bottle, then gotten hooked on drugs. She'd faded bit by bit in front of him—changing into someone he didn't know at all. Then she'd dumped him. Never looked back.

He hadn't really had a good Christmas since his dad's passing. Not like he'd had anyone to celebrate it with over the years. Sure, as an adult, he went through the motions, but...

Just because it was expected. Had to do the whole routine in front of business associates. Colleagues. No, he hadn't really celebrated Christmas in a long time.

Until last year. With Melody. She'd decorated. She'd taken him ice skating. They'd watched *It's a Wonderful Life.* They'd danced slowly to Christmas music in his den, and he'd realized...his life *was* wonderful. The holiday was going to be different. He'd celebrate every year going forward. They'd have a family. Maybe one day he'd even dress as Santa for the kids and then—

Then in a blink, she'd been gone. Everything had been gone. When your heart had been carved from your chest and you walked through a house with decorations everywhere but the person you needed the most was *gone...* there was nothing more brutal.

"Why did I disappear in the first place?" Her soft voice had his jaw locking. "Why would someone make me vanish?"

He had no answer. For the last year, he'd tried to understand, but he couldn't.

"When we were at the estate, Sebastian said...he said it was his fault. You were right there. I know you heard him."

Yes, he had heard him. "Sebastian gets confused, baby." Victor wanted to pull her into his arms. Hold her. But he was almost afraid to touch her.

"He said he was supposed to pay. That he was supposed to get me back, but he didn't. That sounds like ransom to me. Like maybe a ransom demand was ordered but Sebastian didn't pay it." She shifted on the seat. Edged closer to him.

Pull her against you. Hold her. Don't ever let go.

"Was I kidnapped?" Her hair brushed over her cheek. "Did he not pay the ransom? Did he just let them take me?"

The limo drove slowly through the dark streets of the city. "If there had been a ransom, don't you think I would have paid?" Victor would have given every dime he had in order to get her back. "I would have paid *anything*." He needed her to understand that basic truth. "I would have paid any amount of money. I would have done anything to get you back. There was no ransom. No demands were made. You simply vanished."

"But what if the demand wasn't made to you? What if it was made to Sebastian—to my father? Olivia didn't know that we were involved. I don't think anyone did. If no one knew, why would my abductor ever have contacted you? He probably thought you hated me. That seems to be what most people thought. You hated me. Or, at the very least, you tolerated me because of the company and my father."

I don't want to be your dirty little secret any longer.

He pressed his lips together.

"Maybe the ransom demand didn't come to you. Maybe it went to him. *Sebastian said he didn't pay.*"

"Baby..." Shit. It broke his heart to do this. "Baby, you can't believe anything he says."

"I get that he has dementia. Things come and go. But he said—"

He had to tell her. Not like there was a lot of time left. "Sebastian is dying. It's not dementia. It's a tumor, pressing hard on parts of his brain as it gets bigger and bigger."

She sucked in a breath. Her hand pulled away from his. It hovered over her heart.

"Inoperable." He *hated* telling her this. Dammit. "He may have a month left. Maybe two. He says things...hell, he's said things for the last year that make no sense. I took over the business because he'd driven the company to the brink of bankruptcy." Something most people didn't know. "I...bought it out." And Sebastian had raged. Only to then forget. To celebrate at the company party last year like it had bene a planned partnership. "He was going to lose everything. So I had to take control." And when he said everything, Victor truly meant it. "There is no Mage estate any longer. It's mine. I own the house. I own all the property." He'd kept it all...

For you, baby. I kept it for you.

"Sebastian has no money. He couldn't pay anyone for anything. And he hasn't had contact with anyone outside of a very select circle in...hell, since last year. Since the big company party where he announced that I was taking over." *And you vanished.* "He doesn't check emails. Doesn't read any texts. He doesn't leave the estate because he gets confused and angry in new environments. And he—he says things...things that don't always make sense. Things that aren't always true." He'd been down that rabbit hole so many times. "That wasn't the first time Sebastian said it was his fault that you were missing. I checked through every phone record, checked all emails—checked everything. He never received a ransom demand for you."

"He's...dying?"

The doctors were honestly surprised that he hadn't passed already. "He gets confused about time. It comes, and it goes. Like I told you before, he'll have good days." And some really, really bad days. "He's on strong meds to help. But there is nothing that can fix him. There is no magic cure waiting in the wings. I was at the estate this weekend because he'd been having a few good days." The doctors had even warned him that maybe, right before the end, Sebastian would seem perfectly normal. Lucid. And then...

Gone.

"I wanted to have one last goodbye with him. Dario wanted to push about changes to the will." What Dario didn't get—those changes had been made with Amaya's assistance long ago. There was nothing left to inherit.

But they hadn't discussed the will or any future plans because the Ghost of Christmas Past had walked through their door.

"He's dying." Not a question this time from Melody. A statement. Sadness. Her hand fell onto the seat.

Victor nodded. "I'm sorry, baby." There was more he should tell her. But, fuck, he'd just broken her heart, and he knew it. Couldn't the rest wait?

She didn't make a sound, but Victor reached out anyway. His fingers skimmed her right cheek. He felt her tears. "Melody..."

"I don't know him," she said. "Don't remember him. So why does it hurt so much?"

He pulled her onto his lap. Wrapped his arms around her. And held her against his heart.

SEBASTIAN MAGE STARED out his bedroom window. He stared into the darkness.

He'd thought that Melody was home. He'd asked to see her. Been so excited...

But his nurse had told him Melody was gone. He must have gotten confused again. Melody...she'd been gone a long time.

So had her mother. Her beautiful, lying mother.

His hand pressed to the window pane. So cold.

"It's really late, Sebastian."

Ah, the nurse. He looked over his shoulder. Light spilled around her, making the blonde look like an angel. To him, she was an angel. Always helping him. Always looking out for him. Softly reminding him when he forgot things.

Things like...names.

Places.

Who the hell I am.

Sebastian Mage. *I am Sebastian Mage.*

"Melody is gone," he told her.

"Yes, but she'll be back."

No. "She's been gone a long time. Dario says she's dead." He could remember that. Dario, in his den. Saying that he had to change the will because Melody was never coming home. "I wanted to give her everything."

"You wanted your daughter to have your fortune." She nodded.

What was her name? He struggled to remember. But it had been such a long day. Had the sheriff been there?

No, no, surely not. The sheriff must have been there another time. One of the many times when Sebastian had wanted to find Melody. "I wanted my daughter to have everything." He saw her picture on the dresser. A young Melody, in a black ballerina tutu.

Her mother had been a dancer before she'd become an actress.

Such an incredible actress. The critics had never given her enough credit for her talent. *She even fooled me.*

"You need to get in bed, Sebastian."

His gaze lingered on the photo. "I loved her."

"Melody?"

No. "My wife." He shuffled toward the bed. His right hand gripped a cane. He needed that cane. Sometimes, he fell. Didn't he?

"I'm sure your wife loved you, too."

He shook his head. "Lying bitch."

A swift inhale from the nurse.

"She's dead. I did it." He eased into the bed. Left the cane close by. He sighed.

She brought the covers up to his chest. "You killed your wife?" Mild, vaguely curious.

"She was cheating on me." Had been, for so long.

"So you killed her?"

His eyes had closed. Now, though, he opened them. The lamp by his bed had already been turned off. He stared into the darkness. He couldn't see the nurse's face clearly. "I need to get everyone to the house this weekend," he said, determined. "The will has to be settled."

She tucked the covers in around him. "Everyone was here. You just forgot. Sometimes, you forget things. We all do."

Yes, yes, he did forget things. Especially late at night. But some things...some things he remembered. "I killed her."

Another careful tuck of the covers near his hip. "Your wife?"

No. "My daughter." A tear leaked down his cheek.

Sebastian had fallen asleep. She opened his door. Crept outside—

"What in the hell are you doing?"

Olivia Hatcher jumped. Her right hand flew over her racing heart even as her left still gripped the doorknob. The doorknob that led to Sebastian's room.

"Why were you in Sebastian's room?" Tracy demanded. The light from the hallway fell on her glaring features.

"Jeez." Olivia heaved out a breath. "Talk about nearly scaring someone to death."

Tracy took a hard step toward her. "Why were you in Sebastian's room?"

"Uh, because he was calling out for help? Because he's an old, confused, and *sick* man? And his *nurse* was nowhere nearby so when I heard him, I went in to assist, like the amazing person I am?" Olivia sniffed. "I don't need this third-degree bullshit from you when I was just trying to help out. Sue me for doing a good deed why don't you?"

Behind Tracy, she caught the hulking presence of a guard. The bodyguard that Victor had sent to keep watch on Sebastian. Only that guy hadn't been in the hallway earlier. When Olivia had come creeping toward Sebastian Mage's room, the area had been deserted. Thankfully.

She'd figured everyone had to take a bathroom break, sooner or later.

"He was supposed to be sleeping," Tracy snapped.

"Yes, well, he wasn't." Or, he *had* been. Until he'd woken up and found her poking through the drawers of his dresser. "He called out, and I helped him like the Good Samaritan I am. End of story." Nope. It was not. Not even close. "Now, if you don't mind, I am going to bed. Dario and I are leaving first thing in the morning. We had our not-so-fun, grilling time with the sheriff." He'd treated them like suspects. As if she'd been running around in the cold, shooting at people. "The sheriff said no one had to stay any longer. The roads are clear out of this countryside retreat from hell, and I'll be getting back home come first light." Olivia strode forward, intending to return to the bedroom that she shared with Dario.

But Tracy moved into her path. Her eyes were narrowed. "Sebastian gets more confused at night. Particularly if he wakes from a bad dream. He will say things—things that aren't true."

"I'm aware of his condition." Now that she and Dario were an item, she was fully ensconced in the Mage inner circle.

"The confusion has gotten significantly worse. If he spoke out and said anything, ah, odd to you—" Tracy wet her lips. "He doesn't mean what he says."

"You sure about that?" Because the man had seemed pretty certain to her.

Tracy's pretty features hardened. "Stay out of his room. I am his nurse. If he needs help, it's my job to take care of him."

Olivia leaned toward the other woman, as if imparting a secret, and whispered, "Then you should do a better job." With that parting shot, she skirted around Tracy. She headed for the end of the hallway. Her gaze darted over the guard. Big, tall. Silent. Kinda lickable. If you went for that type. The dangerously intent and sexy type.

"Hello, John Henry." He'd been introduced to her earlier.

He inclined his head. His gaze raked her. Lingered a moment on her silk robe. She winked at him because she did like that type. But she kept going because she also really, really liked the super-wealthy-and-due-to-inherit type. Though, for fun, she let her hips do a little roll. Why not throw the big guard a little treat?

Soon—finally—she was back in her room. She opened the door, slipped inside and—

"Well?" Dario demanded as he sat on the edge of the bed.

She tucked a lock of hair behind her ear. "I'm pretty sure your stepfather is a murderer."

He nodded. "Always did wonder..."

Really? No other response? "So what are we gonna do about that?" Olivia wanted to know.

Dario smiled at her. "I've got a plan."

Wonderful. "I hope it's better than your last plan. Because that one went straight to shit, didn't it?"

Chapter Twenty

"We have a problem," John Henry told him.

Victor stood in his den. The house was silent. Cold. Melody was upstairs. He'd taken her to the guest room. Made sure she had clothing. Following Victor's instructions, Jenner had stopped by her place before he'd come to the station. He'd packed bags for her. Brought over everything she needed.

When they'd arrived at Victor's house, she'd seemed so small. So fragile. So *breakable*. He'd wanted to pull her into his arms.

But hadn't he already pushed her too much? He'd *taken* her at her house. He hadn't been able to stop. When she'd offered herself to him, his control had shattered.

He'd intended to play the gentleman. To charm her. To prove to her that she'd always be safe with him.

Only he'd fucking feasted on her.

Then nearly watched her die right in front of him. Like he'd ever get over that moment.

He'd been in the upstairs guest room with her when the phone call had come. He'd carried up her bags and put them down just as his phone had pealed with a call from John Henry. And he'd known that he had to slip away.

"I've got quite a few problems," Victor murmured. "You're gonna need to be way more specific." *A man died in front of me tonight. After he nearly killed Melody.*

Right. In. Front. Of. Me.

"The nurse just caught Olivia Hatcher sneaking out of Sebastian's bedroom."

John Henry had his complete attention.

"She was only inside a short time. Very short."

"Where the hell were you?" He'd given orders that Sebastian was to be protected.

"I swear, I'd only left my post for moments. The guy had been sleeping, and I needed to piss, all right? But she must have been waiting for me to leave. Gave some BS story to the nurse about him calling out. The woman looked guilty as sin." An exhale. "No way she just *happened* to hear him calling out. Her room with Dario is on the other side of the house."

Yes, it was. "Anything else?"

"Sheriff grilled everyone. Didn't turn up any evidence at the estate. The truck was stolen. I did get that much intel from the deputies."

And Benny Turner was good at boosting trucks. "I'll follow up with the sheriff in the morning. Make sure that Sebastian has no other unwelcome visitors, would you?"

"Thought I was supposed to be guarding him from attacks. The woman in the see-through robe didn't have a weapon on her."

"Looks can be deceiving."

John Henry grunted. "Olivia is leaving in the morning. Heading out with Dario."

"I'm sure they will be paying me a visit at the first

opportunity." He'd be ready for them. "Appreciate the update." He lowered the phone.

It was the second update he'd gotten that night. The first had been from Hunter McQueen, a call that came during Angus's unfortunate interrogation session. It had been short.

The fingerprints match. Used one of Declan's new tech systems, it's five times more accurate than a human expert. The woman with you is Melody Mage. Ninety-nine percent accuracy. That is your missing fiancée.

As if he hadn't already known that fact.

He'd been balls deep inside of her. He'd heard her moan. He'd felt her come. There were some things that could not be faked in this world. The way Melody acted and the way she looked when she broke apart for him?

I know her. Inside. Out. I know my Melody.

Even as he gripped the phone in his hand, it rang again. A soft peal followed by a quick vibration. He glanced down at the screen. Sure, why not take another late-night call? Victor put the phone to his ear.

"You were supposed to check back in with me," Hunter chided him. "This is my call to confirm that you are still in the land of the living. Doing my due diligence and whatnot."

Victor had to unclench his jaw. "Sorry." Clipped. "Had a situation to handle."

"What kind of situation?" Then, harder, "Is Melody all right?"

He looked upward. Was she crawling into bed? Already sleeping? Or wide-awake as she replayed the events of the day and night? "We were ambushed."

"*What?*"

"When we left the police station, the bastard was

waiting. My tires were slashed. This kid, Benny Turner, was waiting with his knife. He swung at Melody."

"You stopped him?" A pause. Then, with certainty, "*You stopped him.*"

"He's dead."

Hunter cleared his throat. "Yeah, you stopped him."

"He was running away. He ran straight into the path of a van. Died before he could tell me anything."

"And Melody?"

"She's upstairs."

"Damn." Softer, "Damn." He cleared his throat. "Tell me about the attacker. Every detail you've got."

"Benny was a former foster kid who was in and out of trouble for years." Like that could not be a description of himself. Hadn't Victor bounced around? Only to wind up taking care of himself? And, yeah, he'd crossed the line and broken the law a few times.

But that sonofabitch Colton Crane, he'd truly deserved what he got. *Don't think about him. Not right now.* Victor forced his grip to ease on the phone. "Benny was a repeat offender. One who was apparently good at boosting cars."

"This a random attack?" Doubt filled Hunter's voice.

"He went for her, not for me. There was nothing random about it."

A low whistle. "Someone definitely wants Melody Mage to stay gone."

Too fucking bad. "I need you to dig into Benny's life. See who his contacts were."

"I'll do more than dig. I'll rip his life apart." A pause. "Next time, remember to *call* when there's an ambush. Think you can handle that? You're not flying solo on this one."

Yeah, he got it. "I wanted to kill him." There. Done.

said. "As soon as he swung at her with the knife, he was a dead man."

"*You* didn't kill him." Maybe a faint question underscored those words. Or maybe not.

"I was chasing him. Me and the detective—Angus Clinton. The perp had on a ski mask. He didn't stop when he burst out of the alley we were in. He just ran right into the road."

"Hell."

"I've never seen a hit like that. You could hear the bones crunching. His scream kept echoing. And there was so much blood." And all Victor had thought was...

It was like this for Melody? This is what she went through? Hunter had already gotten her medical records emailed to Victor. A bit of not-necessarily-legal probing without a medical release. But he'd scanned those reports while they'd been at the station.

Medically induced coma. She'd been in a medically induced coma because there had been so much swelling in her brain.

Was it any wonder she didn't have a memory?

Brutal truth, he didn't care if her memory ever came back fully. He would take her any way he could get her. Fuck the past. They'd build a better future together. Maybe he wouldn't screw up and make all of the same mistakes that he'd made with her before. Maybe this time, he could do things better.

"I know what it's like when the screams won't stop." Hard words from Hunter. "Be prepared for that shit to chase you into your dreams."

Victor knew Hunter's past was twisted. He'd glimpsed the scars the other man carried but had never asked specifically about them because Victor hadn't wanted to cross lines. A person's pain was private. You didn't dig it up and show it to the world.

"Your lady okay?" Hunter wanted to know. "Seeing that accident had to be like getting an up-close view of her own hell."

His exact worry. "She's resting."

"Is she?"

Fuck. He feared she wasn't. He feared she was replaying the scene in her head over and over again. Wasn't he doing that?

"I'll check in tomorrow," Hunter promised. "Until then, try not to get hauled to the station or attacked, okay? Sure would appreciate that."

Victor hung up the phone. Shoved it in his pocket. He whirled and rushed toward the stairs, but...

Stopped.

His backpack had been tossed near the entranceway table. He remembered dropping it there earlier. His gaze lingered on the backpack before he looked up, following those winding stairs to the next level of the house. *Maybe Hunter is wrong. Maybe Melody is asleep. Or maybe...maybe she just doesn't want me around her right now.*

Again, a person's pain was private. You didn't dig that shit up, not without an invitation. And yet...

Unease slithered through him. His stare shifted to the backpack once more. Things weren't adding up for him. One of the things bugging him? *Why the hell had Sebastian held onto the old sheriff's file for so long?* And was a teenage joy ride really worth blackmail money?

He opened the backpack. Took out the manila file. Began to thumb through it and read it in more depth and—*sonofabitch.* His breath left him in a whoosh.

Sebastian had been sitting on *this*? He'd kept this news

secret for years? Victor yanked out his phone once more. He had Hunter back on the line in about three seconds.

"Missing me already?" Hunter wanted to know by way of a greeting. "I get it. I'm cool. But, still—"

"Brant McKee," he gritted out the name.

"Brant McKee," Hunter repeated. "Brant McKee...why in the hell is that name familiar to me? Wait, wait, he's the guy running for attorney general in Maryland, isn't he? Gonna be the next big gun there."

"I need you to look into him. *Hard.*"

"Uh, dude, I think you misunderstand my role with the Ice Breakers. I was supposed to help you find your lady. She strolled back herself, so I didn't exactly hold up my end of the deal there, but as far as helping you with any weird vendettas that you might have against politicians, you're gonna need to count me out."

"When he was seventeen, Brant beat up Melody so badly that she had three broken ribs." Rage nearly blinded him.

"*What?*"

"She broke up with him after she found out that he stole a ride. The prick attacked her in response." He wanted to find the bastard and rip him apart. He *would* be destroying Brant McKee. Only a matter of time. "Hatterson found them." That had been in the file.

"Wait, her dad's guard? Or butler? Or whatever the hell the dude is?"

Hatterson was all of the above. "He pulled Brant off her. Called the sheriff." A man who'd died...last Thanksgiving. In a hunting accident.

They always called the sheriff's office for estate business because it was outside of the city's jurisdiction. The local sheriff—the previous guy, Sheriff Tom Jenkins—had been running the county for years. After his death, fresh blood had finally come in the form of Jamal Wroth. Victor liked Jamal. Respected him. A former Green Beret, Jamal didn't stand for BS. Unlike the previous holder of his position... "The old sheriff took down a report." There had even been references to pictures in the report. *Where in the hell are the pictures?* They weren't in the file Victor had. "But from what I can tell, no charges were filed. Sheriff Jenkins kept the details private." *If Tom Jenkins blackmailed Sebastian, he probably blackmailed Brant's family, too.*

"Her ex beat Melody when she was a teen? She never told you about this?"

*A person's pain was private. You don't...*Her smile flashed in his mind. That wide smile. The dimple in her cheek. "She never said a word." But she'd opened two shelters for abused women and children. He'd hadn't asked Melody why she'd done that. He'd just thought, hell, he'd thought that she had a big heart. That she liked to help people.

Now he realized that she'd probably opened those shelters because she knew what it was like to be a victim.

"Tell me what you're thinking," Hunter ordered him.

Oh, that was easy. "I'm thinking Brant McKee is a dead man." The prick just didn't know it yet.

"*Victor.* Dammit, I was afraid of that. You can't just go after and *kill* the lead candidate for attorney general in Maryland! We can leak the file you have, all right? We can wreck his life. Working with Declan Flynn, I've learned that there are a thousand ways to destroy a person. But you don't get to murder someone. Repeat after me, 'We do not murder—'"

"The sheriff who originally investigated is dead," Victor snapped. The piece of shit who should have locked Brant away. Who should have protected Melody. *And what about her father? Why the hell didn't Sebastian help her? Why didn't he punish Brant? Destroy him?* "The photos showing what happened aren't here. The vic who could tell the world what Brant did..." *My Melody.* "She was taken a year ago. Nearly killed. Call me crazy, but I'm seeing a fucking pattern here. All of this is happening as the SOB is revving up interest in his run for attorney general." The election would be held the upcoming November.

"You think Brant is making his past disappear."

His gaze lifted to the ceiling once more. There had been no sound from upstairs. "It's a possibility." A pause. "She won't disappear again."

"I know."

"Even if Brant is not involved in her disappearance, that sonofabitch will pay." *Three broken ribs?* What. The. Fuck? Three? And where was the medical report? There had been a notation of three broken ribs, but to know that information, then Melody must have seen a doctor.

There were no medical records in the file.

"You don't just stop," Hunter muttered. "Perps never do. You don't abuse one girl, then treat the rest you meet with the utmost care for the rest of your life. That's not the way those pieces of shit operate. You hurt someone once, you hurt other victims over and over again."

Victor agreed. "There will be other victims." Victims who had stayed silent. Probably because they were fucking terrified. Or maybe Brant had done something to *ensure* their silence. "Fuck," he breathed. "Do you think anyone else close to the would-be attorney general has gone missing?" Because that would be one sick pattern.

"If so, we'll find them." Hunter seemed certain. "After all, that's what the Ice Breakers do."

Yeah, it was. It—

"Victor!" Melody's scream echoed through the house.

Chapter Twenty-One

SHE WAS COLD AND WET.

Something brushed against her cheek. So chilling. The icy touch of death.

I know this dream. No, I know this nightmare. It was all so familiar, because it just would not stop.

Her eyelashes fluttered. She stared straight up. Softness rained down on her. Softness. Cold. *Snow.*

Her breath shuddered out. A white cloud appeared before her mouth. And pain pierced through her body.

Her hands flew down, touching her stomach. It was wet. Not wet like snow, though, more...soaked. Her dress stuck to her skin and when she pulled at it, she felt the tear in the material. Her fingers lifted. She saw the red on her skin.

But...this time, she paused. Focused harder on the dress. A red dress. Like, a cocktail dress. Beautiful fabric. Soft. The dress was red in the white snow. And she was bleeding because something had sliced along her stomach.

He sliced me. He'd had a knife, and he'd been coming at

her. But she'd gotten out of the ropes, and she'd lunged up. She'd rushed past him.

But the blade had sliced across her stomach.

Her head pounded. Throbbed over and over, and her blood-covered fingers rose to touch the left side of her head. Her head hurt because—he'd tackled her. They'd fallen in the cabin. And he'd taken the side of her head, and he'd rammed it into the floor. Once. Twice. Three times? She'd screamed and begged.

He hadn't stopped.

But she'd...

Gotten away. Gotten the knife. She'd stabbed him. Aimed for his heart. Missed, but...

I got away.

This dream...it seemed different.

Surrounded by the snow, she turned. Her icy toes sank into the snow. Bare toes because she'd long since lost her high heels. "H-help..."

Her face hurt. Her cheekbone. *Because her cheekbone had been smashed into the floor.* Her lips were busted. Parched. "Help!" she cried again. She spun around, looking at the snow. No tracks to show where she'd been. Nothing around her but snow. So much snow in every direction. Trees heavy with the weight of the snow on their branches. Woods that waited in the distance. No person. No cars.

Fear settled deeper around her. One hand shoved against her bleeding stomach.

Run. Get away. Because if she didn't get away, he would kill her. That was what he wanted. To kill her. To enjoy her pain.

She slogged through the snow. She had to keep going because she had to get back home. Something—someone important waited at home.

She turned, spinning once more, and her blood spattered onto the snow. Where to go? Which direction? She had to escape.

She sank deeper into the snow. Stopped feeling her toes. Tremors shook her body. Her hand lifted to shove wet hair out of her face, but she paused, staring at her hand. Her left hand. *He took my ring. Ripped it off me. Said I'd never be a bride.*

"*Melody!*" A roar.

She whimpered.

He doesn't usually call my name in this nightmare. But she could hear his roars, and she knew he'd seen her.

Go, go, go. She *had* to keep going. Couldn't stop. If she stopped, she'd be dead.

She plowed forward. Straight ahead. No stopping. No hesitation.

Brakes screeched. Tires squealed. Her head whipped to the right. The darkness had grown. When had the night come? How long had she been walking? It had been lighter before, when she'd first woken. Light enough to see the blood.

But now darkness was everywhere. Darkness except...

Except for the two headlights that stared back at her. And there was no time to move. Only a split second to realize that she'd reached a road, that she'd stumbled right into the path of a vehicle.

Then it hit her, and she screamed—screamed desperately for, "*Victor!*"

He threw open the bedroom door. "Melody!" His hand

flew out and hit the light switch. Illumination immediately flooded into the bedroom.

She lunged up in bed, her breath heaving and one hand whipping up to cover her heart. Her head swung toward him. Terror covered her beautiful features as she gaped at him, and her lower lip began to tremble.

In a heartbeat's time, he was across the room. He shoved the tangled covers out of his way and pulled her into his arms. He held her tightly, needing to feel her against him. "You're safe," Victor told her. The words were an absolute promise. "I've got you." *I will not let go.* "You're safe. You're all right, baby. You. Are. Safe."

She shuddered against him. "I was back in the snow. Wearing my red dress. I didn't have my high heels."

He stiffened. Had she mentioned those details of her nightmare to him before? He didn't think she'd spoken of the dress or heels. He could remember both perfectly in his mind. She'd been absolutely gorgeous in the red dress that had clung to her curves. Her heels had been sexy as hell. Then again, he'd always found her to be sexy as hell. Always.

"I...I'd gotten out of the ropes."

His grip tightened even more. *She definitely did not mention the ropes to me before.*

"He had a knife. He wanted to kill me."

Sonofabitch. Sonofabitch.

"He slammed my face into the floor until I felt something break along my cheek. And, I...I think that's when I got my head injury? Because I was bleeding from my left temple. He slammed the side of my face and head into the floor. He was so strong."

Victor wanted to *kill*. For a moment, everything went dark around him as a killing fury consumed him. Rage nearly choked him. Some bastard had taken his Melody. Attacked her.

Abducted. Melody was abducted. He'd screamed those words at Detective Clinton so long ago. At the other cops. At anyone who would listen. But they'd refused to use the term "abducted" in their investigation. She'd "disappeared" —that was how they'd termed it. "Vanished" one night. They'd often said she'd "gone missing" when they described her.

Bullshit. She'd been abducted. He'd known it. Had known that she would not leave him and her father without glancing back.

Melody had loved him. She wouldn't disappear, vanish, or just fucking *go missing* for shits and giggles.

Abducted. Attacked. Nearly killed.

She'd been through hell, and he hadn't been able to help her.

Never again.

"I got away," she whispered as she shivered in his arms. "It was so cold in the snow."

Fuck that shiver. He rose, holding tightly to her, and when he sat down on the bed again, he'd repositioned their bodies. With one hand, he tugged the thick comforter up over her. He needed her to be warm.

"I walked and walked through the snow until I couldn't even feel my toes any longer." Her head tilted back. Her eyes had narrowed as she peered at him. "I had frostbite," she suddenly said. "In the hospital. I remember them telling me that. They said...said I was lucky I hadn't lost any toes but with everything else happening, I just..." A sigh. "Frostbite seemed like the least of my worries when they were telling me that I'd been in a coma. That they'd worried about permanent brain damage. Everything they discussed seemed to hit me in a haze. Then I was just staring at them and realizing I had no idea who the hell I was supposed to be."

Fuck. This. "You are Melody Mage," he told her. Was he aware that his voice was deep and harsh? Yes. Could he do anything about that? No. *"You are the woman I live and die for."*

Her lips parted. Her eyes searched his. "I screamed for you."

She had, and he'd come running.

A little furrow cut between her brows. "When the car was barreling toward me, when all I saw were headlights in the dark...even as it hit...I screamed." A pause. *"For you."*

Did she understand how those words utterly carved the heart from his chest? She'd screamed for him, and he hadn't been there to help her.

"You came running tonight..." That furrow scrunched a little deeper. "Because I screamed your name, didn't you?"

He nodded.

"I..." A blink of her incredible eyes. "I screamed for you when we were at the Mage Mansion, didn't I?"

"Yes."

"I didn't realize—" Melody stopped, shaking her head. "How long have I been waking up, screaming for you, and I didn't even realize it?"

Yes, his heart had just been completely carved out. Going forward, Melody would have an army of guards around her. She would have every bit of protection he could give to her. She would have his entire fortune at her beck and call. "Marry me."

Her lips parted. "What?"

Okay, dammit, he hadn't meant to spit out the proposal. Or maybe he had. Not like he was in full control at the moment. "Marry me. As my wife, you will have full access to everything I own. Every resource I have. You can stay protected, always. I can have so many guards around you that you never have to be afraid again." And he'd have her tied to him. Melody would be linked to him. Forever. "We can leave," Victor told her because he wanted her *safe*. If safety meant getting the hell out of that city and never coming back, then *done*. He was ready to board the plane with her. "We can fly to Paris. To London. We can go to some tropical island where we will have complete privacy." Hell, he'd buy her an island, if she wanted. "I can make sure you're protected twenty-four, seven. You don't ever have to fear again. I can have you so surrounded—"

"I don't want to hide for the rest of my life." A slow, negative shake of her head that sent her soft hair brushing lightly over him. "And I don't want the monster who hurt me to get away. I can't let him hurt someone else. I can't let him do this again. I will not run from him. I will not let him destroy me. I *can't*."

He wanted to take her away. To force her into hiding. But...

That wasn't him. And he understood her desire for justice.

He wanted justice, too. Okay, fine, fuck it. What he wanted was vengeance. Good, old fashioned, *I-will-fucking-kill-you-for-what-you-did-to-her vengeance*. "I'll put him in the ground for you." A simple offer. A quiet promise.

She sucked in a breath. "Victor." But, rather than look horrified, she stared at him as if he'd just said the sweetest thing in the world to her. "You love me."

He could not speak. A lump had risen in his throat, choking him.

"You offer to kill for me in the same quiet tone that you

use when you offer to whisk me away to Paris." A faint smile curved her lips and lifted some of the terror from her eyes. "I actually think you would do both if I said yes."

He would. The truth was that he would do anything she asked. "All you have to do is say the word." But, frankly, she did not even have to do that. He fully intended to kill the prick who'd taken her, no matter what. That bastard didn't get to hurt her and then just keep living. A cage wasn't good enough for the bastard.

Hunter McQueen wasn't the only resource that Victor had. He still had his own PIs who were working for him. He'd sent them texts while at the Mage estate, and he'd keep giving out orders about her abductor. He had plenty of money and resources, and he would find the man who'd taken Melody.

When she talked about the attack, she'd said... "He slammed the side of my face and head into the floor. He was so strong."

Melody had remembered her attacker. He needed to question her more, carefully. Maybe she hadn't even been fully aware of her words.

She remained in his lap, her body pressed to his, with the comforter pulled over them both. Warm and soft.

"Melody." With an effort, Victor kept his voice quiet. Calmish. "The man who had you, the one who hurt you... you said you got away from him."

"I stabbed him." Her eyes were on Victor as she tilted back her head a bit more. "He had a knife, and he used it on me, but I got it and I stabbed him." She wet her lips. "I aimed for his heart, but I missed. The knife went into his chest, though. I know it did. Slashed down diagonally. He fell back. And I got away. That's when I ran. I ran and ran and...the car hit me."

"In Canada."

A nod.

"You were tied up," he said.

She twisted a bit in his lap. Her head dipped down as she stared at her wrists. "Yes."

"Where were you tied up?" Victor didn't want to scare her. Hell, not more than she already was scared. So he tried to keep his prompting very gentle. "Did you...see anything around you?"

"A cabin." Slow. Thoughtful. "I was in a cabin. It was dark. Lantern light. So cold in there. A...a hood had been over my head for the longest time. I just saw darkness for so long that I thought I was blind."

Tied up. Kept with a hood over her head. He had to unclench his teeth. "How did you get to the cabin?"

"I..." She bit her lower lip. "I don't remember. It was just so dark for so long. I...*tight*," Melody suddenly said. "It was tight, and there wasn't a lot of room, and we were moving and it felt like *forever*."

Victor didn't let his expression change, but it sure sounded to him like she might have been in the trunk of a car. He'd looked up Hamilton, Ontario, after she'd first mentioned the hospital in that city. Hamilton wasn't far from Toronto. From Richmond to Toronto, that was about an eleven-hour drive. She could have been in the trunk of a car that entire time. Her abductor would have needed to be careful when sneaking over the border, but, hell, yes, it could be managed.

Her abductor could have taken her from Mage Industries. Or right after she left Mage. He could have forced her into the trunk of a car. Then driven out of Richmond as fast as possible. So by the next day, the day after she'd vanished, when Victor had been ripping the town apart for her, she'd already been in Canada.

Already been stabbed? Been hurt?

In the days that followed, he'd followed BS leads and turned up nothing. *While Melody was in some damn coma.* Unable to reach out for help. After the Christmas party, Mage Industries had basically been shut down for the holidays. Only a skeleton staff had remained. Everyone had gone their own way.

He'd gotten stonewalled at every turn by the authorities. *It's the holidays. She wanted to get away. There is no crime in that.*

Fucking hell, yes, there had been a crime.

He eased out a slow breath. "You said a man hurt you. What did he look like?"

"I—" She stopped. Tilted her head back once more to gaze up at him. Her green eyes held confusion before she blinked. "I don't know."

"It's okay." *Don't push her. She's remembering. Be patient. Use care.*

"No, no, it's not okay!" Her voice sharpened. "I don't know. I don't know what he looked like. I-I can't see him. I *can* see the cabin, in my head. I can see the knife. *But I can't see him.*"

"It will come to you," he tried to soothe. She'd already remembered so much more than before. They were making real progress. "We'll give it time and—"

Melody jumped from his lap. The comforter fell to the floor. "I don't want to give it time. I gave it a whole year!" Her hand angrily sliced through the air. "I want to see him and be able to say more to you than just the fact that he was wearing a big, gray coat." Her eyes widened. "Gray coat," she repeated. "I..."

Victor rose. "What else, baby?"

"Gray coat. Black boots." Her hand didn't slice the air again. It rose, going over her head. Hovering near Victor's head. "That tall," she whispered. "He was bigger than me. Wide shoulders. *Strong.* H-he had to be strong...because when he was shoving my head against the wooden floor..." She swallowed. "Your height. Your build. Big and strong and..." Her head tilted. "Couldn't see his face. He had on a —" She broke off and gestured toward her features. "Covering. Over his head. Most of his face. It went all the way down his neck."

Even as more tension tightened his muscles, Victor maintained his position near the bed. "A balaclava? That kind of face mask?" They'd been out in the cold, so a balaclava made sense to him. He knew they were often used in cold weather. The material could cover a person's head, neck, and face. When she frowned, he pulled out his phone and did a quick search. Victor turned the phone toward her. "Did the thing over his face look anything like this?"

Her finger curled over the phone. Over his. A soft, hesitant touch even as she nodded quickly, eagerly. "Yes. That's it. The black one."

Victor checked the screen. There was no eye covering with the balaclava mask. She would have seen the abductor's eyes. She'd said there was lantern light, so maybe she'd gotten a glimpse of their color and shape. "What did his eyes look like, sweetheart?"

She blinked. "Me."

A frown pulled at his lips. "I'm not sure I'm following."

"I just see me reflected." She let go of the phone and backed up. "Not goggles but not sunglasses, either. Sort of both. He shoved open the door to the cabin. He rushed inside, and he came at me with the knife." Fast words. "He

232

said he was going to kill me. There would be no going home. Then—then he attacked. But I'd worked the ropes loose. I jumped out of the chair. The knife sliced me, and I fought and I fought and..." A ragged exhale.

"You got away." He tossed the phone onto the nightstand. "You got away, and you found your way back to me."

She pulled in deep breaths. She'd changed into a black nightgown, a soft, silky one with spaghetti straps and a lacy hem that skimmed her thighs. He'd seen her wear that nightgown dozens of times. He'd removed it from her body, dozens of times. Carefully tugging the delicate straps from her shoulders, letting the silk slide over her and fall into a puddle at her feet.

"I came back to you," she whispered.

He nodded. Victor closed the distance between them. His hand lifted and curled under her chin. "He spoke to you."

"S-said he was going to kill me."

"Not gonna happen." *He'll be the one who dies.* "What did his voice sound like?"

"Hard. Grating."

"Did you..." *Ask.* "Did you recognize his voice?"

Her smile was sad. "I have no idea."

"It's okay. You are remembering more. The memories are returning. Tomorrow, we'll go back to Mage Industries." Tomorrow—hell, had they already passed midnight? He didn't even know. It was late. That was all he understood. "The office is closed for the holidays. Only security is there now." And it was a Sunday. Wasn't it? Fuck, he was confused on his days. "I'll make sure the security guards know we are coming. We'll search, and maybe something else will come to you. Another piece of the puzzle." She appeared so uncertain. He hated that. "We will figure this out. We will find the bastard who took you." He searched her eyes. "Do you remember anything else about your life? Other than the attack? Have more memories come back to you?"

A sad shake of her head.

"It's okay." He edged ever closer and pressed a kiss to her forehead. His mouth lingered against her skin. *She is back. She is safe.* "You've had one hell of a day, baby," he murmured against her skin. "You want to try and get more sleep?" He forced himself to step back.

But she shook her head. "I don't know if I can sleep. Too —too scared. Too hyped up."

Okay. He nodded. "How about we go down to the kitchen? You used to love hot chocolate." It had always been her go-to favorite. "I've still got the machine I bought for you last year. It froths for you." The frothing had delighted her. A necessary requirement, she'd called it. "I even have the hot chocolate mix ready to go."

"Do...do you drink hot chocolate?"

"Nah. Can't stand the stuff."

"But...you have the mix ready to go?"

Yes. "I bought some fresh supplies a few weeks ago."

Her lower lip trembled. "For me."

"For you." He swallowed the lump in his throat and caught her hand. His fingers twined with hers. "Come on, sweetheart. Hot chocolate and some Christmas music always perk you up."

But when he tugged her hand, she didn't move. "You know me better than I know myself, don't you?"

No, he didn't. Because he hadn't known that Brant McKee had hurt her. He hadn't known that she'd started the shelters for abused women and children because of her own past. And he couldn't help but wonder, what other secrets had she kept from him?

A year ago, Melody hadn't told him that the detective had come to her and spouted off about Colton Crane. But, apparently, she'd just defended Victor to the cop. Told the detective that she trusted him.

I kept secrets, Melody. Dark truths that I never want you to discover. Because he was afraid that if she discovered the truth that he'd concealed for so long, he would lose her again. Victor wasn't sure he could survive her loss, not for a second time.

"Did I know you just as well?" Melody asked him. "Before I lost my memories, did I know all of your secrets?"

He stared into her eyes, and he lied, "Yes." He choked down the lump in his throat. "I swear, you knew everything that mattered."

Because the dark parts...they didn't matter. Not any longer. His plans had changed. His life had changed. And maybe, just maybe, she would never, ever need to know the truth about him.

Chapter Twenty-Two

"YOU ASKED ME TO MARRY YOU."

Victor's broad back was to her as he poured the hot chocolate into a mug. A smiling Santa mug. Melody bet the mug didn't belong to him. No way. The winking, smiling Santa was probably something else she'd brought to the house. Something he'd kept.

His broad back stiffened. "You were my fiancée."

"I'm not talking about last year." She stood in front of the large, marble island in the middle of the kitchen. "I'm talking about five minutes ago. Upstairs. In the bedroom."

The hot chocolate had frothed, but he moved toward the refrigerator. Opened the door. Pulled out a can of whipped cream. "You always liked a little on top," he said. "Told me it made the hot chocolate even better." With a few twists of his hand, he sprayed the cream onto the hot chocolate. "There." He even reached out and drizzled a few chocolate chips onto the top. "All done." He brought the mug toward her.

She stared at it, and she wanted to cry. "Yes."

"Uh, yes?"

Her gaze lifted to collide with his. "Yes, I will marry you. You asked me five minutes ago. Or maybe you told me. Hard to say for sure because the words didn't really sound like a question." They had not. And, now, he was just staring at her, with those sexy lips of his slightly parted as stubble covered his hard jaw. "Um, you know," Melody prompted, "when you were offering to fly me to Paris or jet me off to some private island." She reached for the mug. Her fingers slid over his. She could feel the heat of the hot chocolate, but, more, she could feel the warmth of his touch.

"Melody..." If possible, his jaw hardened even more. "Baby, you don't remember—"

"I scream for you when I have nightmares." Not just nightmares. When she'd been terrified—both in that cold, snowy hell from her past and earlier, when they'd been near the police station and the attacker had come at her, she'd screamed for Victor. "I scream for you because I know you'll help me. I may not remember our time together, but the more I am around you, the more I know how I *feel*."

He backed away.

Slowly, deliberately, she raised the hot chocolate as she kept her gaze on him.

"Be careful," he rasped. "You don't want to get burned."

She brought the hot chocolate to her lips. And, being careful, she just lightly licked the whipped cream. Then she blew down, cooling the hot chocolate before she took a sip.

Utter perfection. "You know what I like."

"Melody."

"*I* like the way you say my name. *I* like the way you look at me."

"You told me that when you saw me at the estate, you were afraid."

Another careful sip. Another lick of the whipped cream. *Delicious.* "I'm still afraid."

"And yet, you say you're going to marry me?"

Yes. "For a year, I felt like I was frozen on the inside. And with you, in such a short time, I'm coming alive again." It was like waking up. Did that even make sense? "I'm afraid that I will lose you, I will lose the me that I'm finding, and I'll go back to the ice." Another sip. Then deliberately, she put down the mug of hot chocolate. "I don't want to lose you. Not ever again. So, yes, I'll marry you. As soon as possible. Because I may not know everything about my life before that snowy hell." A mocking laugh escaped her. "*Everything* is certainly a stretch, huh?" Because she barely knew *anything*. The smile left her. "But I know I was desperate to get back home, and I think it was because I was desperate to get back to you." She squared her shoulders. "I love you, Victor Alexander."

His dark eyes burned with intensity, but his hands clenched. His body tensed.

"Um, I kind of thought you'd have more of a reaction." Her own hands twisted in front of her. She'd hoped for the kind of reaction where he rushed to her, swept her into his arms, and kissed her as if his very life depended on the task.

"I'm *trying* not to jump you."

Relief swept through her. Now, that was better. But... "Why are you doing that? I want you to jump me."

He lunged forward. His mouth took hers. Warm. Hard. Possessive and strong. Devouring and delighting, and joy filled her. Real joy. The kind that she hadn't felt since— well, she had no clue. But joy pumped in her blood as she wrapped her arms around him, and he pulled her tightly against him. Then he lifted her up with that sexy strength of his that seemed so effortless, and Victor carried her. Not too far, though. Only a few steps.

He put her down on the kitchen table. A big, sturdy, white, farmhouse table. The bottom of her nightgown hiked up, barely skimming the tops of her thighs, and his finger slid under the material, working up higher and higher until he touched her sex.

His mouth pulled from hers. "You taste delicious."

Probably the whipped cream.

"Sweetheart, you aren't wearing panties."

Good of him to, ah, notice. His fingers slid over her clit, and she choked out a moan.

"Baby, baby, baby..." A sigh. "I am not going to be able to hold on long."

He had on too many clothes. "I don't want you to hold on at all. I want you to go wild for me."

He stared down at her with glittering eyes. "Only if you go wild first."

Pretty sure she could guarantee that.

He kissed her again, dipping his tongue into her mouth. Stealing her breath and feeding her lust and making her arch against his hand because she wanted those fingers *in* her. She wanted his dick in her. She wanted to forget pain and fear and just feel the wild pleasure that he gave her.

He'd been right.

Best lover ever.

"You taste so good." Deep. Low. Rough.

"That's the whipped cream," she whispered back.

He smiled at her. "Is it?" And he backed away.

Wait, why was he backing away? She needed him. "Victor!"

He grabbed the whipped cream. "Get comfortable. Spread out."

Wait. There? On the table? "Um, should we go upstairs?"

"No, we should stay right here. Ease back, love. Spread out for me."

On the kitchen table? Really? But, ah, okay. She eased back. Her shoulders pressed to the wood. Her legs hung off the side of the table. Her eyes locked on the small chandelier that hung over the farmhouse table. "What are you doing with the whipped—*Victor!*"

She'd just felt the cold spray between her legs. Her mouth opened wide, but she didn't get to call out again because in the next breath, he was between her legs. Licking away the whipped cream. Swiping his tongue over her. Into her. Driving her to the edge and beyond, and there was no slow build up. There was just a quick, frantic frenzy as her hips slammed against his greedy mouth because he was feasting on her like he was starved. A hot, wild sexual frenzy, and she came right there, right then, rocking against him as he tasted and took and possessed her with his wicked, wicked tongue.

Her breath heaved in and out. In and out. She blinked, dazed, and tore her gaze from the chandelier. She stared down at him. His hands had slapped onto the table on either side of her. Slowly, his head rose. He licked his lips once more. "The whipped cream is good," he said, voice thick and deep. "But you're better." He pulled back so that he could toss away his shirt. Victor shoved the pants and his underwear out of the way. The broad head of his dick lodged at the entrance to her body as he positioned himself against her. "Gonna come for me again?"

She had no idea. Her body was still vibrating with aftershocks of pleasure. When his dick began to push into her, she gasped because those aftershocks just hit *harder*.

"So tight," he growled. "Fucking...*missed you.*"

"I missed you." Maybe it seemed crazy to say she'd missed a man that she didn't fully remember, but she had. A hole had been in her life, and that emptiness hadn't been filled until she'd worked her way back home. She'd felt like someone was missing.

Victor.

He drove deep into her, and she had no more words. She was too lost to feeling and need and a lust that grew stronger with every deep drive of his cock into her. Her sex clamped fiercely around him. Her hands grabbed for his shoulders as she held on tight.

As tight as possible.

His hands curled around her hips. He urged her up against him, pulling her until they were sealed tightly together and for a moment, he stilled.

Her breath shuddered out. She yearned. She needed. She was caught on the edge and so ready to go over.

"Promise that you'll never leave me again."

She gazed into his intense eyes. So much darkness. "I promise."

He let go. Pistoning, thrusting frantically. One of his hands slid between their bodies. Caught her clit between his fingers. Stroked. Squeezed. Sent her careening into a release as she shouted out his name.

He lifted her off the table. Her legs wrapped around him. Her arms twined around his neck. His hips pounded and pounded, and he came inside of her. She tightened around him because she loved the way he felt within her. She loved being connected to him. Held so close to him. Loved everything— "I love you," she whispered. And it was true. She *felt* it in her heart. Some things, you did not have to remember. You could *feel* the truth. She loved this man. He was hers.

HE DIDN'T TAKE her back upstairs. Instead, Victor carried Melody to his room. He wanted her in his bed. Needed her close.

Tenderly, carefully, he cleaned between her legs, using a warm cloth on her delicate core. Then he ditched the cloth, turned off the lights, and climbed into the bed beside her. Automatically, his arm reached out and curled around her stomach as he pulled her against him.

She was warm. Soft. Safe.

His.

I love you.

The three most precious words in the world. Had he even understood how precious until he lost her?

"Did we do this a lot?" Sleep teased at her words.

He smiled at the faint slurring. "Have sex on the kitchen table?"

"No." Husky laughter. "Though I may not ever eat on that table again, just so you know."

His smile stretched. He'd rather enjoyed *eating* at that table.

"I mean..." Her hand curled over his. "Sleep together. In here. Just curl up and drift away."

"Sometimes." She was the first woman who'd ever spent the night in his home. He'd never been the long-term type, until her.

Actually, in the beginning, his plans for Melody had been quite different. Guilt stirred and tried to steal some of the happiness he'd been feeling. "I'm sorry," he whispered.

He didn't think she'd even heard those words. He knew sleep had pulled at her but...

Melody turned in his arms. She faced him, their heads close on pillows that were separated by inches. "For what?"

For too many things. "I wasn't always...good enough for you." Who the hell was he kidding? He still wasn't good enough.

Her hand rose and pressed to his cheek. His stubble had to scrape her skin.

Did I scrape her thighs?

"I think you're plenty good enough," Melody assured him. "Actually, I think you're pretty incredible."

I think you are the most important person in my world. Victor sucked in a breath. "I love you."

Again, soft laughter. Her hand lingered against his cheek. "I know. You don't keep hot chocolate ingredients for people you don't love." She snuggled closer. Yawned. Then she stiffened. "Oh, no! Victor!"

"What is it?" Had she remembered something else?

"Your arm! The graze!" Her fingers fluttered over the bandage he wore. A damn unnecessary one, in his opinion. "Did I hurt you?"

Yes. When you left, you destroyed me. "No. Not at all." He exhaled slowly. The darkness surrounded them. The quiet. The bed had felt so empty without her. He'd missed her more than she would ever realize.

She hadn't known about him for the last year.

He'd thought about her every single day. And night. The nights had been the hardest.

He'd lived with grief. He'd lived with rage. And he'd lived with guilt. Because there were words he hadn't said to her before, words that he damn well should have said. He would never hesitate with her again. "I should have told you a thousand times that I loved you."

"V-Victor?" Soft. Again, sleepy. She'd probably been about to drift off when he spoke.

"Sometimes, I think I should have told you the first day that I met you. But I didn't." Instead, he'd schemed and planned and tried so hard to get her to belong to him. "I even proposed, and *you* said that you loved me." Just saying the words left an ache in his heart. "Baby, when you said you loved me, those were the best words in the whole world. *You loved me.* I was stunned. Over the moon. You took the ring I had for you." Three diamonds. The biggest one had rested in the middle, framed by two matching diamonds on the side. "You said for me to meet you at your house." The words wouldn't stop. "I was going to tell you that I loved you as soon as we got to your place. Only you weren't there. *I never got to say the words to you.*" Victor stopped.

Silence.

Hell. Had she fallen asleep? Missed his big confession? There was no light to see her face. "I love you," he said again. He wouldn't hold back this time. Everything would be different. "I've always loved you. Since the first moment." There. Done. "And I always will."

The silence stretched.

Yes, she was asleep. He should close his eyes, too. They had a long day ahead of them.

"I love you, too, Victor."

His heart stopped. She was awake. She'd heard everything.

"And I think I always will," she said.

"THERE's something you need to know." Victor reached into the briefcase that he'd carried into the back of the limo.

Jenner drove the limo. Melody sat near Victor. She'd changed into gray dress pants. Boots. A warm, green sweater.

Victor wore all back. Pants. Sweater. Gleaming dress shoes.

He handed her a manila file. "That came from your father's estate."

Frowning, she reached for the file. She could see the CONFIDENTIAL stamp on the side.

"Your fingerprints were inside the file. That's what Hunter used for a point of comparison with you, but, fingerprints or not, I know who you are."

The limo slowed for a traffic light. It was early, and no other cars were on the slick road. They were bound for Mage Industries. Would more memories come to her once they got to the building? Melody wasn't sure. But going there was certainly worth a shot.

They were being tailed by a black SUV. Two guards were inside. Those guards had been waiting outside of Victor's house that morning. Calista Connors and Luis Ortega. Victor had explained that Luis was former FBI while Calista had worked as an agent with Wilde Security for years before branching out on her own.

Did Melody think it was overkill to have the guards trailing them? Um, no, she thought it was awesome. But her fingers fluttered through the papers. A frown tugged at her lips as she realized that she was reading an arrest report. "I stole a car?" She hunched over the records. "Brant McKee..." Her stomach seemed to do a little dip as she read the name. "I..." Melody glanced up. "This was a long time ago."

Victor nodded. "Keep reading."

She shuffled through the papers. "I can't believe I stole a car."

"You didn't, sweetheart. Brant did. The asshole didn't tell you that he'd taken a stolen ride until after the sheriff pulled you both over. No charges were filed against you, but the sheriff kept those details that you see, and I think he used them to blackmail your father."

She scanned through the report and...wait. *A second incident assessment.* She read the details. Twice. "I had broken ribs?" That dip in her stomach turned into a twist. "How did my ribs get broken?" She kept reading, faster.

"You broke up with Brant," Victor told her. "Guess you didn't like hanging out with a thief."

"He hit me." Her grip tightened on the file. "Hatterson was there. Hatterson stopped him. Called the sheriff and— *what?*" There. The incident report ended. Just ended. There were no notes. No pictures. Nothing. She thumbed through the file, searching desperately for info that wasn't there. "What happened after that? Did the guy go to jail?"

"No, he went to military school."

The limo turned to the left.

"Military school?"

"And he's currently running for attorney general in Maryland."

"Bastard," she breathed.

"Yeah, I think he is."

She stared down at the notes in the file. "I don't remember any of this."

"You never mentioned it to me."

Her head snapped up.

"I found out about it when I got the report and the fingerprints from your father's safe. You never told me that you'd been hurt." A pause. "If you had told me, I would have wrecked him. Now that I *do* know, I've already taken steps to make sure that he will not be the next attorney general in Maryland."

"Taken steps? How?"

"While you were sleeping last night, I made a few phone calls. His big donors will no longer be interested in him. Hunter and some private investigators I know are digging hard into Brant's recent relationships. I want to know who else he hurt. I want to know if—"

"If he had anything to do with my disappearance?" Her temples throbbed.

"Yes."

"Had I—had I talked to him, I mean, before my disappearance?"

"No clue, baby. I didn't even know that you'd talked to Detective Clinton before your appearance." He scraped a hand over his jaw. "Speaking of the detective, aren't you going to ask me about Colton Crane?"

Her lashes fluttered. "Am I supposed to ask about him?" She was rather busy dealing with one bombshell at a time. *This Brant McKee jackass hurt me? And now he's going to be some attorney general?* Except, Victor was saying that wouldn't happen. He was saying he'd stopped the man's whole political future with just a snap of his fingers.

She tried to process everything. Consider possibilities. Had Brant been involved in her disappearance? Just the thought of the guy had unease pricking at the nape of her neck.

"You are supposed to ask about Crane. Seeing as how a detective told you I nearly beat the man to death, I thought you might be somewhat curious."

She held the file tighter. "Okay. I'll ask." Her gaze

drifted over his hard features. Lingered. "Did you attack this Colton Crane individual?" Melody fully expected him to say no—

"Yes."

"Pardon?" She must have misheard.

"Yes, I beat the hell out of him. Left him in a crying, bleeding heap on the floor. If others hadn't pulled me off the SOB, I might have killed him." One eyebrow quirked. "Got any other questions for me?"

Chapter Twenty-Three

He should have been more tactful. One hundred percent. The shock and horror on Melody's beautiful features showed him that truth. She'd just been dealing with the bombshell about Brant McKee. He should have been way more careful as he told her about his own past. It was just...

Victor had woken up, feeling as if he was running out of time. He'd kept secrets from her before, and he'd hated doing that. As much as he could, he wanted to tell her the truth.

As long as I don't lose her.

But the way she was staring at him right then...

"Yes," she told him, voice firm, "I do have other questions. The main one would be *why*? You're not some vicious predator. You don't go around hurting people."

"I can be quite vicious." And he could not wait to hurt the bastard who'd abducted her. When he got his hands on that bastard, Victor would be incredibly vicious. *He will die.*

"Victor! Stop trying to scare me." She shook her head, as

if in confusion. "Why would you want to scare me? I told you, I love you. All of you."

He wasn't trying to scare her. Wait, was he? Was *he* afraid because she'd said she loved him and she— "You don't know all of me." Gruff.

"Yeah, shocker. *Amnesia.*" She rolled her eyes. "But I think I know that you're not some sadistic killer. I'm holding the file about an asshole who broke my ribs. Pretty sure you'd cut off your own arm before you'd hurt me."

Hell, yes, he would. And wasn't that why he was clinging so tightly to one particular secret? A secret he feared might shatter her? Victor wanted to tell Melody as much as he could about himself, but he did not want to hurt her. Ever.

"So, who were you protecting?" Melody waved toward him with her left hand. "Come on. Just spill it. You're not a monster. But I have noticed you tend to have some big, hyper protective tendencies." She bit her lower lip. "You know what? I think those tendencies might be what drew me to you in the first place."

Now she'd surprised him. His eyebrows climbed.

She leaned toward him. "What happened with Colton Crane? I refuse to believe that you're some horrible villain."

"Not to you," he rasped. "Never to you."

She smiled back at him. Her dimple winked. "I know."

She did, he realized. She knew, because she trusted him. She'd trusted him a year ago when the detective had paid her that secretive visit. She trusted him now. So he'd dig up the ghost from his past for her. "Colton Crane was an asshole who got off on hurting people weaker than he was. We wound up in the same foster home. Baby..." An exhale. "I bounced around those homes so many times. I was labeled as having oppositional defiance. I was flat-out called a troublemaker. No one wanted me. There was no permanent place for me."

She put down the file on the seat next to her and reached for his hand. Her soft fingers curled over his. "I want you. Your place is with me."

He knew that was exactly where he belonged. With her. But he had to tell her the rest of the story. "That home... the foster parents had a biological daughter who lived with them. Shannon. A sweet kid. Always smiling. Always warm and welcoming. She was the first person who'd really welcomed me anywhere. And Colton..." Fuck, he didn't like going back to that dark time. But he would, for her. "Shannon was barely ten years old. The sonofabitch slipped into her room. I heard her crying, so I burst inside. He was—holding her down. Trying to hurt her. When I saw what he was attempting to do—" Victor stopped. "I beat the hell out of him."

She nodded.

He spoke slowly, clearly, as he said, "I ripped him off her. I drove my fist into him again and again. His face, his stomach. Torso. He fell, and I was still going to attack again because she was crying, and she was just a damn kid. A sweet as hell kid. The only innocent, sweet person I'd ever met, and he was trying to destroy that innocence. So I wanted to destroy *him*."

She stopped holding his hand. Instead, she threw her arms around him and wrapped him in a fierce hug. "*Victor*."

"My foster parents came in. They'd heard all the screams. *His* screams. They pulled me off Colton. Called the cops. The cops had already locked me up before Shannon managed to get everyone to listen to her. To tell them what had happened." He felt Melody's lips press to his neck in a soft kiss. He was telling her about one of his most violent times, and instead of being horrified, she held him.

His eyes squeezed shut. "I do not deserve you."

She just held him harder. "What happened to the little girl?"

He opened his eyes. "Shannon grew up to become a nurse. She works in the Neonatal Intensive Care Unit. She helps premature babies live. It's perfect for her. She was always so loving and just *good*."

"You kept track of her."

He'd done more than that. He'd paid for her college. "She saved me from going to jail. I felt it was only right to look after her."

She pulled back, and her solemn gaze studied him. "Define 'look after' for me, would you?"

Not like it was a big deal. "I set up a fund to pay for her college. I wanted to help sooner, but it took me a while to get established. For a long time there, I was dragging myself up. Fighting fucking hard for every crumb I got."

"And what happened to Colton Crane?"

"He's been in and out of jail most of his life. Currently, he's serving a ten-year term for a gas station robbery. Prick pulled a gun on the attendant over four dollars and fifty-seven cents."

The limo slowed once more. Victor glanced out of the window and saw that they were pulling into the parking garage. They'd made it to Mage Industries.

"How did you do it, Victor?" Melody asked him. "How did you go from the life you had then...to everything you have now?" She dipped her head to indicate the limo.

He'd fought. Every single day. "Shannon's dad was grateful when he realized what could have happened to his daughter." Victor hadn't wanted the man's gratitude. He'd just wanted Shannon safe. "I didn't go back to that house. Her parents didn't want either me or Colton around Shannon, and I don't blame them."

"But you didn't do anything wrong."

"I nearly beat a man to death right in front of her. Not sure that falls into the *right* category." An exhale. The limo had stopped. "Her dad got me enrolled in a pilot program in a school the next town over. It was an engineering and science focused high school, only it was also a *boarding* school. The kids accepted into the program lived on campus. That's where I wound up." Things had changed then. "A boarding school in Mobile, Alabama. I worked my ass off. I'd always been smart, when I fucking tried, anyway, and I was more motivated than I'd ever been in my life. I'd almost gotten locked away. Almost saw everything end in one night. I knew I had to change. And I did." Short version of the story.

The long version? It had taken hours, years of work. Sleepless nights. He'd gotten into college, but the scholarship he'd received hadn't covered everything, so he'd worked two jobs around his classes. He'd kept working his ass off, shifting his focus from engineering— which he'd always loved because once upon a time, he'd wanted to be an inventor—to business. He'd eventually gotten his MBA. His law degree. Practiced business law as he positioned himself in just the right way, at just the right time...

For Mage Industries. Because Mage had been the goal.

Until I met you, Melody.

"You've come a long way," she murmured.

A long way from that sad kid who'd been waiting in a trailer park for a father who never came home.

The limo stopped. He heard the engine die. Jenner

opened the driver's door, and Victor knew the guy would be coming toward the back.

"Any other run-ins with the law you think I need to know about?" Melody asked.

He swallowed. She wasn't fleeing from him. Wasn't staring at him as if he was, indeed, a monster. She sat beside him. She'd hugged him. She was right there for him. "No more run-ins with the law." His shoulders rolled back. The weight felt a bit lighter, but he still needed to tell her, "I swear, I will never hurt you." Never.

"I know."

Jenner opened the door.

MELODY CLIMBED FROM THE LIMO, and her gaze swept the cavernous parking garage. Only a handful of cars occupied the spaces. The place felt light, actually. Open. Plenty of illumination.

The SUV that had trailed them parked nearby. Calista turned off the vehicle and climbed out, with Luis exiting on the passenger side. Victor had introduced her to the guards right before they'd all left his place that morning. Melody knew she was safe, with Victor and Jenner and the two guards, but, standing in that parking garage, a shiver still skated down her spine.

She found herself looking toward the elevators. Two elevators were at the elevator bank. All the doors were shut. She had the random, sudden thought that they needed to open. *The doors should open. He had to hurry up and appear. He was coming and—*

"You always parked right over there." Victor pointed to a space near a large, white column. The black coat he wore stretched with his movements, sliding over his broad shoulders. "When I came out that night, you were already gone."

She walked toward the indicated spot. It was empty, so she stood in the middle of it. From that position, she had a perfect line of sight to the elevator. Her gaze kept wanting to go to the elevator doors.

Once more, she thought...*The elevator should open.* Fear pulsed. *The doors would open, and he would help—*

"I was supposed to follow right behind you." Grim words from Victor. "But Dario stepped into my path and wanted to talk about the company. Or, more specifically, my plans for the company and where the hell he'd fit into them."

So, Dario had been upstairs when she left. Victor had been upstairs. Her gaze shifted a bit to the left. "Were those security cameras always here?"

"Yes. The footage was reviewed after you vanished. You were seen entering your vehicle. Just you. You cranked it up, and you drove away."

A shiver slid over her. "And my car was never found?"

"Never. I had an investigator tell me it was probably sold, chopped up, and sent out in pieces."

At least I wasn't chopped up in pieces. Except...her hand dropped to her stomach. Slid over the scar that rested beneath her sweater.

"The camera perched on the column gave us a clear view of your front seat," Victor added. "It was just you in the car."

"What about the backseat?" The question pulled from Melody as another shiver worked over her body. "Could you see that?" She forced her hand to drop back to her side.

Victor had followed her to the empty parking spot.

"No." His lips thinned. "And I wondered about that. Was some bastard in the back of the car? Had he snuck in the vehicle? Was he waiting for you? Because you didn't go home. You were supposed to go home, but you never made it there. This is the last place you were seen."

Calista advanced toward them. Her gaze was considering as she surveyed the scene. "Probably would have been easy enough to avoid the cameras and slip into the back of her car. Perp would have just needed to stay low, beneath the line of sight." She pointed to the closest camera. "It wouldn't pick up a ground image from here."

Behind her, Luis nodded. "The trick would have been getting into her car without setting off the vehicle's alarm, but a good booster would know how to get inside, no problem."

Benny Turner had been good at boosting cars. Benny Turner had been waiting behind the police station. He'd had the knife, and he'd slashed at her with it.

Melody's scar seemed to burn on her stomach.

An elevator dinged. She jumped, and her gaze flew right back to the elevator bank. The doors of one elevator opened and—

Dario rushed out. Dario, followed by two uniformed security guards.

What in the world was Dario doing there?

Red mottled his face as he charged forward. "You sonofabitch!" he snarled at Victor. "I know what the hell you've done!"

The two uniformed security guards locked their hands on him and hauled Dario back before he could get within fifteen feet of Victor.

"You stole the company!" Dario yelled. Spittle flew from his mouth. "You took *everything!*"

"Sir?" One of the guards—his name tag ID'd him as Rodney West—fired a fast glance at Victor. "He has his security pass, so he got upstairs, but then he broke into your office. We were gonna escort him back to his vehicle. Didn't, ah, know if you wanted the police involved. We were gonna call you first, once we had him off the premises, since it was a family matter."

"He's not my family," Victor said flatly.

Dario fought the hold of the guards even as Calista and Luis took up protective positions near Melody. Jenner inched closer to Victor, and Melody noticed that Jenner's hand began to rise toward his waist.

Is Jenner carrying a weapon? She'd wager that he was.

"I talked to Amaya!" More spittle flew from Dario's mouth. His hair shoved out at odd angles, as if he'd run his fingers through it. Or as if he'd been yanking at his hair. "I talked to her right before I came here! Demanded to see the fucking will!"

Amaya had the will? Well, she was the chief counsel for Mage Industries so...

"I know what Sebastian did, hear me?" Dario raged. "I know the man is a freaking killer!"

What?

"I told Amaya that I was taking over. Had to, what with him confessing to killing! I had to take it all. The estate, the cars, the bonds, all the accounts—only there *is nothing*, is there? Because you have it! You control it *all!*"

"Take him back upstairs," Victor ordered, his voice as calm as you please. "Secure Dario in *his* office for now."

The guards began to haul Dario back toward the elevator.

"Fuck that!" Dario yelled as he struggled. The struggles didn't free him. "Fuck you!" Dario bellowed at Victor. Rage twisted his face. "You took it all, didn't you? Took every single fucking thing!"

The guards had gotten him back in the elevator.

"Don't trust him, Melody!" Dario shouted. "He conned every single one of us! He took what he wanted! And he's left us with nothing—"

The elevator doors closed on him, muffling his fury.

Chapter Twenty-Four

"Do we need to call the police?" Calista asked.

Why? Because Melody's stepbrother had looked as if he wanted to commit murder? "I want to talk to him first." Talk, not have the bastard scream at him. Victor needed to know what the hell new confession Dario thought that Sebastian had made.

Hell. The web just kept getting more and more twisted.

But, regardless of Sebastian's new confession...

He slanted a glance at Melody. *The truth has come out.* At least, part of it had, anyway.

His phone rang. Melody was still staring at the closed elevator doors. She seemed a bit dazed. Not that he could blame her. Dario had come charging out of that elevator like a maddened bull.

He checked his phone's screen, and sighing, he put the phone to his ear. "The tip-off call could have come earlier, Amaya."

"Did he come to you? I'm so sorry, Victor!" Her words rushed out. "The man was pounding on my door, waking up my kids. I wasn't even thinking clearly and when he

259

started demanding that we transfer property into his name, I just—I slipped up. Said there was nothing to transfer. That everything had been handled. I thought...Hell, I thought you were going to tell him this weekend. That was why you agreed to go out to the estate for the meeting, wasn't it?"

One of the reasons. But then Melody had come back.

Everything had changed.

Melody's gaze left the elevator. Came to him.

Don't hate me, baby. Please. "It's all right," he told Amaya. "I'll handle things."

"Where are you? Do I need to come and meet you?"

"I'm at Mage Industries. Dario is here, too."

"Dammit. Okay, okay, I can fix this. We can fix it. I'll be there as fast as possible."

There was nothing to fix. "I'll handle Dario."

"Victor..."

"Stay with your kids, Amaya." She had five-year-old twin boys who needed her. He could handle Dario. "I've got this."

"But—but what about what he was saying regarding Sebastian? He claimed Sebastian murdered Melody's mother. Dario swore he'd go to the cops. Victor, we can't cover up a murder."

No, they couldn't. "I'll handle everything." He ended the call. With a hard, jerking motion, Victor shoved the phone back into his pocket.

Melody edged closer to him. Her hand lifted and touched his arm. "What's happening?"

Just the past, trying to drag him under. "We'll go upstairs and talk about things." He looked over her shoulder. "Jenner, stay down here, would you?" He wanted eyes on the ground floor, just in case. Sure, there was a

Mage guard at the parking garage's gate, but he needed extra security.

Jenner had never let him down.

Jenner nodded. "Yes, sir,"

"Calista and Luis, come up with us." They could stay close by while Victor and Melody talked. Then when he had his face-off with Dario.

Dario. The guy had been a pain in his ass for years.

The group headed for the elevator bank. A press of the button had the elevator on the left opening. Victor and Melody went in first, followed by the two guards. Instrumental Christmas music played through the speaker as the elevator rose. Heading straight to the top floor. And damn if that Christmas music wasn't an instrumental version of "Last Christmas" playing.

Hell.

Last Christmas had been a fucking nightmare that he never intended to repeat.

He reached out, took Melody's hand, and curled his fingers around hers. He'd had plans for *this* Christmas. Presents, magic, new memories that he'd wanted to give her. He wanted to take away all of her pain and make every wish she had come true.

Instead...

His head turned toward her. "I'm sorry."

"For what?"

He could feel the guards watching them. "For being a bastard."

The elevator chimed. The doors opened.

Calista went out first, checking the scene. Victor followed, still keeping his hold on Melody. He was afraid to let go. Luis followed up as the caboose of their group. The top level—the executive level—of Mage Industries should have been dead silent. It wasn't. He could hear Dario's shouts coming from down the hallway.

But before he went to face-off with Dario, he needed to talk with Melody. Alone. He glanced over at Calista. "You'll stay out here in the lobby area?"

She nodded.

"Thanks. Luis, will you make sure the guards don't need help with Dario?" And by help, he meant *make sure those guys have him under control.*

"On it." Luis spun on his heel. The bulge of his weapon could barely be seen beneath his jacket. Victor had a gun tucked beneath his own coat, too.

Victor guided Melody to his office. He caught her glancing around, taking in all the decorations as they traveled down the thick carpet in the hallway. As always, Mage Industries was decorated to the hilt for the holiday season. Trees everywhere. Glowing lights. Wreaths. Red and gold banners. The company hadn't held the big annual Christmas party this year, though.

Without Melody, he just couldn't.

The door to his office hung open, and Victor frowned. With his left hand, he pushed the door all the way in, and... hell. Files were scattered. Paperwork littered the floor.

The guards downstairs had said that Dario broke in. They'd neglected to say that he'd trashed Victor's office.

"Sorry, sir." Another guard stood behind the big, mahogany desk, trying to pick up some of the chaos. "Dario got in here and wrecked the place. Tried to claim he was searching for some file, but he was just throwing paperwork everywhere."

"Leave everything as it is." That paperwork was confidential. "Get any and all access keys that Dario has to Mage Industries. After I talk with him, he will be escorted from the building." A pause. "He will not be coming back."

The guard—Hayward Young—straightened. "Yes, sir." He hurried from the room, but not before staring, wide-eyed, at Melody. "Good to see you, Ms. Mage," he murmured. He exited, leaving the door open.

Victor glared at the mess.

"Victor." Melody's hand turned in his grip. "I want to know what's happening, and I want to know right now."

He opened his mouth to tell her.

"*I couldn't stop him!*" A yell from the hallway. A woman's yell.

Victor turned, letting go of Melody's hand and automatically moving to stand in front of her. Olivia barreled down the hallway. Her intent was clearly to reach his open office. Where in the world had she been? None of the guards had mentioned her.

Tear tracks glistened on her cheeks. Hayward moved into her path, but Calista had already beat him to the interception. "You need to stop." Calista's hand shoved back her coat to reveal her holster. "Right the hell now."

Olivia screamed and scrambled back. "What in the hell? *No, no!* Don't shoot me!"

"I don't plan to do so," Calista informed her. "Unless you pose a serious threat."

"Victor!" Melody pushed at his back. "Why is Olivia here?"

"Dario must have brought her." Dario had keycards and access materials. Olivia didn't.

"I need to talk to Melody!" Olivia stretched around Calista. "Melody, I have to tell you about your mother. I have to tell you what is happening!" She pointed at Victor. "You're being lied to by him! He's manipulating you. Victor has just been using you all along! Victor knows what your father did, and I think he blackmailed Sebastian into giving him control of the company."

Melody stepped to Victor's side. She peered down the hallway.

Olivia's eyes locked on her. Desperation filled her expression. "Victor never came here to save Mage Industries. Never. He came to destroy it. He wants to destroy the whole family! That's why Dario and I are here now—we were looking for proof! We have to stop him!" More tears poured from Olivia's eyes. "I am your best friend. I have been friends with you since the sixth grade when Mary Hodgins called me fat and you told her to kiss both of our fat asses. You have always had my back, and I've got yours. I'm telling you—*Victor is lying!* He's trying to hurt you!"

"You're leaving," Calista said, voice sharp. "*Now.*"

Hayward took a cautious step forward.

"No!" A desperate screech from Olivia. "Melody, *listen to me!* Listen! When the guards were hauling Dario downstairs, I called Detective Clinton! Told him everything. He's coming here."

Great. Just what Victor didn't need. Another damn interrogation with the dick detective.

"I know you don't have your memory, Melody! I know! The detective told me—he called Dario after he met with you at the station. He told us that you didn't remember anything. Said he was worried about you. That he didn't trust Victor."

The detective had always suspected him. Angus had stonewalled the investigation and suspected Victor and done jack shit to truly find Melody.

Fresh tears trickled down Olivia's cheeks. "That's why

Dario and I had to act! Why we had to search Victor's office. To find evidence for the detective. Melody, please, believe me! Victor is using you. He's been using you all along. Playing some sick game to get revenge."

So they'd *both* searched his office? To find evidence for the damn detective? What. The. Hell?

"Victor?" Melody's hesitant voice. "What is she talking about? What revenge?" Her hands twisted in front of her. "Why would you want to get revenge *on* me? What did I do?"

Not a damn thing. "Hayward, escort Olivia from the building."

The guard snapped his gaping mouth closed. Nodded. "Yes, sir." He shuffled forward.

A door opened down the hallway. Luis poked his head out. "Everything all right?" he demanded.

No, things were pretty fucked sideways.

Calista and Hayward reached for Olivia.

"Do not put your hands on me!" she yelled. "Melody, *Victor is twisted!* Listen to me! You have got to *listen!* I first began to suspect the truth months ago. Sebastian was rambling about a fire. Saying it shouldn't have happened...I did some digging because I was all like...what the fuck is he talking about? What fire? And I found out that there was a horrible fire at a Mage factory in Alabama years ago. It was ruled an accident, but—God, corners were cut! Managers weren't following safety protocols. People died. *Victor's father was one of the people who died at the Mage factory!*"

A sharp inhale from Melody. "Victor?"

Fuck. *Change of plans. The fuck now.* Because his world had just exploded right in front of him. "In the boardroom," he snapped. Dario and Olivia had been far busier than he'd realized. "I want Olivia in the boardroom." Before she blurted out more secrets for even the freaking guards to hear. "Get Dario in there, too. Now." Because too many secrets were coming out, and if he wasn't careful...

"Victor?" Melody said his name again. Confusion. Pain. Fear. Sorrow.

If he wasn't careful, he'd be losing her.

THE DOOR to the boardroom closed quietly.

Melody rubbed her chilled arms. The big boardroom almost felt like—like a tomb to her. It shouldn't have. The place was gorgeous, with floor-to-ceiling windows that looked out over the city. The middle of the room was dominated by what appeared to be a fourteen-foot conference table. Leather chairs surrounded the oval table. A Christmas tree—tall, white lights, green ornaments— waited in the corner to the right.

A little crowd had assembled in the boardroom. A glaring Dario. A tearful Olivia. A silent Victor. Calista and Luis waited just beyond the closed boardroom doors. Melody figured there were some things Victor didn't want the guards to overhear.

She was almost afraid to hear the truth herself.

Victor loves me. He loved me a year ago. He loves me now. He wants to marry me.

"His only goal was to destroy Mage Industries." Dario swiveled in his chair as he jabbed a finger toward Victor.

Her temples began to ache. Her gaze darted around the boardroom. The colors on the tree were wrong. The ornaments shouldn't just be green. They should be a variety of colors. Red. Blue. And an angel should be at the top of the tree, not that red ribbon.

Her breath shuddered out. This place, this boardroom...

I'm done being your dirty little secret. She could almost hear those words. In her voice. Because they were—or had been—her words? From a different time?

"He holds Mage responsible for what happened to his father," Dario continued as rage vibrated in his voice. "His dad died, his family fell apart, and the guy wound up shuffled around in foster care."

Yes, Victor had been in foster care. He'd told her about that time. He'd told her about his father's death, but she hadn't realized his dad had been working for Mage. "Is it true?"

"My father worked for Mage." Victor sat at the head of the boardroom table. His hands gripped the armrests on either side of his body. "He died when I was six. My family did fall apart, yes, my mother turned to drugs and alcohol. I got passed around to distant relatives and eventually wound up in foster care. All completely accurate facts."

"See! *See!*" Dario crowed.

Olivia sniffled.

"He found out that Mage cut corners. Safety protocols weren't followed like they should have been." Dario slapped his hand down on the table.

Olivia jumped.

Melody didn't move. Unlike the others, she wasn't sitting. She stood near the tree, almost seeing two scenes in her head. This scene, with the angry group and another scene...another tree... another time...

Just her and Victor in that scene.

"You're breaking my heart." Again, her voice, whispering through her mind. A memory?

Olivia pushed back her chair. "Victor made it his mission to destroy Mage, by any means necessary. He got a job here. Worked his way up the corporate ladder. Manipulated your father. Manipulated you." Pity flashed on her face. "You asked me if you were engaged to him."

Had she asked? Melody thought she'd *told* the other woman they were engaged.

"I thought it was a joke, but the more I considered things, the more I realized—shit, it's true. Only you don't remember it, do you? The engagement, I mean?"

Melody felt rooted to the spot.

"If you *are* engaged, he tricked you," Olivia informed her flatly. "Part of his effort to really screw over the Mage family."

Her breath shuddered in and out. *"Didn't think you could break a heart that someone didn't have."* That voice running through her head—it wasn't hers this time. The voice—the words—had been Victor's. He'd said those words to her, right in this very room, even as he looked at her with ice cold, dark eyes.

Melody's hand rose and pressed to her chest.

"While you were gone, he took everything." Dario surged to his feet. Both of his hands shoved down against the top of the table. "He doesn't just have the business. He owns the estate. The freaking cars. Hell, I think he even owns *your* home, Melody. That's what I was looking for in his office. Proof. And I found it. Deeds, paperwork. He took everything."

The drumming of her heartbeat seemed to echo in her ears. "Do you own everything, Victor?"

A curt nod from him.

And she had a flash of them. In this room...

"You have everything you ever wanted." She'd worn a red dress, one that left her arms bare, one that fluttered near

her knees. High heel shoes. Her voice had trembled with pain.

"*The hell I do.*" Victor's voice. Hard and grim. As hard and grim as his expression. "*But I will.*" And he let go of her wrist.

He'd been holding her wrist as they faced off in this very room. Then he'd let her go.

Victor...he had everything now.

"Did you want to destroy Mage?" Melody asked through numb lips. All of her just felt numb.

"When I started, yes. All I wanted to do was rip the company to shreds."

She flinched.

"He's a bastard!" Dario declared. "But we'll fight him, Melody. Take his ass to court and take back what belongs to us!"

Her head turned toward him. "How?"

Dario blinked.

"If he has the legal paperwork...if Sebastian signed the company over to him...if—if I was gone the last year and couldn't stop anything..." *OhGodohGodohGod...no, please no.* She shook her head hard. No. Victor couldn't have been involved in her disappearance. He could not have—

The boardroom disappeared. Darkness swam before her eyes, and suddenly, she was inside a vehicle. Back down in the parking garage. Gripping a black steering wheel and staring at the closed elevator doors.

"*This is a gun, Melody. I can blow your brains out here and now, or you can start the damn car.*"

Her hand flew to her temple because, just for a moment, she was sure that she'd felt the muzzle of a gun pressing against her.

"Victor sends his regards." The man with the gun had said those words. Victor, who hadn't come out of the elevator. Victor, who should have been there, but wasn't. *"Drive the fucking car."* An order from the man with the gun.

And, she'd driven...

Melody doubled over as pain knifed through her, cutting as savagely as any knife.

"Melody!"

Pain and betrayal coiled within her. Footsteps rushed across the boardroom floor.

"I have to get out of here." Melody tossed back her hair and looked up just as both Dario and Victor closed in on her.

Both men looked worried. Victor, though...

Fury. It burned in his eyes.

"Dario, please," she heard herself beg, "get me out of here." Because she was going to be sick. Melody could feel the nausea and pain rolling within her.

Dario immediately nodded. "Yes, yes, come on. Let's go." He put his arm around her waist. "I've got you. It's okay."

"Get the fuck away from her," Victor snarled.

Olivia flew for the door. She yanked it open.

Dario curled his body protectively around Melody's. "My sister doesn't want you near her."

"She's not your sister."

"Fine, *stepsister*. Now back off. Melody wants out of here, and I'm getting her out. You know, I never trusted you. Never. Steamrolling into our lives. Always acting so perfect. Smug. Arrogant SOB. And I swear, if I find out that you had anything to do with Melody's disappearance—"

"I *didn't!*" Victor thundered.

Olivia jerked and gasped.

"I'm the one who has been fighting like hell to get Melody back while you just moved right on with your damn life!" Victor snarled. "You and Olivia. You never looked for her. You never did shit but spend Sebastian's money. *My* money." His words fired out with fury and—desperation? "Melody, *listen* to me. Please. I didn't tell you about my past because—"

"Because he wanted to fuck over our whole family," Dario fumed as he pushed her toward the open door.

"Because I didn't want to lose you!" Victor was right beside her.

She couldn't look at him, though. Right then, she just hurt too much.

"No, because he didn't want to lose his position," Dario corrected. "He didn't want to lose his wealth. His power. He didn't want you telling Sebastian to throw his ass out of the company. Sebastian would have done it. Of all the people in Sebastian's inner circle, you are the one he always listened to. You told him to go to the doctor—he refused when everyone else said he needed to be checked out. But one word from you? He went. Done. That's the way it always has been. Sebastian bends the world for you." His hold was tight on her. "My poor sister, with no memory? Why the hell didn't you just tell me? It's okay. I'm going to take care of you."

"*You're going to take your fucking hands off her.*" Lethal.

Melody felt Victor's stare on her. Melody focused on the open doorway. Olivia still held the door open. Through that open door, Calista and Luis peered back at her.

"Is everything all right?" Calista asked, a frown pulling at her pretty features.

"No, no, it's not all right," Olivia snapped at her. "My best friend just found out that your jerk of a boss has been lying to her and using her for ages. We're getting her out of here." A determined nod. "Come on, Melody. You'll be safe with us. Let's *go*."

She stumbled forward, with Dario's grip tight on her. She was almost at the threshold.

"I'm not letting you leave." Victor's voice. A harsh growl. He'd moved into her path.

Dario laughed. Bitter. Mocking. "See what I mean? He can't lose control. He's a possessive, predatory jackass." He let go of Melody and took an aggressive step toward Victor. "What are you gonna do? Have your goons attack us? You gonna *kidnap* Melody? Or, wait, have you already been there and done that shit?"

Melody forced herself to look at Victor. She expected absolute rage to be on his face. But instead...

Sorrow.

"I'm not letting you leave *alone*, baby," Victor gritted from between clenched teeth. His hands were clenched into powerful fists at his sides. "You don't want to be with me, fine, but I can't have you in danger, Melody. Calista and Luis are your guards. Where you go, they go, got it? You need protection. You have to stay safe."

"She is safe with me," Dario vowed. "As if we'd trust anyone you hired!"

"Well, that's just insulting," Calista muttered. "I am exceedingly trustworthy."

"I do feel insulted," Luis agreed.

Victor just stared at Melody. His dark eyes swirled with the thunderstorm of his emotions.

Footsteps thudded down the hallway. Not fast and storming. Hard and determined. Another guard, coming to join the mess in the boardroom? One of the uniformed security guards from Mage? Or maybe—maybe it was the detective. Detective Angus Clinton was supposed to be coming to the scene, wasn't he?

"What in the hell is going on here?" Hunter McQueen's fierce voice demanded.

Not the detective. The Ice Breaker that Victor had been using to find her.

Victor has guards to protect me. He keeps my hot chocolate in his house. He hired PIs to find me. Victor...

"My *stepsister,*" Dario emphasized, "has just found out what a total and utter liar your boss is. You're not gonna be flying her off in some helicopter with him again."

Dario had been watching them all from the estate as they left in the chopper. She'd felt the stares on her.

Victor...

Victor had taken a bullet for her. Well, a graze. One that he still basically refused to acknowledge but...

Her head tilted. The past surged up to choke her. *"Victor sends his regards. Drive the fucking car."* The words seemed to be playing in her head on an endless loop. Only in her head. She didn't voice them. Couldn't.

"I didn't tell you about my past," Victor spoke flatly. "I didn't tell you about my plans for Mage. I didn't tell you because everything changed when I met you."

"Bullshit." A sneer from Dario. "We've wasted enough time. Come on. We'll wait down in the lobby for the detective."

The past pulled harder at her. That stupid, grating voice... *"Victor sends his regards. Drive the fucking car."*

Her breath shuddered out. Her gaze darted around the boardroom. So familiar. So different. *"I'm done being your dirty little secret."* Her words. Her past. Her stare shifted back to Victor. She wet her lips. "I'm done being your dirty little secret." The words were out loud, not just in her mind. She'd spoken them deliberately.

His eyes widened. "Melody?" One of his hands reached for her.

"Uh, Vic?" Hunter cleared his throat. "What the hell is my role here? You the good guy or the villain?"

"Both," Victor snapped. "And if Melody leaves this room, you stay with her every second, understand me? Every. Second. I'll give you a million damn dollars to keep her within sight at all times."

Melody barely heard his words. Her heart pounded too fast. Echoed too loudly in her ears. "You're breaking my heart," she whispered. Again, familiar words and, in response, he was going to say back...

Didn't think you could break a heart that someone didn't have.

But instead of saying those words—the words that she *knew* he'd said in the past—pain twisted his face. "You own my heart," he told her. The hand he'd lifted toward her hovered in the air. As if he was afraid to touch her.

Dario pulled at her. "Enough. Melody, he stole the company. He wanted to destroy us all from the beginning. You can never trust him."

And, yet...Melody jerked away from Dario's grip. She took a step closer to Victor.

Victor, who stood as still as a statue even as his eyes blazed at her.

"You two are *done*." Dario's voice cracked on the last word. "Over. You might have taken the company—for the moment—but you and Melody are over. Hear me? *Done*. She knows the truth about you—"

"*We're not done*." Victor's vow.

Those words—this room—she looked again, almost

dizzy as her heart seemed ready to burst right out of her chest and as her temples throbbed. "Why not?" The words were an echo of the past. "You have everything you ever wanted."

Victor's head shook. One hard, negative swipe from left to right. "The hell I do." Grim. An echo of the past that she could feel flooding through her. "But I will." A vow.

Then he dropped to his knees right in front of her.

Chapter Twenty-Five

"What in the hell are you doing?" Dario blasted at Victor.

Victor ignored the prick, for the moment, because he didn't matter. What mattered was Melody. Convincing her to stay. Proving to her that she was the one who had always mattered to him. She always would matter.

"You're starting to remember, aren't you?" Victor asked Melody. She had to be remembering because she was saying some of the exact words they'd used before in this very room.

Did he remember every fucking conversation of his life? Hell, no. But he did remember *that one*. Because he'd asked her to marry him. Because she'd said yes. Because Melody had said that she loved him. All things that had made the moment play in his head again and again.

And because...

Because she'd vanished after that talk. He'd gone from heaven to hell, and the words before the trip might as well have been tattooed on his freaking soul.

She rubbed her left temple. Dark shadows had swept

under her eyes even as the rest of her face seemed far, far too pale. He wanted to grab her, swoop her into his arms. Run the hell away with her and never, ever look back.

But...

Tread carefully. Because the events in this room would send her running. Either to him or away from him.

Run to me, baby. Always, to me. He pulled in a long, deep breath. "Nothing ever goes according to plan." He'd told her that before, one year ago. Because he'd had such great plans in place for his proposal. Only she'd stood in that boardroom and said they were done.

We can't be done. I need you too much.

"I don't have a ring with me this time." He looked at her left hand. The one that still rubbed her temple. No ring there.

But...she lowered that hand. Frowned at it. "He took my ring away," she whispered. "He yanked it off my finger when he tied me to the chair."

Footsteps clattered. Victor's gaze darted to the door. Olivia had just rushed away. She'd shoved past Calista and Luis.

"I was wearing my engagement ring when he took me." Not a whisper. Stronger.

She had been wearing it. An engagement ring with three diamonds. Two matching square cuts on the side of a large oval. He'd picked out those diamonds for her. Been so nervous to propose, but he'd had his plans in place. He'd been intending to propose on Christmas Eve, beneath the Christmas tree at his house because she loved the holiday so much.

Only she'd been breaking up with him in the boardroom. He'd had to prove that he loved her.

I never gave her those damn words last year. Because he

hadn't said "*I love you*" to anyone back then. He hadn't said those words since he'd been taken away from his mother. Even though she'd been in a drugged haze when the ladies from DHR and the cops came to get him, he'd still raged and begged and...

"*Mom, Mom, don't let them take me! Please! I love you, Mom! It's going to be better! I can make it better!*"

But she'd looked right through him. Muttered something about a cousin who could take him.

Saying *I love you* hadn't changed a single thing that day.

He hadn't been sure that he could actually love anyone. Not until Melody.

I told her this time. I told her at my house, I told her that I loved her.

But she'd just found out about the secrets he'd worked so hard to keep. Maybe love wouldn't matter.

It hadn't mattered before.

She crept closer to him even as Dario wrapped his hands around her shoulders. Victor couldn't control the growl that broke from him. If Dario didn't move those fingers soon, Victor would be removing them for the prick.

Stay focused. Melody matters. Melody. "I have the Mage company." He shook his head. "But I will sign it over to you right the fuck now if you want."

"Yes!" An excited shout from Dario. "It's what she wants. Do it. Do—"

Hunter shoved Dario away from Melody. "You need to settle your ass down."

Victor hated having eyes on them. This moment was for him and Melody alone. "Everyone but Melody, out. Now."

Hunter hauled a protesting Dario to the door.

"No, no, Melody wants me here—"

But Melody turned to frown at her stepbrother. "I want to talk with Victor. Alone."

He broke from Hunter and lunged toward Victor and Melody. "You can't trust him., Melody! What if he is the one who took—"

"No." Certainty. "Victor didn't have anything to do with my abduction. He loves me." Simple. Like she was stating a fact that she knew with complete certainty. "Please leave, Dario."

His jaw dropped. "But—but—"

Victor surged to his full height. "You heard the lady." He grabbed Dario and shoved his ass toward the door—then through the doorway and into the hall. "Don't let the door hit you." Because it was about to be slamming. A snap of his teeth. "Get your ass out of the building. *Now*."

"You sonofabitch!"

"I'll escort him," Hunter offered. He exited the boardroom and took up a position right near a red-faced Dario.

Victor waved to a watchful Calista and Luis. "Go with them. Detective Clinton is probably arriving any damn minute. Keep the cop busy until I come downstairs."

But Calista angled around him to look back at Melody. "Are you sure this is what you want?" Calista shrugged. "Because I don't give a shit who signs my paycheck. You want to leave, then we'll walk out right now."

"I want to stay with Victor."

He grabbed the doorframe because those words *burned* through him. She was choosing him. She believed in him.

"For what it's worth," Hunter said as he wrapped a hard hand around Dario's shoulder. "I think that's a good choice. He never gave up on you."

And I never would.

The fight seemed to go out of Dario. "The whole company..." He turned away, body hunching. "It's all his."

Victor shut the door. He saw the faint tremble in his fingers, and his hand flattened on the wood. "Where were we?"

"I...remember." Halting.

He'd thought as much.

"This room. Being with you. You told me that you almost had everything you wanted."

Now he turned toward her. She stood in front of the boardroom table. Last year, she'd said that she loved him. He'd lifted her onto the table. Wanted nothing more than to fuck her right then and there. He'd *almost* had his dream. Her. A future. A life with the woman he loved.

Then, that dream had been gone in a blink. "You're what I want."

She rocked forward onto the balls of her feet. "You hate the Mage family? Because of what happened to your dad?"

"I thought I did." Slowly, carefully, he went back to her. Back to the woman he loved more than anything in the world. "Hate was my purpose. I was a dumbass kid who was drowning in rage. I had to channel it. Had to get out of the nightmare that kept pulling me under. After Colton Crane...hell, I had to be different. I could feel my own violence and rage, and I knew something had to give. So I made a goal. Get out. Get strong. Go after the company that had sent my life careening into a nightmare."

She watched him with her deep, incredible eyes. Eyes that had stolen his soul long ago.

"I got my education. Became smarter. Sharper. Obtained a job at Mage Industries. Worked my ass off and... got close to Sebastian Mage. Only I realized something as I was working with him."

Melody didn't speak.

"He's a tough bastard," Victor said. "But he was fanatical about safety."

Her eyes narrowed.

"He'd go out and inspect facilities himself. Every single time. Over and over again. Told me that we had to put employees first. People mattered. Lives mattered. It was only after he got sick that I understood the full truth."

"What truth was that?"

"He blamed himself. Guilt has eaten him alive. Guilt for the accident at the factory. Guilt for your mother's death."

"My mother?"

He nodded. "Guilt for your disappearance. He blames himself for everything. The nurse with him? She's there because he's been on suicide watch."

"*What?*"

"I didn't understand why the gun was in his study," Victor muttered. That still bothered him. Who the hell had put the gun in there? "I'd ordered all guns removed from the estate. His nurse keeps a close eye on him. And John Henry has directives to watch him like a hawk right now. Sebastian is not himself any longer. He—he makes mistakes. He says things that he doesn't mean."

"Like...killing my mother?"

Yes, like that. "Dario got it wrong. Your father didn't kill her. But he told me once—before the sickness stole so much of him—that he'd been a shit husband. That he was never home. That he didn't spend enough time with her or with you like he should have done. He felt like he drove her away, and if he'd just been there, been with her more, then the skiing accident would never have happened. You wouldn't have lost your mom. He wouldn't have lost the one woman who made him happy."

"And my disappearance? He said it was his fault. I was there. He said he didn't pay."

"He wasn't talking about a ransom. I'd heard that same rant from him over and over in the last year." The first time he'd heard it, Victor had thought the same damn thing she did...*Holy shit, there was a ransom for my Melody? I'll pay it. I'll pay anything.* But Victor had checked every phone, every text, every computer. There had been no ransom. There had only been Sebastian's guilt. "He's been sick. Very, very sick." Victor thought guilt had been eating the man alive for a very long time. "He thought that he had to..." Hell, how to explain? "Sebastian thinks he has to pay with his life in order to atone for his sins." *For the men who died at the factory. For the wife who'd been taken away in the skiing accident.*

For the daughter who'd vanished and never come home again.

Tears filled her eyes. "Victor..."

"I found out, once I started working at Mage and going through the files, that his brother was the one in charge back then. Jackson Mage. The older brother was the one who pulled all the strings at Mage Industries. Your father was second in command. It was Jackson who had ordered the tight production schedule at my dad's factory. In order to meet that schedule, the managers cut corners. The equipment wasn't inspected properly. The supervisors at the factory checked boxes just to keep things moving, *but there was no inspection.*"

"I'm so sorry."

She'd done nothing wrong. She didn't need to apologize to him. "Your uncle stepped down after the accident. The board voted your father into his position. That's when safety guidelines were stepped up across all properties and ventures. When he realized what had happened at my dad's factory, Sebastian sent money to all the families of the victims."

"Money doesn't bring people back."

No, it sure as fuck didn't. His mother had taken the money and used it on drugs. Almost a million dollars. He'd never seen a dime of it. It hadn't helped him. It hadn't helped her. An overdose had ended his mother's life.

"How much was a life worth?" Melody asked.

He swallowed. "One hell of a lot less than you would think."

"Victor..." She shook her head. A teardrop rolled down her cheek. "*I'm sorry.*"

"Your uncle died of a heart attack a few years later." He'd never met Jackson Mage. Sebastian barely ever spoke of his brother. "Mage Industries has been different since then. Hell, your father was great when it came to safety. Like I said, he was fanatical about it. But he couldn't anticipate product demand and development for shit." Another exhale. "Things got worse with his...condition. I think it had been at play for longer than most people realized. When I took over, it wasn't a peaceful transfer of power." Nothing like they'd all pretended. "I fought tooth and nail for this company. It was going bankrupt. Either I took over, or it ended. By that point, I understood that there were thousands of employees counting on checks. They had families. My job was to take care of them. All of them. So I stepped up. I took the company from Sebastian."

"You had what you wanted."

"No. Yes. Dammit—*I want you.*" She needed to understand this. "I will never be like him." So lost in business that the people close to him paid the price. *So many pay the price.* "I'm running the company my way. Safety will always be a priority. I will do the job. I will take care of my people." He advanced toward her. "But I won't forget my wife. I won't push her to the side. I will cherish her. Every single day." He stood right in front of her. He knew exactly the words he'd given her before. He would give them to her again. "You're it, Melody. You're what I want." His end goal. "No more secrets. No lies. I want you with me, always. I love you." He held his breath. He waited...

"He wanted me to think you were behind the attack."

Victor's eyes narrowed. "What?"

"I remember...being in my car. A blue Benz. My Benz." She bit her lower lip. Slowly let it go. "I was staring at the elevator and waiting for you." Her hand rose and pointed to her temple. "Then he was just there. In the back seat behind me. A gun was pushing against my temple and he told me...he said you sent your regards."

Something broke in him. "*No.*" A snarl. "I didn't! I wouldn't have! I would never have ever—"

The door behind them creaked open. "Not now," Victor snapped without looking back. He'd deal with Dario and Hunter and the detective and whoever the hell else later.

A gunshot blasted. He felt the impact in the next instant as a hammer seemed to pound into his back. Horror filled Melody's eyes. Her mouth opened as she screamed.

Another gunshot thundered but Victor was already hurtling himself forward and onto her. He covered her body as they slammed into the floor.

Chapter Twenty-Six

"Victor?" His weight crushed into her. The boom of the two gunshot blasts echoed in Melody's ears. "Victor?" Her hands grabbed for his arms.

She felt something wet on her fingertips. Wet. Warm. Blood.

"Gun," Victor whispered.

Yes, yes, she'd gotten that someone had a *gun*. Hard to miss that. The person had just shot Victor. The person had—

"Take," he rasped.

Her eyes widened. He covered her almost completely, and her hands slid down his body, moving as quickly as she could. Melody ignored the blood on her fingers as she shoved her hand under the edge of his coat. He'd never even taken off the coat when they came into Mage Industries, and she hadn't realized that he was carrying a gun.

But she felt the holster near his left arm. Her fingers inched toward it.

"I just don't get why you couldn't have stayed gone," Olivia said.

Her heart froze.

Victor's eyes were closed. His body seemed to slump harder against her. *No, no, no.*

"I mean, you weren't dead. It's not like I wanted my best friend *dead*. What the hell am I? A monster?" Olivia shut the door. A soft creak.

Melody had taken the gun from the holster. She gripped it tightly. Victor's body hid the gun.

"We checked in on you a few times. You were harmless up there. Working at a diner, living in that tiny hole of an apartment. You didn't remember anything or anyone, so I thought—why not let you just stay there? Time kept passing. Nothing changed. You didn't have to die. That's what I kept telling him. *You didn't have to die.* Not like you remembered anything." She edged closer. "You could stay there. Sebastian could die. All the plans we had would work. Once Sebastian died, we'd have everything. Except— *there is nothing to have!* All that time! All that energy, and this prick Victor has it all!"

"Victor?" Melody whispered. He didn't seem to be breathing. The gun felt cold in her grip. He crushed her against the hard floor.

"Get the hell from beneath him!" Olivia snapped. "I can't shoot through him in order to hit you. That's not how this is gonna work! It has to look like *you* attacked *him*, and then you're gonna shoot yourself. Like—like you realized what he'd done. You realized that he'd been the one to arrange your kidnapping. So you snapped, and you shot him."

Melody made no move to crawl from beneath Victor. Even as his body seemed to grow heavier.

"You shot him," Olivia said again. "And because you have brain damage and guilt and all kinds of crazy shit happening, you shot yourself, too. That's how the scene will play out. That's the explanation the cops will give the media. I will make this quick, I swear it. You are my best friend, Melody. It's not like I want you to hurt."

Please, please, Victor, be okay—

"You can't just stay beneath your dead lover's body forever, am I right?"

Not dead. He could not be dead.

"Dammit!" A wild cry from Olivia. Her heels rushed across the floor.

Victor's body jerked. Olivia—she was kicking him. Tugging at him. She was—

Victor rolled. Hard. Fast. Not heavy and slack any longer. He grabbed Olivia's kicking leg. Victor yanked her down to the floor. She hit the floor with a scream and landed on her ass. She yanked the gun up, pointed it straight at Victor, and cried, "You bastard! You are dead!"

No, he wasn't.

Melody leapt up. Her shaking fingers were tight around the gun. She stared at the woman who claimed to be her best friend, and Melody fired the gun. The bullet slammed into Olivia.

Olivia's pain-filled scream echoed around them.

"WHAT IN THE hell is happening here?" Detective Angus Clinton demanded as he stormed into the lobby at Mage Industries. He flashed his ID, then shoved it back in his pocket. His gun was holstered near his hip.

Hunter stood beside a glaring Dario. The guards that Victor had hired—Calista and Luis—waited close by. A few of the uniformed security crew from the Mage Industries also shuffled around every now and then, but the building was mostly shuttered.

Quiet.

Safe?

"These bastards are kicking me out of the building!" Dario raged. He gestured toward Hunter. Calista. Luis.

Luis waved at the detective. "Hi. Yes. We are. And, detective, we were waiting for you and planning to make sure Dario leaves and does not return. Pulling double duty. Huh. Maybe triple duty?"

"*Victor Alexander is a lying piece of shit!*" Spittle flew from Dario's mouth. "He has been lying to my sister—"

"Stepsister," Luis corrected.

Dario fired a lethal glare his way. "Victor is trying to destroy Mage Industries! I think—I think he's upstairs right now, feeding more lies to Melody! You have to go and help her, detective. I have proof that he stole the company right out from under me!"

Hunter rolled his eyes. This guy was really a piece of work. One that was getting on his last nerve. He'd never been a fan of privileged, arrogant assholes who thought they were owed the world on a silver platter. Hunter had done his research on all the major players involved here long before he'd ever agreed to take the case.

He knew Victor had worked his ass off for years.

While Dario had just been coasting on his stepdad's fortune.

He also knew plenty about Detective Angus Clinton. The man had been lead on Melody's case for most of the last year. He'd partnered with the Feds, and he'd turned up jack shit. From what Hunter had determined, Angus had never worked particularly hard to find Melody or her abductor. He'd spent too much time thinking Victor was guilty as sin or telling everyone that Melody had left of her own accord—no crime there.

"Detective." Calista sighed as she stepped forward. "This man broke into Victor's private office. I think he should be thoroughly questioned about Melody's disappearance."

Hunter nodded. He thought an interrogation with Dario was a stellar idea. Bonus points for the lady.

"Bullshit!" Dario's teeth snapped together. "Detective Clinton, let me tell you *this*. Sebastian Mage is a straight-up murderer! He confessed to killing Melody's mother. And Victor, hell, we know he nearly beat that Colton Crane guy to death that time!"

Hunter wasn't rolling his eyes any longer. He was narrowing them and sharpening his gaze on Dario.

Dario smirked at him. "Oh? Didn't know that your boss was fucking *unhinged*? He is! You aren't doing Melody any favors by leaving her alone with him." He pointed toward the elevator bank. The younger security guard, Hayward, stood near the elevators, shifting from foot to foot. "Victor is violent, he's obsessed with Melody, and she just found out that he's a damn *liar*. He's up there now, alone with her, and who the hell knows what he is doing to her? You need to get up there, detective, and help my sister. You need to get up there *now*."

"Melody chose to stay upstairs," Hunter said. His gaze weighed Dario. "How do you know about Colton Crane?" Hunter knew about the bastard because he made it his job to be thorough. Before the Ice Breakers had signed on to investigate Melody's disappearance, they had truly ripped apart Victor's life. The guy had been the most likely suspect in Melody's disappearance, after all. But while Hunter had gotten access to info about Colton Crane and the assault, the case reports should have been sealed to the general public. Hunter's *access* hadn't exactly been obtained through legal means.

No way should Dario know about Colton Crane.

"Olivia told me," Dario muttered. He yanked a hand through his hair.

Hunter peered around the lobby. "Where is Olivia?"

"I—" Dario stopped. Seemed to notice her missing for the first time. Unease slithered across his face.

"You say Sebastian Mage committed murder?" Detective Clinton asked. He advanced on them, hands heading to his hips. "You are sure about this?"

"Yeah, yeah." A quick nod from Dario. "He confessed to Olivia. Look, I bet she's upstairs. We need to all go and talk to her, right now."

"No way." Hunter moved in front of him because the guy was not getting back on an elevator and going upstairs. "You are not going back up there. Victor wants you out of the building, and you are getting *out*."

"Everyone, calm down. I'll go up and talk to Victor. And Melody." The detective rolled back his shoulders. "I'll get to the truth." He shot a frown at Dario. "Why don't you go outside? Or, better yet, head to the station? I can take a full report from you as soon as I am done upstairs."

"When you're done upstairs, you'll be arresting Sebastian Mage!" Dario nodded vigorously. "That's what you'll be doing."

Detective Clinton pushed the button for the elevator. "Keep an eye on all of them, will you?" Angus Clinton said to Hayward right before the doors opened. Then the detective ducked inside. He pressed a button on the control panel. His hands went to his hips as he turned back to face them.

The doors began to slide closed.

Dario barreled for the elevator. "I'm coming up, too!" One hand jerked up angrily. Something gleamed in his fist. "That sonofabitch Victor isn't going to get away with—"

"Knife!" Hayward yelled. The kid was sweating, and his eyes were wide as he grabbed for the taser on his hip.

The elevator doors closed, sealing the detective inside.

Hunter surged for Dario. He tackled the bastard even as Hayward fired his taser. And 50,000 volts were suddenly pumping through Hunter's body.

❋

"You shot me! You freaking *shot* me!" Olivia grabbed her shoulder and scuttled backward on the floor.

Victor heaved up to his knees.

Melody raced forward and grabbed the gun Olivia had just dropped, and when she did, Olivia started laughing.

"Now your prints are on it! S-see? Perfect!"

Melody hurried back to Victor's side. He hadn't risen fully, was still on his knees, and there was *blood*. So much of it. She slapped Olivia's gun on the boardroom table but kept the one she'd taken from Victor.

He was far too pale. The lines on his face cut deeper than she'd ever seen them before. "Victor?"

His gaze raked her. "You're not hurt."

No. Two gunshots had been fired from Olivia's gun. She knew one had hit him, in the back, but what about the other bullet? And just *where* exactly had that first one hit? Melody tried to peer around him.

"The room is...soundproof," Victor bit out. "No one will have heard the shots. You...you need to go get help, Melody. Find the security guards. Call...cops." He weaved a bit.

Almost dropped fully back to the floor. "Shit." He caught himself.

Olivia laughed. "Yes, yes, call the cops! I'll say—"

Melody ignored her. One hand gripped the gun and the other feathered over Victor's shoulder. "Victor?"

His head turned toward her. "Go get help." His breath rasped out. "One bullet is in my back, about...ah, maybe two inches from my spine? Can feel the bastard. Hurts like a mother." Sweat dotted his forehead. "The second just... went through my arm. Or, hell, could still be in it."

His right arm. It hung limply at his side. *Covered* in blood. When he'd grabbed Olivia, he'd caught her kicking foot with his left hand.

Tears stung Melody's eyes. She shoved the gun into his left hand. "You can still fire, right?"

A nod.

She rushed to the boardroom door and swung it open. "Help!" Melody yelled. "I need help in here!"

Footsteps rushed toward her.

She spun away and looked at Victor. He had the gun aimed at Olivia. Melody darted back toward him.

Just as he slumped onto the floor.

"Victor!" She flew to crouch beside him. "Victor!"

Olivia laughed.

"What in the *hell* is happening here?" Detective Angus Clinton demanded as he raced inside the boardroom.

Melody whipped her head toward him. She opened her mouth—

"*Shoot them!*" Olivia screamed. "They attacked me! *Shoot. Them!*"

Horror flooded through Melody. Frantically, she shook her head. "No, no, Olivia is the one—"

The detective smiled. *Smiled.* Melody didn't even get to

finish speaking because he was hauling out his weapon and aiming it at her. "Stand down!" he shouted loudly.

They were down. They *were*. Victor was on the floor, bleeding, and Melody wasn't armed.

"Hey, Melody," Angus taunted. "Victor sends his regards."

A gun against my temple. A man's rasping voice in my backseat. "No—"

A gun fired.

The detective's body jerked.

The gun fired again. Again.

The detective stumbled back even as blood bloomed on his chest.

"Yeah," Victor rasped as he held the gun in his blood-stained grip. "Sure do...send my regards...Hope you...enjoy hell, you sonofabitch."

The detective fell.

Olivia screamed.

Victor turned the gun on her.

Olivia's eyes doubled in size. "It was all his idea!" Tears streamed down her cheeks. "He's the one—*it was all Angus! Don't shoot me! Don't shoot, I am begging!*"

More footsteps. Rushing into the boardroom. Only...the detective's slumped body blocked the doorway. Hunter and Calista had to jump over him to get fully inside.

Calista knelt, her hands going to the detective's chest. "Damn." She started trying to cover his wounds. Apply pressure.

Hunter took in the scene, his gaze going from the detective's prone body...to Olivia's crying form...to Victor, who still held the gun. Who was bloody and armed and when Melody looked at him, she saw that Victor's face was twisted with rage and hate.

Hunter had his own weapon drawn.

He's taking in the scene. Victor looks guilty. Victor looks like the villain.

"No!" Melody lunged in front of Victor. "Victor needs *help!* Get an ambulance! Get *help!*"

Hunter stared at her a moment longer, a muscle jerked along his jaw and then...he nodded. Hunter lowered his weapon and yanked out his phone. A moment later, "I need an ambulance..."

Melody's breath choked from her as she looked back at Victor. But rage didn't twist his face any longer. He'd sagged back onto the floor. His facial features had gone slack. His eyes closed. "Victor?" She grabbed for him. "*Victor!*"

Chapter Twenty-Seven

Somewhere, Christmas music was playing.

He could hear the music, could even name the song. "I'll Be Home For Christmas."

Darkness surrounded him. The music kept playing.

"I'll be home for Christmas, if only in my dreams..."

He wanted to be home for Christmas. Home—to him, home was Melody. Melody and her dimpled smile and her green eyes. And the sweet, sweet sound of her laughter. He thought that, maybe, her laughter had been what he missed most over the last year. Her laughter had always been the best damn gift.

He'd wanted to spend his life making her happy. Making her smile. Making her laugh.

He'd wanted a Christmas tree. Wanted decorations and stockings hung by the chimney and kids who laughed and baked chocolate chip cookies with him and Melody. He'd wanted all the joy that everyone else seemed to get so easily.

While he'd had such coldness in his life.

He'd wanted...

Melody.

"I don't know why you think you get to sleep all day, but it's just got to stop. I believe you're the one being Sleeping Beauty right now, so when I kiss you, I fully expect you to wake up, stare straight into my eyes, and vow to love me forever."

Her soft lips pressed to his.

Not a dream. A dream had never felt so real. He should know. After all, he'd had plenty of dreams about Melody over the last year.

"Wake up," she pleaded. "Stare straight into my eyes. Vow to love me forever."

His lashes slowly lifted. The darkness faded. The music kept playing. A light blinked, on and off, from somewhere nearby. And Melody—his Melody—leaned over him.

She smiled. A slow smile that stretched her full, unpainted lips, that made her dimple flash at him, and that lit her gorgeous, green eyes. "Hello, Sleeping Beauty," she told him.

He jerked. Reached for Melody. Hauled her down onto him even as his mouth crashed into hers.

"Victor! Victor, *no!* You had a bullet lodged in your back! You had way too much blood loss!" She pushed at him. Kissed him a bit longer but then pushed again and broke free. "Victor." Her cheeks flushed. Her eyes gleamed with what could have been both tears and joy. "You scared the hell out of me."

He stared straight into her eyes. "I will love you forever."

Her breath caught. "Heard that part, did you?" A nod. "I thought you were waking up. Your breathing changed. And, well, you also whispered my name." Her smile came and went again. Came and...went.

Worry clouded her features. "How do you feel?"

He stared at her. Smudges under her eyes. Tousled hair. Wrinkled clothes.

Absolutely freaking beautiful.

Then he looked around the room. His hospital room. A small Christmas tree had been set up in the corner. The blinking lights came from the tree.

"There wasn't a big selection in the gift shop. The two-foot tree was a real find," she murmured. "When I was staying in the hospital, I hated that my room was so stark. It always felt so cold."

His gaze slid back to her.

"I didn't want it to be cold when you woke up."

How could he be cold? She was there.

"Victor." Her brows pulled low. "Should I get a nurse? How do you feel?"

"I feel like it's Christmas morning."

Her eyes flared with alarm. "It's not. Not yet. We still have a few days left. The doctors warned me that you might be confused coming off the anesthesia, but...I'm gonna get the nurse, just in case." She turned away.

His hand flew out and curled around her wrist. "You're here."

"Y-yes." She seemed even more worried as she glanced back at him.

"You love me."

"Yes." Not as worried. More definite.

He nodded. "Then it feels like Christmas morning." Or, at least, what he imagined a wonderful Christmas morning would feel like. Pure joy. Hope.

For the first time in so very long.

Her breath rushed out. Then she was the one crushing her mouth to his again. Kissing him passionately. Frantically.

And he heard the music playing and he was happy. Finally.

"I'll be home for Christmas..."

For real this time. No more dreams.

THE NEXT TIME Victor opened his eyes...

"Melody is back." Sebastian Mage leaned on his cane and stared down at Victor. Hatterson waited behind him. "So you need to get your ass out of this bed."

Victor blinked.

"Did you hear me? Melody is back," Sebastian repeated as he rammed his cane into the floor for emphasis. "She's telling me that you two are going to get married."

Uh, yeah, as soon as I can get my ass out of this bed.

"She said you loved her." Sebastian beetled his brows at Victor. "Do you love her?"

"More than anything."

Sebastian rammed the cane down again. "Good." His shoulders slumped. "I can't...I can't always be here for her." He licked his lips. "You will, though...you'll be there for her...when I'm not?"

"I'll get my ass out of this bed," he swore. *Where the hell is Melody?* "And I'll be there for her. Count on it."

Sebastian nodded. "She was gone..." His gaze shifted to the Christmas tree. The lights flickered on and off. On and off. "Gone too long. I...thought she'd forgotten me."

For a time, she'd forgotten them all.

Sebastian's gaze returned to Victor. A big smile lit his features. It was a smile that Victor had not seen in months. "She loves me."

Victor grabbed the bed's railing. Pulled up with his left

arm. He felt a burn in his back. Along the right side. About two inches away from his spine.

Thank Christ that bullet didn't get closer to my spine. Thank—

"I don't think she should love me." Low. Sad. "But she does." Sebastian heaved a sigh. "I...miss her mother."

Was the older man going to confess to her murder again? Because a nurse had just bustled in and that could be tricky to explain right then—

"I wish I could go back in time. Show Helena that I loved her. Show her how much she meant to me." Sebastian swallowed. His Adam's apple bobbed. "Show my daughter, will you? Every single day. Show her."

Hatterson edged forward. "He's having a good day," he told Victor.

Yes, yes, Sebastian clearly was.

Hatterson curled his hand around Sebastian's shoulder. "Victor took two bullets for Melody," he informed the other man. "I think he's doing a good job of showing her how he feels."

"Technically three bullets," Victor said, cocking his head to the side. "If you count the graze at the estate." A graze that he now saw had been carefully bandaged by someone at the hospital. Maybe by the nurse who was bustling closer? "Ah, can you give us just a minute?" he asked the nurse.

She frowned but nodded. Quickly, she backed out. The door closed behind her.

Sebastian's grip tightened on his cane. "I know about your father."

Victor felt shock roll through him.

"You think...you think I never checked you out? Before I gave you my whole company?"

Behind him, Hatterson inclined his head. "I did my research on you."

"Why the hell didn't you say something?" Victor demanded.

Sebastian shrugged. "Why didn't you?"

Because at first, I wanted to destroy you.

Sebastian nodded. "I always planned to give everything to you. Just didn't realize you'd be taking my daughter, too."

"I love Melody," Victor stated. He wanted to be very clear on this point. "I'm going to marry her."

Something that looked very much like peace swept over Sebastian's features. "Then I can rest. I've been...tired."

He could see the other man fading. "I know." Softer.

"I'm sorry," Sebastian told him. He stared hard at Victor. "I'm so sorry about..." But his words trailed off. He blinked. Looked around the room. His breath rasped out a little harder. "I'm sorry about..." His eyes scrunched. He glanced at Victor. "I—"

"I know," Victor said. He did. "Everything is okay." It would be.

Sebastian exhaled. Silence ticked past. Then, "Melody is back."

Victor swallowed again. Smiled. "Yes." An exhale. "I'm gonna get my ass out of this bed and marry her."

Sebastian's eyes gleamed. "Good. Good. Always thought...she was sweet on you." He shuffled for the door. The cane banged against the floor.

It opened before he could reach it. Not the hospital nurse this time, but, instead, Sebastian's personal nurse, Tracy Ryder. She reached out for him. "I've got some coffee ready for you outside."

Hatterson began to follow them out.

"Hatterson!" Victor's voice came out like a hard bark.

Yeah, he was already feeling better. Feeling better and he had one focus.

Where in the hell is Melody?

Hatterson glanced back at him.

"A word. Alone."

"I've got him," Tracy murmured.

Sebastian and Tracy slipped away.

Hatterson ambled to the foot of Victor's bed. "Melody is with that Ice Breaker guy, Hunter," he said, clearly reading Victor's mind. "They've got loose ends that they are trying to tie up. And you have two guards stationed outside your room. Calista and Luis. Melody insisted that they stay close."

He didn't need guards. He needed information. "Brant McKee."

"What?"

Not a what. A who. "Brant McKee."

Confusion first, then understanding appeared on Hatterson's face. "That prick from when Melody was a teen? Why the hell are you asking about him?" But he leaned over the bed. "Did he have something to do with this mess? Because I warned him—Sebastian and I both told that little prick that if he *ever* came within fifty feet of her again, he was dead."

Victor locked his jaw. "He hurt her."

"Broke three of her ribs." Flat. "So I broke twice as many of his. You don't hurt our Melody and just walk away." He shared a long look with Victor. "Guessing the detective learned that fact, didn't he? Word is that he's the one who took her. Melody said—said she remembered him. Being in the car with her. And when the EMTs were trying to save him, they ripped open his shirt. The bastard had some kind of scar on him that Melody was freaked about."

Because she'd stabbed her attacker when he'd held her in that cabin so long ago.

"The detective didn't make it, FYI," Hatterson informed him bluntly.

No, Victor hadn't thought that the man had. "I aimed for the heart." Only fair, since the bastard had tried to take Victor's heart.

You took Melody.

"Haven't thought about Brant McKee in years." Hatterson rubbed a hand along his beard. "Was he involved? Did he help? Thought we taught that prick a lesson. You never, *ever* put a hand on a woman. I showed him what pain felt like."

"He's running for attorney general in Maryland."

"Oh, the fuck he is." Hatterson dropped his hand. "That can't happen."

"It won't." Victor grimaced as he twisted on the bed. "Time to get my ass out of here."

"Yeah, well, in spite of what Sebastian said, good luck with that," Hatterson informed him. "Don't think the docs intend for you to be home before Christmas. Your ass is gonna be staying here for a bit."

Victor stilled. "Then the docs need to think again. I *will* be home for Christmas." He'd be with Melody. This Christmas and every Christmas that came after.

Chapter Twenty-Eight

"DID YOU REALLY GET TASED?" MELODY ASKED HUNTER as they stood in the hospital corridor.

He quirked a brow. "Did you really shoot your best friend?"

Her *former* best friend. Before Melody could respond, the door to the nearby hospital room opened—the door for her *former* best friend's hospital room. Olivia Hatcher was in that room, and Melody intended to see her. But, first, she had to get past...

Detective Laila Williams. The detective stood in the room's now open doorway. Melody and Hunter met her before, when she'd arrived at Mage Industries with a team of uniforms to find chaos waiting. Her dark hair framed her glowering face in a short pixie cut. The detective's displeasure was plain to see. "This is damn unusual," Laila began.

Hunter just sighed. "Yeah, look, your captain gave the all clear for us. The Feds are on their way down here. Before we can all blink, they are gonna be sweeping in and taking over, and if we can get a nice, neat confession for you before they barge in, then how about we do that? Wins all around, am I right?"

"There is nothing neat about this," Laila crossed her arms over her chest. "And there is no win involved. Detective Angus Clinton is dead."

"Yes." Melody ignored the twist in her gut. When she'd seen that slashing scar on his chest as the EMTs had worked on him... "Detective Angus Clinton is dead. He's also the man who kidnapped me. Who tried to kill me. If Victor hadn't fired and stopped the detective, I'd be the one in the morgue right now." Her *and* Victor. The fact that they were both alive? Damn straight she considered that a win. "Give us five minutes with Olivia. Please." Because she had questions that had to be asked.

"She's gonna be transferred out of the hospital in less than half an hour..." Laila pursed her lips. But then she nodded curtly. "So you had better get in here now."

Melody's eyes widened. Hunter had said he'd pull strings to get her this visit with Olivia, but, wow, the man must have some seriously powerful connections.

"I can't leave you alone with her, so don't even ask." Laila backed up a step. Then another as she waved Melody and Hunter into the room. "And if she wants a lawyer..." Her voice rose as she looked at the woman in the hospital bed. "You have been informed that you can have a lawyer, Ms. Hatcher, and that anything you say can and will be held against you—"

"He made me do it!" Olivia cried out, cutting through the detective's words. Her left hand was cuffed to the bed railing. She wore a green hospital gown, the same kind of gown that Victor wore. Her right shoulder looked bulky, probably because of the bandage from the bullet wound. "I had no choice! The detective forced me! I'm a victim, too! A victim just as much as anyone else!"

"Oh, is that the story she's going with?" Hunter muttered as he followed Melody inside the hospital room. "Got to give the woman credit for trying, huh?" He shut the door.

"It's not a story!" A screech from Olivia. "It's the truth." Olivia's wide eyes locked on Melody. "You're my best friend."

A best friend she'd tried to kill. Yep, sure. Why not go with that song and dance? Melody edged closer to the hospital bed.

"I didn't want you dead, Melody! Listen, listen—"

"You have the right to remain—" Laila began.

"*I'm not being silent!*"

Obviously.

Laila shrugged, as if to say...*Fine, it's your funeral.*

Olivia yanked on the handcuff even as her gaze remained on Melody. "Do you think I wanted you hurt?"

Uh, considering that Olivia had fired a gun at Victor's back and had been *planning* to kill her, too...Yes, Yes, Melody did think her *best friend* wanted her hurt.

"I didn't want to hear any of the stories about what Angus had done to you. He *forced* me to do everything, don't you see? It began when he was first sniffing around, trying to dig up dirt against Victor. He'd found out about Colton Crane. The guy thought he could blackmail Victor or some shit. See, before he approached you, Angus and I met. H-he wanted to know what I thought of Victor. What I thought of you."

That faint stutter—had it been Olivia lying, pausing as she tried to figure out what BS story to tell? Because Melody feared that her friend might have been the mastermind the whole time. *Maybe Angus wanted to blackmail Victor, but you came up with an even better plan, didn't you, Olivia?*

Olivia's desperate gaze pinned Melody. "You blew off Angus when he tried to warn you about Victor. Angus didn't understand why you were so certain of him, why you trusted Victor so much, but I got it. After all, I knew you were seeing Victor secretly." Another yank at the cuff. "You were suddenly so happy. You hadn't been that way in years. And trying to hide an affair? Oh, come on." A mocking sigh. "Not exactly your strong suit. You didn't have casual flings. If anything, you were way too standoffish with men. After you and Brant broke up years ago, you barely ever dated anyone." Olivia's head cocked to the side. "It's kinda funny." Olivia wet her lips. "Before your disappearance, you were suddenly talking about him again. Saying that you were getting some PI in Maryland to look into him."

"I was?"

A pleased glint lit Olivia's eyes. "See? I can help you." Another yank on the cuff. "Tell her to take these off." A fuming glance toward Laila. "We can all work together. Make a deal." A nod. "Because you don't remember very much at all, do you? But I do. I remember everything about your life because I was your best friend. I was there for every big moment. I was beside you for holidays and special occasions. I was always there for you."

Olivia hadn't been there when Melody had been stabbed in the cabin. Or when she'd woken up, alone and confused, in a Canadian hospital bed. Melody stepped forward. "You were aware that I was kidnapped. That I was taken and nearly killed in that cabin in Canada."

"You..." A slow exhale. "Victor was—*is* violent. Angus

and I were just going to set things up so that it looked like he'd been behind the abduction."

Wheels spun in Melody's head. Hunter was silent beside her. He just kept glaring at the woman in the bed.

Meanwhile, Melody's heart felt heavy in her chest. "You mean you were setting Victor up for my abduction *and* my murder." There. Done.

Olivia licked her lips once more.

"You were using Dario." Melody put those pieces together as she saw the flush deepen on Olivia's cheeks. "You were using him and Angus. Manipulating them both. Something I do remember about you is the fact that you were always very good at getting what you wanted."

"*I-I didn't—*"

"Angus knew about Victor's past. He told you. Maybe you did meet him when he was first investigating Victor or maybe you'd met him long before that. I don't know what story is true, but I believe you knew an opportunity when you spotted one, didn't you?" She didn't wait for a response. "When you learned that Victor had nearly killed Colton Crane, you decided that a pattern could be established. Colton, then me. You timed my disappearance to fall right after Victor was announced as the new head of Mage." Oh, but she had to give Olivia credit. She'd worked so much to her advantage. *Even as you shattered my life.* "It would look like we fought, right? That I was furious with him after he took the company. That he turned on me." It all made her so sad. "I vanished. And I'm thinking that Angus meant to kill me, didn't he? And eventually my murder would have been pinned on Victor. How could it not be? The detective on the case was sure of Victor's guilt."

"But you got away." From Laila.

"I got away," Melody repeated. "And suddenly, I was in

a hospital. There were new witnesses. New problems. It spiraled, didn't it? I started working at a diner. Made some new friends. What were you going to do? Come all the way back up there to kill me? Make me vanish a second time? Perhaps that's when it became easier to just leave me there. After all, I didn't know what had happened. I didn't know who the hell I was. The docs said I might never know. If you could marry Dario and get me declared dead, then you'd still have everything you wanted without the trouble of coming for me again."

Olivia's expression slowly shifted. Hardened. "Do you think I enjoyed being your fucking poor best friend all those years? The pity pal that you loaned your dresses to because I couldn't afford to fit in with those stupid, pretentious assholes that were all around us?"

Melody pressed her lips together.

"I wasn't going to be some hanger-on for the rest of my life. I was going to have everything." Olivia's eyes blazed. "I deserved to have all the things that you did! I *deserved* my turn!"

"Speaking of all the things that I had..." Melody rolled back her shoulders. "I notice that your rings are gone. Those sparkly diamonds I saw you wearing at the estate. Did the police take them into custody?"

"We did," Laila stated. "Bagged and tagged."

"I'm pretty sure they were mine." Something Melody had realized in the boardroom. Her stare didn't leave Olivia. "You're trying to act like you were forced to do so much. Who forced you to wear my engagement ring? You had the diamonds separated. You put them on your own fingers, and you *wore* them like some kind of sick souvenir."

Laila whistled. "Well, that will sure be handy evidence."

Disgust—and fear—flashed on Olivia's face. "Why the hell did you have to come home, Melody? *Why*? We were just going to leave you there! You could've had a life."

"I already had a life," Melody snapped back. "You took it from me. I came to get it back, you bitch."

Olivia's mouth dropped open.

"Really have to know." Melody had to choke down her rage. "The big plan of yours—it involved you marrying Dario, huh? What were you going to do, kill him eventually? Then live happily-ever-after with your detective? Or was the detective gonna die, too?" She tapped her chin as she pretended to consider things. "If Dario died, did you believe that you could get all the Mage money and the property? The business?"

"There is no money any longer. No property. Victor has it all!"

"Bet you wish that you'd known all of that before you started spinning your plans."

A knock sounded at the door.

"Come in," Laila called.

Uniformed officers entered. A male and a female in dark blue.

"We're here for the prisoner transfer," the male announced.

Olivia began to cry.

"Guess it's time for *her* to go home," Hunter said, finally speaking. "But I don't think she's going to like the new digs."

"You fucking asshole!" Olivia shouted at him.

"I get that a lot." Hunter rolled one shoulder. "Merry Christmas to you, too, sunshine."

"I THINK you should have stayed in the hospital for another day," Melody fretted as she stood on the front porch of Victor's home. Snow fell lightly, fluttering in the air around them. She'd bundled into her coat and a warm, red scarf wrapped around her neck. "We could have celebrated Christmas there. I had a tree in your room."

Victor turned. Frowned at her.

She smiled at him. Happiness surged inside of her. Sure, her best friend had tried to kill her. There had been a million questions to answer. Details to sort out but...

Victor was alive. He'd gotten cleared from the docs at the hospital so that he could actually be home for Christmas. Her father was safe. She'd been talking to him more and more. Yes, his mind slipped. Sometimes, he would forget her.

She could certainly understand forgetting...

But sometimes, her father would look at her with such love that it stole her breath.

And someone *else* who looked at her with love? The big, tall, dangerous man before her. The man who was currently frowning. Frowning with love. It was a thing.

"We are *not* having Christmas in the hospital," he growled. "We're having it at home, together. I'm going to make love to you all night long..."

"Ah, Victor, I'm not sure the docs said we could do *that* yet." He was clear to go home but not clear to engage in "vigorous activity." As per his release paperwork.

He just stared at her.

"I don't want you to wind up in the emergency room," she mumbled.

"It would be a small price to pay." He unlocked the front door. Swung it open. "Ladies first."

Yes, about that price... "You winding up in the ER is not

a price I want to pay..." But her words trailed off as she crossed the threshold.

She'd just become aware of the music playing. Instrumental Christmas music. And when she paused... Melody was pretty sure that she knew that song. Correction. Not pretty sure. One hundred percent. She even found herself whispering, *"I'll be home for Christmas... if only in my dreams..."*

The foyer was decorated. Green, gorgeous garland. Red bows. She could smell freshly baked cookies. Her feet rushed forward, she almost stumbled, and then she was speeding down the hallway. Bursting into the den.

A decorated tree. So many ornaments. Presents stacked beneath the tree. Stockings were carefully hung near the fireplace. A red stocking with an embroidered M. A green stocking with an embroidered V. The whole place smelled of pine. Well, pine and chocolate chip cookies.

It was beautiful and warm and happy and...home.

"I cheated," Victor announced.

She spun around.

He stood just inside the den. He'd pulled off his ski cap. His dark hair was tousled. His dark eyes so very intense.

"Last year, you did all of this yourself. This year, I was stuck in the hospital, so I had to get a little help."

"Help?" She felt oddly numb. At least on the outside. But deep inside, a spark of joy was growing. Getting bigger. Warmer. Stronger.

"Hatterson." His lips twisted into a half-smile. "I know, I know. You probably wouldn't think he is a decorating expert, but, seriously, the man can do just about anything. Guard, butler, cook, decorator. He is truly a jack of all trades. Though, full disclosure, I'm pretty sure he hired a staff to help out here."

She whirled back around, looking at the tree. The mantel. The presents. "When..." Melody stopped and exhaled. "When did you have a chance to buy presents?" Or had Hatterson done that, too?

"Bought them last year. Saved them for you. Just like I saved all the decorations. I mean, the tree is new. The garland, too. Can't have a dead tree and garland in the house. Kinda doesn't fit the mood. But, ah, the tree and garland are just like the ones you had last year." The floor squeaked as he advanced into the den. "I just wanted everything perfect for you."

She shook her head. "I don't need perfect." Slowly, she faced him once more.

He stared at her with such absolute love on his face. "You are not my secret," he told her. "You're my world."

The last of the numbness—the ice—that had seemed to surround her for so long vanished. She didn't have all of her memories. Maybe she never would. But she had her life back. She had her future. She had this man. A man she loved with all of her being. A man she'd cherish for the rest of her life.

Melody ran to him.

His arms opened for her.

And Melody knew that she was truly home.

Epilogue

"Did you buy me a Christmas present? Seriously?" Hunter stared at Victor as if he had two heads. "Dude, you did not have to do that."

It was Christmas Eve, and Victor was the happiest that he'd been in...

Ever.

Melody was in the kitchen. Baking more cookies. He could hear her singing, slightly off-key. He freaking loved her off-key singing.

Hunter opened the bright red box. "Sonofabitch." He glared at Victor. "Did you give me a taser?" Then he laughed, the sound booming from him. "A taser and chocolate chip cookies." More laughter. "Thanks, man." He offered one hand to Victor.

Forget the handshake. Victor pulled him in for a hug. "You didn't fire your gun at me."

"Uh, why would I have done that?"

Victor let him go. "Because you walked into a damn murder scene where I'd just gunned down a detective. A bleeding woman was shouting that I was trying to kill her. And I was the one still holding the weapon."

Hunter shook his head. "Yeah, but I know you."

You know that I always intended to put the man who'd hurt Melody in the ground. "He used a knife on her. Chased her into the path of a car. Left her to die." Victor paced toward the Christmas tree. Hatterson had done one fine job. That man was getting a big bonus.

"Now the detective is the one going in the ground."

Victor glanced over at the Ice Breaker. At his friend.

"Funny how that worked out, isn't it?" Hunter pulled out a chocolate chip cookie and took a bite. "Damn. That is delicious. Did Hatterson make these or did Melody?"

"Melody. But she was using Hatterson's recipe."

Hunter laughed again.

"You can stay for Christmas dinner, you know," Victor told him. "Sebastian and Hatterson will be here, too." The person who hadn't made the guest list? Dario. The guy was still coming to grips with the fact that he'd been used and betrayed by Olivia. The woman had been a master at playing with everyone around her. "You're welcome to join us."

"Nah. Got a plane to catch. Or, rather, one to fly. Have some friends at home who are waiting on me. But I do appreciate the offer." He took another bite of the chocolate chip cookie and sighed in bliss. He chewed a bit, then added, "Just wanted to come by and tell you that, as far as the Ice Breakers are concerned, the case is closed. Angus Clinton abducted Melody. He and Olivia were working together. The shots fired at the Mage estate? Benny Turner was the perpetrator." He began to amble around the den. "Turner's prints were recovered inside the abandoned pickup. Got that detail from your sheriff buddy, Jamal Wroth. I think Angus had him watching the house."

"And Angus ordered Benny to shoot when Melody came back. Then, when he missed Melody, Angus had Benny waiting outside of the police station for another attack." How had Benny gotten away from the scene of the pickup's crash? *Hell, maybe Angus arranged a ride for the guy. A ride. Some kind of damn pick up from the scene.* They'd learn more when the full investigation was completed. Victor knew that all of Detective Angus Clinton's call logs, emails, and case files were currently being thoroughly reviewed.

The Feds had already found the cabin up in Canada. The damn place where Melody had been held captive. Turned out, the place belonged to Detective Clinton's great aunt. No one had gone to the cabin in years, so the bastard had known it would be the perfect spot to use.

Only Melody got away from you. She sliced you with the knife you wanted to use to kill her. She got away.

Now the detective was the one who was lying stone-cold in the storage locker of a morgue.

Hunter had finished one cookie. "I suspect the detective used Benny to do his dirty work plenty of times. In exchange, Angus went easy on the guy anytime Benny was tagged by the cops."

Now Benny was dead. Angus was dead. And Olivia was locked away.

Finally, Melody was safe.

And singing off-key.

"Hope you enjoy Christmas," Hunter told him. His gaze held Victor's. "You know how lucky you are, right?"

"Fuck, yes."

Hunter smiled. He turned to exit the den. But then he

stopped. Glancing over his shoulder, he said, "Heard an interesting news story on my way here. Seems Maryland's attorney general dropped out of the race."

"You don't say."

"Yep, I say it. I also heard that Brant McKee might be under criminal investigation."

"Huh."

"You wouldn't have anything to do with that, would you?"

Actually, Melody was the one who'd had something to do with that. Thanks to Olivia's tip-off, they'd found the PI that Melody had contacted in Maryland about Brant McKee before she'd vanished. The PI had thought that Melody lost interest because he hadn't heard from her. But, he *had* turned up useful evidence. And Melody had never lost interest.

Now, Brant McKee would be paying. "Guess he made the naughty list this year," Victor said.

"Guess he did."

Victor followed Hunter to the front door. When he opened the door, snow was falling. A chill swept into the house. "So, what's next?" Victor found himself asking Hunter. "After Christmas, you got another case to work?" Because after searching desperately for a year, after seeing what so many families faced as they fought not to give up hope...

Maybe he might want to become a part-time Ice Breaker, too. He certainly had the money to invest in the cause. But it wasn't just him. He and Melody were a package deal.

"There's always another case." Hunter's face darkened. "Always. Something I've learned since joining the crew."

Victor took a deep breath. "I want to help." No, change

that. "*We* want to help. Melody and I are interested in doing whatever the hell we can to assist your team."

Hunter had his red box tucked under his arm. "Thought you both might feel that way." His head tilted to the right. "Changes you, doesn't it?"

Yes. He'd never forget what it was like to lose the woman he loved. But Hunter was right. He was lucky. One of the very, very lucky ones.

He'd gotten her back. "We have resources to use. Mage Industries has a charitable arm. We have investments—*we can help*. We can make a difference."

"I'll call you after the holidays," Hunter told him. "Welcome to the team."

VICTOR WALKED INTO THE KITCHEN.

"*Dashing through the snow, in a one horse—*" Melody stopped. Her dimple flashed. "Victor!" And she rushed toward him. She kissed him. A warm, sweet kiss. One that tasted of cinnamon.

Love.

She pulled back. A dash of flour marked her right cheek. "Where is Hunter? Is he staying for dinner?"

"He had to go. Said thanks for the cookies."

"Aw." Her face fell. "I was hoping to say goodbye. To tell him how grateful I am for all of his help."

"He knows, baby, and it's not goodbye. We'll be working with him again."

"We?" Delight flashed on her face. "So you told him that we want to work with him?"

Because it had been Melody's idea for them to start helping the Ice Breakers.

"What did he say?" Melody asked.

"Welcome to the team."

She threw her arms around him again. Did a little happy bounce.

"Merry Christmas, sweetheart," he told her. *I love you.*

The Christmas music kept playing. The cookies kept baking. And Melody kissed him.

Finally. *Finally.* The kid who'd been looking through the windows and dreaming of a home like everyone else for so long—he'd grown up. He'd fought for what he wanted.

Melody was his family. His life.

"Merry Christmas," she whispered against his lips.

CHRISTMAS MORNING...

With a smile already curving his lips, Victor opened his eyes and reached for Melody.

But she wasn't there.

Unease slithered through him, but he blinked it away. Darkness surrounded him as he turned to face the bathroom doorway. He climbed from the bed. Crept for the door. Knocked lightly. "Melody?"

No answer.

He reached for the knob. Swung the door open. Darkness. Silence.

His heart began to beat faster. A glance at the clock on the bedside showed it was only four thirty. He'd woken early. Excited. Happy. Like a freaking kid.

But...

No Melody.

The unease inside of him grew stronger. He hit the

switch on the wall, and illumination flooded through the bedroom. "Melody!" He hadn't meant to shout. Had he?

He found himself racing out of the room. They'd fallen asleep in his bed. She'd been in his arms, and now she was just gone. His heart heaved in his chest, and fear bloomed because he'd just gotten her back.

He'd— "Melody!" He ran toward the front door.

"In here." Soft.

From the den.

He stopped mid-run. Breath heaving, he spun toward the den. His feet pounded over the floor as he rushed to find her. Victor had a desperate need to see Melody.

And he did see her. As soon as he entered the den, soft lights from the Christmas tree spilled onto her. Melody wore a red robe. Red was her favorite color, after all. She had on reindeer slippers. He'd given those to her, a present she'd opened last night. Slippers that had been wrapped and waiting for over a year.

Melody stood near the stockings. His stocking, he noticed, was full. Chocolate candy bars peeked out from the top. A candy cane hooked over the edge.

"Melody?"

"Surprise." She bit her lower lip. "I, um, thought it would be fun if I filled your stocking. A new tradition, you know, I wanted to do something nice—"

He scooped her into his arms. Ignored the pull of the damn stitches. His body shuddered against her as he buried his face in her neck.

"Victor? What's wrong?"

You were gone. For just a moment, the whole world stopped again. Maybe he'd never fully get over the fear that she'd vanish again. Maybe he'd always be hyper protective where she was concerned. But maybe...

His head lifted. "I love you."

She beamed at him. "Wait until you see what's in your stocking."

He didn't really care what was in his stocking. The best gift of his life was right in front of him. In his arms.

But...

Maybe in a little bit, after he'd kissed her senseless and he'd made love to her underneath the Christmas tree, maybe Melody would take a peek in her stocking. It wasn't empty. There was a small gift inside. A present he'd carefully tucked in before she'd gone to bed with him last night.

Olivia had stolen Melody's engagement ring. The diamonds were evidence. That ring—even if they ever got the pieces back, it was tied up with pain in Melody's mind. She deserved better. She deserved everything.

He'd gotten her a new ring.

A new ring. A new start. A new life. For them both.

She wasn't the Ghost of Christmas Past knocking at the door. She was his present. His future. And he would spend the next fifty Christmases making every dream she had come true.

THE END

Ready for another romantic suspense read? Don't miss WHEN HE GUARDS.

He made a fatal mistake.

He lusted after the wrong woman. Let his need take over. Cassius "Cass" Striker knew that he should have never touched the sexy FBI agent, but he gave in to temptation and had the best one-night stand of his life with Agnes Quinn. It should have meant nothing. He should have been able to walk away...

He can't walk away. If he does, she's dead.

His enemies know about Agnes, and they plan to use her against him. He's the leader of one of the most notorious motorcycle clubs in the US. His name stirs fear into the hearts of nearly everyone...and he has a giant target on his back. Those who want to bring him down have been looking for a weakness to use against him—they think they found that weakness in the form of Agnes. Now he either saves her or he watches her die.

She doesn't need saving, but it's super sweet of him to try.

She fell for the bad guy. Not something that typically happens given her occupation, but Agnes couldn't quite help herself. She'd been drawn to Cass from the first moment, and now the world—uh, the "underworld" thinks that they are hot and heavy, that she's a way to break the unbreakable leader of the Night Strikers. Cass is vowing to protect her, but the only way to do that?

Enter his world. Accept his claim. Eliminate all the threats that exist to them both.

She has to go in undercover, continuing to pose as Cass's lover as they embark on a cross-country trip. She has to follow his rules. She has to seemingly sever her ties with the FBI. In other words, Agnes has to go deep and hard in an undercover mission as she and Cass take out some seriously bad guys. No worries, though. Agnes does love an undercover mission, so this should be fun.

The case is a nightmare. It is not fun. And if Agnes flashes her sexy smile at him one more time…

Cass is sure that he's lost his soul, and he's not even sure where his criminal life ends and the real man that he'd once been begins. He knows one thing, though. Agnes is trouble —and he wants her. Wants her so badly that maybe he'll let the dark side of his nature off the careful leash he holds. And he'll take what he wants as he damns the consequences. Threaten her? Try to use *her* against him? Worst mistake his enemies could ever make because Agnes is *his*.

Cass was never meant to be a protector, but he sure is one hell of a hunter.

Author's Note

Do I still look up at the sky on Christmas Eve and search for Santa? Yes. Will I always believe in magic? Absolutely. Because anything can happen at Christmas. Anything—second chances, true love, redemption.

Thank you so much for taking the time to read ICE COLD CHRISTMAS. I always love to release a Christmas-related romance each year (it's a tradition for me!), and, this year, I wanted to tie in my Christmas tale with my cold-case solving Ice Breakers. I greatly appreciate you reading Melody and Victor's story. Thank you!

I hope that you enjoy an amazing holiday. May it be merry, bright, and filled with lots and lots of books that bring you a ton of delight.

If you have time, please consider leaving a review. Reviews help readers to discover new books—and authors certainly appreciate them!

If you'd like to stay updated on my releases and sales, please join my newsletter list.

I'm also active on social media. You can find me on Instagram and Facebook.

Again, thank you for reading ICE COLD CHRISTMAS.

Best,

Cynthia Eden

cynthiaeden.com

More Books By Cynthia Eden

Protector & Defender Romance
- When He Protects
- When He Hunts
- When He Fights
- When He Defends

Ice Breaker Cold Case Romance
- Frozen In Ice (Book 1)
- Falling For The Ice Queen (Book 2)
- Ice Cold Saint (Book 3)
- Touched By Ice (Book 4)
- Trapped In Ice (Book 5)
- Forged From Ice (Book 6)
- Buried Under Ice (Book 7)
- Ice Cold Kiss (Book 8)
- Locked In Ice (Book 9)
- Savage Ice (Book 10)
- Brutal Ice (Book 11)
- Cruel Ice (Book 12)
- Forbidden Ice (Book 13)

- Ice Cold Liar (Book 14)
- Ice Cold Christmas (Book 15)

Wilde Ways

- Protecting Piper (Book 1)
- Guarding Gwen (Book 2)
- Before Ben (Book 3)
- The Heart You Break (Book 4)
- Fighting For Her (Book 5)
- Ghost Of A Chance (Book 6)
- Crossing The Line (Book 7)
- Counting On Cole (Book 8)
- Chase After Me (Book 9)
- Say I Do (Book 10)
- Roman Will Fall (Book 11)
- The One Who Got Away (Book 12)
- Pretend You Want Me (Book 13)
- Cross My Heart (Book 14)
- The Bodyguard Next Door (Book 15)
- Ex Marks The Perfect Spot (Book 16)
- The Thief Who Loved Me (Book 17)

The Fallen Series

- Angel Of Darkness (Book 1)
- Angel Betrayed (Book 2)
- Angel In Chains (Book 3)
- Avenging Angel (Book 4)

Wilde Ways: Gone Rogue

- How To Protect A Princess (Book 1)
- How To Heal A Heartbreak (Book 2)
- How To Con A Crime Boss (Book 3)

Night Watch Paranormal Romance
- Hunt Me Down (Book 1)
- Slay My Name (Book 2)
- Face Your Demon (Book 3)

Trouble For Hire
- No Escape From War (Book 1)
- Don't Play With Odin (Book 2)
- Jinx, You're It (Book 3)
- Remember Ramsey (Book 4)

Death and Moonlight Mystery
- Step Into My Web (Book 1)
- Save Me From The Dark (Book 2)

Phoenix Fury
- Hot Enough To Burn (Book 1)
- Slow Burn (Book 2)
- Burn It Down (Book 3)

Dark Sins
- Don't Trust A Killer (Book 1)
- Don't Love A Liar (Book 2)

Lazarus Rising
- Never Let Go (Book One)
- Keep Me Close (Book Two)
- Stay With Me (Book Three)
- Run To Me (Book Four)
- Lie Close To Me (Book Five)
- Hold On Tight (Book Six)

Bad Things

- The Devil In Disguise (Book 1)
- On The Prowl (Book 2)
- Undead Or Alive (Book 3)
- Broken Angel (Book 4)
- Heart Of Stone (Book 5)
- Tempted By Fate (Book 6)
- Wicked And Wild (Book 7)
- Saint Or Sinner (Book 8)

Bite Series
- Forbidden Bite (Bite Book 1)
- Mating Bite (Bite Book 2)

Blood and Moonlight Series
- Bite The Dust (Book 1)
- Better Off Undead (Book 2)
- Bitter Blood (Book 3)

Mine Series
- Mine To Take (Book 1)
- Mine To Keep (Book 2)
- Mine To Hold (Book 3)
- Mine To Crave (Book 4)
- Mine To Have (Book 5)
- Mine To Protect (Book 6)

Dark Obsession Series
- Watch Me (Book 1)
- Want Me (Book 2)
- Need Me (Book 3)
- Beware Of Me (Book 4)

Purgatory Series

- The Wolf Within (Book 1)
- Marked By The Vampire (Book 2)
- Charming The Beast (Book 3)
- Deal with the Devil (Book 4)

Bound Series
- Bound By Blood (Book 1)
- Bound In Darkness (Book 2)
- Bound In Sin (Book 3)
- Bound By The Night (Book 4)
- Bound in Death (Book 5)

Stand-Alone
- Waiting For Christmas
- Monster Without Mercy
- Kiss Me This Christmas
- It's A Wonderful Werewolf
- Never Cry Werewolf
- Immortal Danger
- Deck The Halls
- Come Back To Me
- Put A Spell On Me
- Never Gonna Happen
- One Hot Holiday
- Slay All Day
- Midnight Bite
- Secret Admirer
- Christmas With A Spy
- Femme Fatale
- Until Death
- Sinful Secrets
- First Taste of Darkness
- A Vampire's Christmas Carol

About the Author

Cynthia Eden loves romance books, chocolate, and going on semi-lazy adventures. She is a *New York Times*, *USA Today*, *Digital Book World*, and *IndieReader* best-seller. She writes romantic suspense, paranormal romance, and fun contemporary novels. You can find out more about her work at www.cynthiaeden.com.

If you want to stay updated on her new releases and books deals, be sure to join her newsletter group: cynthiaeden. com/newsletter.